Hazard
Night

Also by Laura Vaughan

The Favour

Let's Pretend

Hazard Night

LAURA VAUGHAN

CORVUS

Published in hardback in Great Britain in 2023 by Corvus, an imprint of Atlantic Books Ltd.

Copyright © Laura Vaughan, 2023

10 9 8 7 6 5 4 3 2 1

A CIP catalogue record for this book is available from the British Library.

Trade paperback ISBN: 978 1 83895 708 7
E-book ISBN: 978 1 83895 709 4

Printed in Great Britain by Bell and Bain Ltd, Glasgow

Corvus
An imprint of Atlantic Books Ltd
Ormond House
26–27 Boswell Street
London

WC1N 3JZ

www.corvus-books.co.uk

MIX
Paper | Supporting
responsible forestry
FSC
www.fsc.org   FSC® C007785

For my mother.

One day I'd like to be as good a reader as you.

EVE

The first Arrivals Day, Eve had felt exactly as she was supposed to. She hadn't had to fake the warmth in her voice or the welcome on her face. Even her nervousness was the kind to be approved of: it showed a proper sense of responsibility. Of course, it was Peter's day, marking his debut as Wyatt's housemaster. But, as everyone kept telling her, Eve was to be the power behind Peter's throne. And she'd found the idea flattering as well as amusing because everything had seemed possible, exactly as it was supposed to on the first day of a new school year.

Arm-in-arm, she and Peter had waited brightly on the steps of Wyatt House, watching as the funeral procession of SUVs slunk up the chestnut avenue. In the car park, each new student stood nervously by the family car as parents unloaded luggage, already looking abandoned despite themselves. This batch of eleven year olds were children still, but only just, already lumbered with braces or out-size feet or with legs spindly from a recent growth spurt. Some jittered and fidgeted. Others waited with numb acceptance, as if stunned.

The next day, the older boys would return and take possession of the place. The dorm of sixty boys would reverberate with drumming feet and pounding music, whoops and yells echoing in the stairwells. There would be wrestling matches and water fights, the shrilling of the single payphone by the common room. But for now the place held on to the orderly hush of the holidays. The new boys murmured rather than spoke, cowed by the sense of occasion and its limitless scope for embarrassment. The parents kept up a cheerful patter, one or two mothers trying to hide a treacherous welling in their eyes.

Eve had felt a tenderness, then, for all of them. She had felt it towards even the most peevish of the mothers and pompous of the fathers, towards even the most sly-eyed of the boys. It didn't last. Now, three years later, when she sees the littlest boys haul their luggage up the stairs … fragile, hopeful, trying to be brave … yes, she feels a pang. But she doesn't trust it, or them, because she knows how soon they will begin to coarsen and harden like the rest.

Charm, of course, is what the public school system is known for. It's the most expensive of polishes and burnished onto every Cleeve alumnus. But Eve thinks of the accumulated years here as like the cheap varnish on wooden desks, underlaid with the print of sweaty hands, obscene graffiti and wads of greying gum. It's *this* gnarly carapace that lies beneath the gleaming Cleeve veneer. So when Eve glimpses – very occasionally – a trace of childhood softness in a student, she finds it unsettling. She doesn't intend to be disarmed by these boys.

Cleeve is not for everyone. Full boarding is an all-embracing existence, and our staff are expected to involve themselves in every aspect of college life. But if you are excited by the chance to help shape lives, have energy and ambition, and are willing to throw yourself into our hard-working and vibrant community, we would love to hear from you.

Cleeve is not for everyone. Surely that's the whole point, Eve had said to Peter, laughing, when he first showed her the ad. Cleeve is only for those who can afford it. And, even better, those who are born to it. Those who grow up in expectation of a life lived amidst velvety lawns and aged brick and confident masculine voices in wood-panelled rooms. The boys even sang about it in chapel. *The rich man in his castle, / The poor man at his gate; / God made them, high or lowly, / And ordered their estate.*

All things bright and beautiful indeed.

Eve should have paid more attention. She should have wondered about the tightening of that 'all-embracing' grip and at what point it might leave one gasping for air. But the warning was lost amid a flurry of enticements. Everything was generous – Salary! Accommodation! Benefits! Access to outstanding sports and leisure facilities, a rich and varied cultural programme – all to be enjoyed in five-star scenic surrounds. And then there was her husband's face as he read and re-read the advertisement. Peter looked hopeful, yes, but also stern with purpose. The slackness of the last few months was suddenly gone, and he was handsome again. He'd had his call to arms.

Long before Eve came to Cleeve, she knew it intimately.

The Lake. The Lawn. The Hall. Simple words, as from a child's storybook. *The Avenue. The Chapel. The Clock Tower.* Words that assumed the unshakeable authority of an archetype.

These words and the landscape they possessed (all three hundred acres of it!) had been the backdrop to the best years of Peter's life. He'd said this to Eve not in a burst of nostalgia, but as an admission of pain. As the only child of a depressive alcoholic and his explosively volatile wife, school had been Peter's only escape. A lost boy, he had found sanctuary at Cleeve. There had been a kindly housemaster, to whom he still wrote regularly; a cricket coach who helped him channel his rage into sportsmanship. He had been uplifted by the friendships and anchored by the old-fashioned value system. 'Cleeve saved me,' he said simply. 'It protected me. Sheltered me. It believed in my best self.'

Peter knew his privilege. He knew that in a different

setting the bewildered child he'd been would have grown up to be an irredeemably broken, perhaps dangerous, adult. That's why he spent the early years of his teaching career in schools where many of his students came from homes blighted by poverty and chaos, or worse. He sincerely believed that the ideals of the public school system – the honour code, the respect for authority, the veneration of fair play – could raise both the standards and spirits of schools without any of the resources of a place like Cleeve.

But Peter, with his earnest face and guileless smile, his soft RP tones, was easy prey. In the classroom, he was faced with indifference or rebellion – and indifference was the more relentless of the two. In the staff-room, he was met with weary tolerance. A naive idealist of a conservative bent was, at best, a curiosity. At worst, he was a Tory stooge. Either way, Peter's colleagues were not prepared to waste their near-exhausted energy on coaching him in survival tactics. Night after night, he'd come home to the cramped Kentish Town flat he shared with Eve and his face would be grey with exhaustion, his shoulders slumped with defeat.

The irony is, she was the one who pushed him to go private.

'The world's full of unhappy kids from broken homes – in *all* sections of society. You know that better than anyone. If you want to make a difference it shouldn't matter where you do it.'

And then an old school pal passed on the news that Wyatt's was looking for a housemaster and sealed both their fates.

Public schools were alien territory for Eve. She'd grown up in a bog-standard 1930s semi in the bog-standard suburbs of a bog-standard Midlands town and had never met anyone truly posh until she went to university. There, she and her friends would occasionally recoil from a honking pack of floppy-haired boys in red trousers, cashmere blondes braying at their sides. The wider student body regarded them as exotic irritants, but Eve could tell these people didn't mind being the punchline to a joke. Why should they? Their birthright was predicated on having the last laugh.

Peter was not like this in any case. He was twenty-eight and Eve was thirty when they met. Eve's previous boyfriends had been scruffy and argumentative, displaying the assorted chips on their shoulders like badges of honour. They were men who travelled adventurously and worked creatively; the more untrustworthy ones described themselves as feminists. She was introduced to Peter at a house party, where her friend pointed him out as 'the world's only Tory sin-bin teacher'. He was sandy and freckled, solidly built and attractive in a way that suggested bracing walks on wet hillsides. Not her type. And yet …

Despite Peter's diffidence, he had an old-fashioned courtliness that Eve was secretly rather thrilled by. When he looked at her, his happiness was unselfconscious and open for all to see. His decency made her feel protective, a better version of herself.

Eve's parents were dead. They had both died within a year of each other while she was at university – her father of cancer and her mother of an epileptic seizure not long afterwards. She told Peter on their first date that she was an adult orphan, trying to sound wry rather than self-pitying, but he had taken her hand in his and his own eyes were wet. He understood. When his old headmaster had died, he told her, he'd gone to the funeral and wept like a child, not just out of grief, but from the guilt of knowing that when his own parents passed he would be dry-eyed.

Peter's parents still lived in the same ramshackle Salisbury house he grew up in, still entwined in a knot of mutual loathing; Peter and Eve's visits there were as brief and infrequent as decorum would allow. Cleeve was the closest thing Peter had to a family home, and on their first visit, six months after they married and the day before Peter's final-round interview, a part of Eve wondered why it had taken him so long to introduce her.

Certainly, he was nervous. He'd had anxiety dreams about the application process, and she'd heard him mumbling unhappily in his sleep. 'It's been so many years. I hope I'm doing the right thing,' he said more than once, brow furrowed. 'I hope this isn't going to be a mistake.' And she felt a rush of tenderness towards him.

As they drew near to their destination, Peter apologised for the local town, whose quaint olde-worlde centre had been swallowed up by an ugly shopping development and boxy estates. The road narrowed as they left the desultory outskirts behind and then, just a couple of miles further on, the woods began. The breeze pushed gently through the heavy trees, their closeness oppressive even in early summer. It was easy to miss the plain white sign between two stone posts: *Cleeve College*. Now the dark wall of trees had mown grass at its feet, a pristine lawn lining either side of the road until it curled over the Bridge and became the Avenue.

Everything was as Peter had described. The wide sheltered bowl of the playing fields. The stately red-brick mansion crowning the hill. Sunlight melting against the Chapel windows, the sonorous tolling of the bell in the Clock Tower. Even the students, seen from a distance, seemed to have a scholarly sense of purpose as they to-and-froed. Eve realised her sense of recognition wasn't simply because of Peter. It struck her with new force how much institutions like Cleeve have become part of the English collective unconscious: whatever one thinks of them, everyone inherently knows what they are like. 'Are you still frightened of the Clock Tower ghost?' she asked, and Peter looked at her in surprise. How did she know? And Eve had laughed. Places like Cleeve *always* have a Clock Tower ghost.

Admittedly, the boarding houses weren't so picturesque. They were mostly 1930s institutional gothic, with the exception of the sixth-form girls' dorm, a modern block at the far edge of the campus. Wyatt's had prime positioning near to the Hall; the housemaster's quarters was a large annex, with three bedrooms and its own generous garden. Peter and Eve stayed there overnight as guests of the incumbent housemaster and his wife, who were retiring after eleven 'wonderful, *wonderful*' years.

In her naivety, Eve didn't realise that their chatty kitchen supper was an unofficial part of the assessment process. It was probably just as well, because when she was nervous she could be abrasive. That night, however, the usual pleasantries flowed. 'You've made a lovely family home,' she said to their hostess. 'It must be a great place for children.' Eve didn't mean anything particular by it, but husband and wife exchanged archly approving smiles and Peter blushed over his potatoes.

To change the subject, she asked about the washing line of lace panties she'd spotted strung between two trees on the Lawn. The housemaster's wife had rolled her eyes. 'It'll be one of the leftovers from Hazard Night.' Eve knew, hazily, what Hazard Night was – Peter had described it as a night of pranks once exams were done. She would come to look back on those leftovers as an omen, yet another of the warning signs she'd been so wilfully blind to. Wisps of lace fluttering among the leaves. A spill of bright paint along the ground. A blow-up doll, deflated and mangled in the mud. But – 'I always knew it was a mistake letting girls into the sixth form,' said their host, shaking his head with mock solemnity. 'Place has gone downhill ever since.' And they'd all laughed.

Girls aside, little appeared to have changed since Peter's school days, though their tour took in the new facilities for science and sport. These additions had been expensively designed to maintain visual harmony within the eighteenth-century parkland and were named in honour of the Old Boys who'd funded them or had otherwise distinguished themselves. The Clitheroe Centre for Science and Technology, an oval structure set around a paved quad, was thus linked to the modern languages block by a covered walkway named Havod's Walk. Jack Clitheroe had made a fortune in biotech; Maurice Havod had been a nineteenth-century explorer.

Later, Eve learned that the boys had rechristened these structures in line with the iconic simplicity of other landmarks.

The Clit and the Slit.

ALICE

I think I knew from the start that the new beard at Wyatt's was a hopeless case.

(*Beards* are what the boys call the campus wives. *Gogs* – as in pedagogues – are the teaching staff. *God* is the name for my father, the chaplain. *Fishface* is what they call me.)

I'd been roped in to help on the Winslows' first Arrivals because the kitchen was short-staffed and so Pat B – head of catering – asked if I'd lend a hand at Wyatt's welcome tea. These teas are always served in the housemasters' gardens, and although the kitchen staff do most of the baking and serving, it's a tradition that the housemaster's wife makes her own contribution. When Mrs Winslow unveiled her Tupperware boxes of gingerbread men, she flushed defensively. 'I'm not much of a cook,' she said, attempting a laugh, 'but icing covers a multitude of sins.'

The biscuits were lavishly smothered in pink and blue frosting, presumably an approximation of the school colours of claret and navy. It must have taken her hours, putting in the little currant eyes and those tiny little silver balls for buttons. Anyway, the gingerbread gave her away. Not because the biscuits were blackened and misshapen and tasted like burnt sawdust, or because they were more appropriate for a kid's birthday party than a public school induction. It was because she was already resenting having had to make them. It was obvious from the stiffness with which she got them out of the box. Later, I watched her mingle with the parents and boys, making self-deprecating remarks over her tray of mangled little men, and I thought: *I give it a year.*

I don't know. Maybe I didn't think this at all. It could just be hindsight. After all, who could have possibly predicted the Winslows' tenure would end with two dead bodies and a tabloid sex scandal? And even *that* was only the half of it.

———————————

My father was one of the old-timers who'd been at Cleeve since Peter Winslow's schooldays. He's known as God because he looks like one in an old-master painting, with his flowing grey hair and lordly eyebrows. And his clothes do billow as he walks. But the nickname's not an accolade and it's not particularly affectionate, either. Other school chaplains promote Jesus as everyone's big brother, his arms always open for a celestial hug. Their Jesus is as matey as he's omnipotent. But the God of my father is the Cloud of Unknowing variety, and gets cloudier by the year.

Anyway, Pa remembered Peter Winslow. 'Sad and angry at first, like a lot of the boys from difficult homes,' he said, after such a long pause I thought he wasn't going to speak at all. 'Then keen and grateful. A little fervent. I thought he might fall hard for religion, as it happens. His type often do.'

I waited for more. But, as is usual with Pa, it wasn't forthcoming.

Anyway, there they were: Mr Winslow, tanned and freckled and Tigger-ish, and his narrow, dark wife with the guarded smile. She was easy to spot among the Cleeve mothers, who are generally variations on a theme of Princess Di in mummy mode. The new wife was too plainly dressed for that and a bit too long in the face, maybe, for prettiness. Still, I could tell the boys were bound to jerk off to her. Eve Winslow was attractive enough for that.

The boys don't jerk off to me. I'm a fixture of the place in the same way Pa is – but I'm more of a curiosity than an institution. Like the Hall gargoyle with the painted red nose. Or the ever-present smell of weed in the passage behind the Laundry.

My mother died when I was born, which if I was a different kind of girl would make me tragic and interesting. Here I am, raised by an ancient priest in an ivory tower, amidst a sea of blue-blooded testosterone. A squalling baby, flailing my fists in the Chapel vestibule … A squat toddler, pissing all over the Lawn … A moony ten-year old, dawdling along the Avenue …

13

A dour teenager, trudging back and forth from the bus stop in my cheap school uniform. Flat-chested, goggle-eyed, my mouth permanently downturned. Fishface.

'It will be so nice for Alice to have some other girls on campus,' one of the beards had exclaimed brightly at a faculty barbecue, shortly before the debut of the Monstrous Regiment, which was what some of the staff – only half-joking – had christened Cleeve's first intake of female students in a hundred and sixty years.

'There are girls at my school,' I'd mumbled.

'Yes, but this will be a very *different* sort of girl,' said the beard. I think it was Mrs Riley, from Hawkins House, the latest in a long line of campus busybodies who had tried and failed to take me under their wing. 'More of a kindred spirit, don't you think?'

I was eleven at this point and the oldest campus brat after Mrs Riley's own boys (both Cleevians, thanks to the generous staff discount on fees). A couple of the younger kids went to a private prep the other side of town. Meanwhile, I had attended the local state primary and was about to start at St Wilfred's, the big comprehensive in town. My enrolment was assumed to be some quixotic gesture of my father's (What Would Jesus Do? Send his children to the comp!). Actually, it was my choice.

Quite a few of my classmates also have parents who work at Cleeve. Or else uncles and aunts and older siblings. Cleeve is one of the biggest employers in these parts. But the locals aren't teachers. They're cleaners, laundry maids, dinner ladies, groundsmen. They're the people who looked out for me as I was growing up. They let me tag along, do odd jobs and ask stupid questions. Put plasters on my knees when I fell down the Library steps, saved me an extra helping of chocolate pudding.

This is why I'm tolerated at school. I'm not a posh twit like the Cleevians who strut through the town centre on Saturday afternoons, taking up the entire width of the pavements, sucking up all the oxygen in the shops and cafes. No. But I'm not a townie, either, living as I do in a Hansel and Gretel cottage on the school estate with my dad, the weird vicar. At school, I am known to be clever and assumed to be odd. Back at Cleeve, meanwhile, I'm just … odd.

I knew from the start that having more girls around wouldn't make any difference, at least not to me. Two or three times every term bus-loads of girls are imported from neighbouring public schools for socials in the Hall. These visitors, I observed, uniformly wore crushed velvet sheaths that barely skinned their arses and all had huge quantities of hair which they were constantly flicking about into lopsided quiffs. And they were always pawing each other, mouths nuzzling at each other's ears. Breathy whispers, breathless giggles. An occasional shriek of hilarity or disdain. As they tottered out of the coaches, I'd watch them peep out at the waiting Romeos from under their silky manes, some coy, some malicious and all with the same sort of pretty-kitten face. They were as alien to me as the swarm of scuffling, swaggering males I'd grown up with. More so.

The first year's intake were treated like celebrities. That was inevitable. But they were like celebrities who had suffered some kind of public fall from grace. Sure, they were coveted and venerated and gossiped about ... but also somewhat despised. 'Desperate virgins or mad slags' was the verdict at St Wilf's and maybe they had a point, because why else would these girls be pioneers? It can't have been for the academics. Cleeve is what's known as a 'solid' educational establishment, which essentially means that Oxbridge offers aren't in great abundance.

Anyway. After five years of lady sixth formers the novelty's mostly worn off. I watch them, sometimes, sunning themselves on the Lawn or idling by the Lake, and they're not a part of the landscape yet. They're too aware of the effect they're having, or trying to make. I don't envy them. It looks exhausting.

EVE

For her first few months at Cleeve, Eve commuted to her job in London four days a week. It was a slog, no doubt about it – first the bus, then the train for an hour, finally the Tube. But she liked her work as a copywriter at a small liberal think-tank, and her boss was accommodating. And though the days were long, and the hours she spent travelling were generally cramped and unpleasant, she felt her heart lift as she took her first steps through the glimmering, whispering arch of the Avenue.

Soon, of course, the nights drew in. But even then, Eve had loved to see the trees rise like plumes of smoke against the waning light. Never having lived in the countryside before, she was quietly amazed by the vastness and gentleness of its nights. She used to dawdle outside of Wyatt's, taking a moment before going in to look at its grid of lit windows like an opened-up Advent calendar. She would listen to the hiss of the showers, music from competing stereos, the laughter. Someone might be practising a violin or flute, and a stammer of Mozart would turn into a ripple, then a soar of sweetness through the dark. That was the point when Eve would push open the door to the Private Side – it was never locked – and there would be supper, kept hot in an actual Aga, from the school kitchens.

True, she and Peter saw very little of each other. Peter's day started before seven and usually finished around eleven, when he did a final check on the boys, and by which time Eve – exhausted from her commute – was already in bed. In addition to Peter's housemaster duties, he taught a reduced timetable in his subject, history, and coached cricket on Saturday afternoons. There were sports fixtures and socials and cultural outings to be chaperoned too.

Eve told herself they just needed to settle in. The assistant housemaster, a gawky twenty-something who lived in a tiny flat at the top of the building, would gain in confidence and Peter would be able to delegate more. He'd stop volunteering at quite such an enthusiastic rate. He was still the New Boy, she reasoned, looking to prove himself.

Then Eve fell pregnant. It was not an accident, exactly, but it was certainly a surprise. Her morning sickness was violent and lasted most of the day; quite early on, it was obvious the travel would be impossible, never mind the job. Eve didn't know anyone who 'telecommuted': by Christmas, she was officially unemployed.

Never mind, Peter told her. Cleeve was a wonderful place to raise a child: she'd said so herself. Why not take a year or two out to have the baby and enjoy motherhood on her own terms? Then she could look around, hopefully find something local, or maybe even retrain. They'd work it out.

They decided to keep the sex of the baby a surprise, but Eve was secretly convinced she was carrying a girl. When Milo was finally torn out of her, in a furious, frantic birth, her disappointment that he was a boy was something she worked to hide; at the beginning, she even hid it from herself. It might have been easier if he'd taken after her. There were people who looked at Eve's slanting dark eyes and sallow skin and assumed some intriguing ethnic mix (if so, it must be a very distant ancestral throwback). Milo, however, was pure Peter. He was stolid, freckled, with a frank, open gaze.

'An angel baby,' said the health visitor, for Milo was from the start contented and plump. The first months, which everyone told her were the hardest, were the easiest for Eve. She took simple pleasure in her baby's swaddles of fat, in his miniature velociraptor cries, the vinegary tang of his excretions. Even once Milo was on solids, the smell of his shit was a secret delight. She would press her nose to his wiggling backside and breathe in through the nappy the warm reassurance of his stink.

Motherhood changed when Milo was about eight months old. He would no longer entertain himself or stay safely put when placed on the floor. His three naps a day shrank to one. He wanted her, desperately, all the time. To rattle shakers and turn cogs and stack rings; to remove items from cupboards and turn pages of books. Whenever she left the room he exploded into howls of primal anguish. One morning Eve felt tears prick her eyes and realised she was, quite literally, crying with boredom.

Eve had always found other people's children tedious or faintly alarming. She had assumed this changed once you had your own. She'd quite liked the idea of a child, or at least assumed she did. Peter, meanwhile, had longed for one. 'He'll make the most wonderful dad,' people kept telling her, and this had reassured her when faith in her own maternal instincts faltered. But Peter was already a parent: to sixty teenage boys. Somebody was always crying or sick or fighting, playing pranks or on the verge of a breakdown. Somebody's parents were always on the telephone.

Soon all of Eve's time was spent waiting, waiting, waiting for the day to pass. The long hours had no landmarks except chores; when she did them, she felt resentful; when she neglected them, the house filled with a depressing slurry of toys and laundry and half-eaten food.

Worse, she had the lurking dread that she herself would never outgrow this phase – that from here on she would always find her child a burden. She looked into Milo's eyes, and the bright expectancy of his gaze was frightening. The development of likes and dislikes, of moods and personality, all these things a parent rejoices in … they made her heart quake with love, yes, but they were also the terms of a new imprisonment.

She couldn't shake off the feeling that somewhere, somehow, a terrible mistake had been made.

'I think it's a mistake,' said Nancy Riley righteously, over coffee in Eve's living room.

Cleeve's latest bid to ingratiate itself with the local populace was to open up the school swimming pool for family swims on Sunday mornings. It was the hot-button topic *du jour* but Eve found herself distracted by a stain on the wallpaper just above Nancy's head. It was rust-coloured, in the shape of a spider, and its position meant it appeared to be squatting on a blowsy pink rose. Their predecessors had be-sprigged the house in Laura Ashley-style florals, and although there was a redecoration allowance, Eve and Peter had agreed to put off home improvements until Milo was of a less destructive age. Milo was now nearly three and Eve was still staring at the same faded spread of fat, smug roses. But the spider-stain was new. Or was it?

It took an effort of will to turn her attention back to her visitor.

'Sundays are so special at Cleeve,' Nancy was lamenting. 'Convivial yet quiet. It's when school life feels the most *intimate*, don't you think? All that will be spoiled with strangers tramping all over the place – those dog walkers in the woods are more than enough to contend with. There'll be litter too. And,' she said darkly, 'I dread to think what will end up in the water.'

'Mm.' Eve found it hard to believe the purity of the pool was under threat – not when one considered the pustule-laced adolescents who usually marinated in it. 'Do you know the First Lady's view?'

The First Lady was Mrs Parish, the headmaster's wife. She was cosy and diminutive, with round pink cheeks and twinkling blue eyes. Uptight parents, and fathers in particular, immediately softened in her presence. Eve had soon learned that the twinkle was actually a chip of glittering ice. It was rumoured that nothing official at Cleeve happened without her say-so.

'Oh, Madeleine's very supportive *publicly*, of course. *Privately* I'm sure she feels the same as we do.' Nancy deferred to the headmaster's wife in all things, but Eve suspected she chafed a little under her sovereignty. Nancy herself had the appearance of an attractive squirrel: bright-eyed and toothy with bristling reddish hair. The more helpful she was, the more squirrelly she became.

And Nancy had been exceedingly helpful to Eve, especially when Milo was first born. She'd held a welcome tea-party for Eve and another one close to her due date and had been generous with baked and knitted goods, not to mention advice, once Milo was born. It was she who'd prompted Eve to put Milo's name down for the 'only acceptable' nursery in town. And she'd helped Eve get her current job – working part-time in the archivist's office.

Since then, she had been assiduous – or relentless, depending on how you looked at it – in involving Eve in extracurriculars. Game nights. Charity bakes. Supper parties. Eve would have felt beholden in any case, but she had a nagging feeling that Nancy was positioning the two of them as particular friends. She was only five or six years older than Eve but had recently waved the youngest of her two boys off to university and was, Eve could admit in her more charitable moments, probably feeling somewhat at a loss. Meanwhile, Eve was mourning her old friends back in London, who, on the increasingly rare occasions they met up, seemed to want nothing more from her than smutty and amusing anecdotes about life in her 'posh Borstal'.

Nancy didn't only have updates on the swimming pool wars: a new head of Classics had been appointed. 'Gabriel Easton, the name is. He's terribly grand and an actual Cambridge don. He's written several books. Quite a coup for the school.'

'This man left Cambridge for Cleeve? Why?'

'Apparently his wife wanted a change of scene. Nobody's met her yet – she's a bit of a mystery. Let's hope she's not one of those snobby bluestocking types.' Nancy gave a toothy smile.

Eve had never considered herself an intellectual, but she found it frustrating how determinedly the faculty wives set themselves apart from anyone – and especially women – of even modest academic ambition. There were only three female teachers, two of whom lived out and one who taught (Music) alongside her husband (Geography), who was in every way her whiskery fuss-pot twin.

Eve thought of her old friends again, with their ooh-err jokes about matrons and fagging. She wondered if Nancy had come up against this too. Perhaps that's why she and the other women here huddled so determinedly together. They were like forgotten colonialists in some unfashionable backwater of the Empire, congratulating each other on their good works and frontier spirit. Meanwhile, the natives went on about their business, completely ignoring them. Or possibly fomenting revolt.

The students are revolting! Eve had a hazy memory of scenes from *If …*: of floppy hair and starched collars and public school boys with machine guns, insouciantly mowing down the establishment from the school roof. They should remake the film, perhaps, but put the teachers and support staff on the roof instead – the wives could lead the charge. Now, *that* would be subversive.

'What are you thinking about, Dolly Day-Dream?' Nancy asked.

'Firing squads,' said Eve, and went to fetch the shortbread.

ALICE

The day the Eastons arrived was a significant one for me, in any case, because it also marked my third meaningful encounter with Henry Zhang.

Henry was one of the recent wave of Hong Kongers who'd been packed off to British boarding schools by parents anxious about the upcoming handover of the territory to China. There were a smattering of such students at Cleeve, but they seemed resigned to their foreignness, which was of the intrinsically unglamorous sort. Their shoulders were permanently slumped and their eyes were anxious; the furtiveness with which they spoke to each other in their native tongue only seemed to confirm their alien status. Henry Zhang, however, was different. One of his grandfathers was English, which helped; then he was captain of the cricket team, which helped even more. Plus he was six-foot tall with cheekbones that could cut glass. Once, I overheard somebody refer to him in passing as 'the Yellow Peril', and one of the other boys had drawled, 'Yellow? Nah, that dude is *golden*.'

Still, he didn't start off that way. When Henry first arrived, he was bespectacled and skinny, wearing an obviously second-hand uniform. This represented everything the two alpha male types on campus were not. Type Ones had lions' heads, all tawny manes and gnashingly bright teeth. They captained sports teams and were a regular feature of both the school prospectus and the Bystander pages of *Tatler*. Type Twos were druggy and piratical, with baggy clothes and shadowed eyes. They were permanently on the verge of expulsion. Both types were referred to by their peers, without irony, as legends. Even in his golden age, Henry was more … circumspect.

Our first encounter was in his first term at Cleeve, which was the spring term of Henry's and my third-form year. I'd seen him being dropped off at Wyatt's, and the only reason I noticed him was the same reason everyone else did – because his mother, a very small and very exquisite Chinese woman, was 1) bundled up in a slightly woebegone fur coat instead of the usual cashmere, and 2) sobbing loudly and uncontrollably while hanging on to his neck. Few boys would have recovered from this in a hurry, and especially not some Hongky joining Cleeve halfway through. I suppose I might have felt sorry for him if I'd bothered to think about it.

Anyway, exeat weekend came up and the school abruptly emptied. I love exeat weekends even more than the holidays. During the holidays, the place is pimped out to language schools or music festivals or drama courses, and throngs of strangers with clip-boards are endlessly traipsing about. Maintenance work steps up and something is always being noisily built or demolished. But on exeat weekends nothing much happens. It's as if the bricks and lawns and trees exhale a long, slow breath. The dorms are dark at night, and the paths and passageways are mostly empty except for shadows and a flurry of leaves. Best of all, hardly anyone's around to use the swimming pool.

Swimming's my thing. I started late – I was nearly seven when the rowing coach took pity on me and taught me alongside his four year old on Sunday afternoons. It's thanks to him I have good technique. And, OK, I'm not strictly allowed to be in the school pool by myself, but I know the codes to get in, and the staff are generally fine to look the other way.

This particular Saturday, I let myself into the pool just before four. It was a late January afternoon, dank and cold, and the sky outside the windows was leaden. I hadn't bothered turning on the main lights, so most of the illumination came from the pool, which shimmered a chemical turquoise. I was cruising up and down, luxuriating in the easy roll of my shoulders and hips. *Catch, pull. Flow. Breathe.* I came up for a pause at the shallow end and rubbed the steam from my goggles. That's when I realised there was somebody – a boy – a student – one of the Asians – standing by the side.

He was in his navy school trunks, a white towel slung around his shoulders. He cleared his throat. 'Hi. Hello. I, uh, thought we had to wait for the lifeguard?'

His voice echoed off the tiles. It was cut-glass, but also slightly old fashioned somehow.

I shrugged. Rudely. I was pissed off by the intrusion.

We looked at each other for a moment, each clearly wondering what on the earth the other was doing there. I saw a quiff of black hair and strong black brows. Reflected water dappled his face: not yellow, not yet tanned to gold. Ivory. He was frowning a little, trying to work me out. Or maybe he was just struggling to see without his specs.

Whatever relative or friend he was supposed to be staying with for the exeat must have fallen ill or had some kind of emergency, and he was still too much of an unknown to be scooped up by one of the other boys. I didn't care. The swimming pool's probably the one place in the world where I don't get self-conscious. I like the sleekness of my body in my sports costume, the way my straggly mouse hair is tucked safely away, and my skull feels hugged by my swimming cap. And I know how well I move through the water. With grace, with strength. He was the interloper here, not me.

Perhaps he sensed this. He blinked. 'You know, uh, you're a really good swimmer.'

'Yeah. Thanks.' I spread my hands out in the water. Was this boy going to swim too? Or was he just going to wait and watch me until the lifeguard they'd found for him turned up? The dim lighting, the humid warmth of the air, made our solitude oddly intimate. Water rippled suggestively. Around us, there was a sense of pipes and filters thrumming away. The boy made an awkward gesture, and I realised he didn't know what to do either.

He cleared his throat for a second time. 'I'm Henry, by the way.'

'Alice.'

'You look familiar … I'm sorry … have we …?'

I smiled. 'I'm the child of God.'

Now he looked really confused. I guess he hadn't yet picked up on my father's nickname. I bit back a spurt of laughter.

I was fourteen and had, up until then, always been indifferent to Cleeve boys. The lions, the pirates. The beastly and the nerdy and the nice-but-dims in between. The boys at school, too, with their gelled hair and tracksuits, their quick eyes and surly mouths. But now I looked back at Henry Zhang – at his long, smooth body, at his hair and his skin. Ebony and ivory. Soon, I knew, he'd get over his hesitancy. He'd stop clearing his throat before he spoke. He'd fill out, learn how to compensate for his foreignness and his second-hand clothes. Soon he'd build up some ease, then some popularity, and he'd disappear into it.

What was I waiting for? I pushed off, swimming down the lane at a furious rate. Let him look at me. I wasn't Fishface – I was a water nymph, a mermaid. Daughter of a sea god! But when I came up for air again, the boy had gone.

After that, Henry Zhang would always say hi if he saw me in passing. Quite openly, as if we actually knew each other. I always had a mad fear that he'd be able to hear the thumping of my heart when he smiled at me. It helped that he was at Wyatt's, which is the dorm nearest to mine and Pa's.

We live in a funny little half-timbered house that was once a gamekeeper's cottage on the edge of Cleeve Woods. My parents only lived here together for a couple of years before my mother died. The two of them met while studying Theology at university. Both were mature students; my mother was in her twenties, but Pa was pushing forty – a self-described 'evangelical atheist' who'd had a Damascene conversion after some kind of crisis at work. He used to be a family lawyer. 'Lawyers already think of themselves as priests,' he likes to say. 'So in some ways it was a natural transition.'

My mother, by contrast, had always been very devout. She had an underlying heart condition and was warned that pregnancy would be dangerous for her, but she said that the outcome was God's will. During my own brief phase of religious zealotry, which lasted for about six months between the ages of nine and ten, I asked Pa if my mother's death had caused him to doubt his faith. He'd given me a scorching look. 'God is not happiness. God is love. Which is a different thing entirely.'

In the photographs, my mother looks exactly as you'd expect a chaplain's wife to look – mousy and well-meaning. I'm sure she'd have been a very nice mum. A little over-protective, probably. Pa is not given to fussing, or indeed noticing much, but no doubt my mother would have fretted over my coming-of-age in Cleeve and whether I'd be susceptible to the wrong type of boy. A misplaced fear, as events proved, since it turned out the wrong type of girl can be every bit as dangerous.

As it happened, my second significant encounter with Henry Zhang – nearly two years after the first – was on account of dangerous girls. I'd gone to the cinema on a Saturday, only to find that my solitary expedition coincided with a load of Cleeve squits (as the first years are called) on their weekly jaunt round the shopping centre. I came out of the back entrance to avoid them, only to spot a couple of strays in the alley that runs up to the bus stop. Squits are strictly confined to the mall during their hour off the leash, but these two had either taken a wrong turn or made an ill-advised break for freedom. I watched as three townie girls who'd been loitering by the bus stop moved to block their path.

Two of the girls went to my school, and everyone there knew to give them a wide berth. They had shark eyes and grey teeth, their faces pulled tight by their scraped-back hair, and mottled bare legs as thick as tree trunks. The other one, who I didn't recognise, was curvaceous and tanned, and might have been pretty under the pancake make-up. All three were swigging from bottles of Diamond White.

'What the fuck are you looking at?' demanded Skank One.

'N-nothing,' the bigger squit said.

'We just want to get past,' faltered the smaller one.

Skank Two bared her teeth. 'What's the password then?'

'We – uh – we don't – we –' Consternation all round.

Skank One cackled. 'Try "I'm a posh twat and I want my mummy". Go on. Say it.' The third girl, the one I didn't recognise but who had kept quiet until now, tapped ash from her cigarette onto the little one's head. It was an oddly graceful motion.

Reluctantly, I went over. 'Give it a rest.'

'What's this?' Skank One demanded. 'The nanny?'

Skank Two looked at me with narrowed eyes. 'No, I know her. She goes to our school but she lives in *theirs*.'

'Oh yeah.' Skank One nodded. 'Her dad's that weirdy-beardy vicar.'

'He's probably a paedo, then. One of them paedo priests.'

'That's the Catholics.' I smiled. Just a bit of friendly banter. 'Boys, Mr Prentice is looking for you.' I pointed back to the mall. 'Get a move on.'

The squits scuttled off without so much as a backward glance.

'Boys, Mr Panty-piss is looking for you,' one of the skanks mimicked in a hoity-toity falsetto. The other one doubled over in laughter. The third girl, the silent one, had a sleepy, cat-like smile on her face.

'Well,' I said, too brightly, 'see ya.'

I moved to walk past.

Skank One reeled extravagantly and clutched at her heart, as if I'd shouldered her in the chest. She opened her fist, and the bottle of cider hit the pavement. There was only a dribble of liquid but an explosion of glass. 'Look what you've gone and done now!'

I stared. 'Are you kidding me?'

'You *owe* me. Compensation. Premium liquor, that was.'

'And assault!'

'Then there's the cost of hurt feelings.'

Skank Two made a grab for my bag.

A hand clamped over hers.

'I wouldn't do that if I were you,' said Henry Zhang.

All of us froze. He was so very tall and so very male. And then there was the sureness, the aloofness. Once upon a time this effect would have been something he'd had to practise. Now it was second nature. I felt, despite myself, a little pang.

Skank One recovered first. 'Mine's a sixty-nine,' she sneered. 'And make it snappy.'

'Egg flied lice!' shrieked Skank Two.

'I don't get told what to do by Cleeve twats,' said the third girl coldly. 'Or chinks.'

'No? Perhaps you should start getting used to it. A thousand years ago, my people were busy inventing gunpowder and the compass, whereas yours were living in mud huts and picking fleas out of your pants.' He smiled pleasantly. '*Plus ça change*, one might say.'

The third girl gave him her sleepy cat's smile, followed by the finger. She seemed almost appreciative. Her sidekicks were furiously huffing and shuffling. *Lesbo. Wok-face. Shit-head.* But it seemed the confrontation was over. With the skanks still spitting insults, the trio moved off, and it was just the two of us.

My heart was doing gigantic skips again. I told myself it was because I'd been about to get mugged. 'You didn't need to do that.' In my effort to keep my cool, I realised I sounded ungrateful. 'But thanks.'

'Do those charmers go to your school?'

'Two of them. But most of the kids aren't like that. They're pretty normal. And not, you know, racist.'

'There are plenty of racists at Cleeve. Ask Chidi Abimbola or Simon Chowdhury.'

In spite of everything, I was still a little shocked that Henry came right out and said it.

He wouldn't have done so, I thought, if I'd been an equal in the hierarchy. A popular boy. A pretty girl. It was one of those unspoken rules about unspeakable things. You didn't call out racism at Cleeve, at least not the common-or-garden kind. The same went for the other -isms and -phobias. Doing so was regarded as hopelessly gauche. Or, rather, *unsporting*.

'I'm sorry,' I said awkwardly.

'Don't be. At least, not on my account. Haven't you heard? I'm golden, not yellow.'

The arrogance of his smile was pure Cleeve. But it was also performative: he was letting me in on the joke. In our different ways we were both inside-outsiders, and we'd shared a moment of subversion.

It wasn't much in the scheme of things. I know that. And our third encounter of note was even more fleeting, though it was the start of everything, in the end.

―――――――――――

The Eastons moved into their campus lodgings at the last possible moment, which was lunchtime on Arrivals Day, and so only an hour or so ahead of the new batch of first years. Henry Zhang was there too because, as house prefect at Wyatt's, he had to be on site to help the new squits get settled in. From my vantage-point on a bench in the Lavender Walk, I spotted him walking purposefully up from the Lodge, no doubt engaged on some welcome-party-associated errand.

That particular bench is my favourite people-watching spot in Cleeve. A lot of the benches have dedications to dead

Old Boys carved into the backs, but this bench is one of the few to bear a woman's name. *Margaret Mumford, In Memoriam.* Some loyal retainer or dearly departed beard, I suppose. My mother didn't get a memorial bench, so when I was quite small I decided to adopt Margaret Mumford's instead. As a result, I got weirdly affronted when other people sat on it.

'Is it just me,' I heard a girl say in a throaty drawl, 'or is that guy really fit for an Asian?'

A couple of lower-sixth formers were dawdling along the path to the right of me. The new girls also arrived a day ahead of the rest of the school; these two must have got rid of their parents early and were on a campus orientation all of their own. I could sense them looking at me and wondering if I was one of them, and if so, why I was so badly dressed.

As Henry hurried along, someone called out to him from one of the faculty cottages to the north of the Lodge. A woman was standing by a beaten-up car, her face obscured by the box of books she was holding. Her words were indistinguishable, their tone plaintive yet playful. Assorted bags and boxes were stacked up on the drive; after a brief exchange, Henry lifted an unwieldy wooden easel out of the car boot, following the woman into the house. He emerged about five minutes later.

On an impulse – and partly, I admit, to show off to the new girls – I got off my bench and fell in with Henry as he resumed his walk back to Wyatt's.

'Was that the new Classics' beard?' I wasn't actually interested, but the question seemed marginally less lame than asking Henry about his holidays. 'What's she like?'

I was proud of how casual I managed to keep my tone.

Henry seemed amused. 'She's ... different.' He ran a hand through his hair; he'd had it cut shorter at the sides, with an untamed quiff falling over his eyes. His teeth flashed white against his summer tan. 'She asked me if I'd read *Journey to the West*. Here.' He passed over the battered paperback he was carrying; I was very conscious that our hands touched. 'Another well-meaning white lady trying to enlighten me about my heritage. You're a bookworm, aren't you? Tell me if it's any good.' And he set off at a jog.

I looked down at the delicate Chinese painting on the book's cover and skim-read the blurb. The story was described as a 'towering classic of Chinese literature', both a comic adventure and a spiritual allegory, recounting the mythic pilgrimage of a Buddhist monk. On the inside of the cover, the owner had written her name in a florid cursive. *Fenella Easton.* I opened a page at random.

Suddenly he caught sight of two female fiends bailing water from a well. How did he know so readily, you ask, that they were female fiends? Because he saw that each of them had a chignon on her head, about fifteen inches tall ...

If I were the superstitious type, I might have said this was an omen.

EVE

Eve was wholly uninterested in the 'Enigma of Mrs Easton', as Nancy Riley insisted on calling it. In the week before the new school year started, Gabriel Easton had attended the requisite department meetings and training days, and one or two of the mixers that followed, but of his wife there had been no sign. Peter had described the new Classics master as a 'nice' fellow, but Peter thought everyone was nice. 'A little austere' was how he qualified it. 'Fearfully bright, obviously.'

Since there were no Easton children, and Gabriel Easton was an academic, Eve pictured his wife as the tweedy, greying sort. Doughty. Her name was Fenella, for God's sake.

On the first Saturday of Advent, the autumn term, Mrs Parish always held a drinks party for the wives. Strictly speaking, it was for faculty partners in general, but the male other halves of the few female teachers never came. 'The First Lady knows us girls have to stick together,' said Nancy, the first time Eve received her invitation. 'More *oblige* than *noblesse*,' was how Eve described it afterwards to Peter.

Mrs Parish was said to come from money. At any rate, the furnishings in the east wing of the Mansion, where the headmaster's family were housed, were of a different quality to the lugubrious Victorian furniture in the main function rooms. There was a sparkling clutter of crystal and chinoiserie, offset by the choicest blooms from the school gardens. Silver-framed photographs of the Parish offspring crowded every surface, tracing their progression from winsome tots to willowy twenty-somethings. In the midst of all this, Mrs Parish seemed to embody the benevolent mother from an old-fashioned children's book, with her doll-bright cheeks and pretty laugh. 'Ah, Mrs Wyatt,' she said when Eve arrived, clapping her little white hands. 'What a *treat*.'

It was one of Mrs Parish's whimsies to name the wives of housemasters after their husbands' dorms. Eve gritted her teeth and collected a wine glass.

The wine was even cheaper than that served at functions for parents or Old Boys, and the nibbles were the supermarket-brand crisps given to students in their occasional packed lunches. In a corner by the fireplace, Penny Hammond (Miles House) gave her a wave. Penny was sturdy and plain, with a forthright sense of humour that Eve had warmed to, but she had four children under ten who commanded most of her attention. Eve went over and they briefly commiserated over their respective holidays – Eve's in a cottage in Exmoor, where it had rained every day, Penny's at her in-laws' farm in Yorkshire – before Nancy Riley bustled over and claimed Penny's attention with plans for a bake-athon.

From the window, Eve watched a troop of boys make their way towards the Manson-Green Lecture Theatre for the evening's film club. Peter would be there on chaperone duty, helping to man the projector and serve the popcorn. She had a flashback to one of their early dates, at a cinema in Brixton, where they'd spent the whole film necking in the back row like a couple of horny teenagers, Peter's hand sliding under the thin cotton of her dress, and up her thigh to the damp heat between her legs. What had the film been? She couldn't remember. Something French and melancholy, though it had made them laugh. Everything made them laugh in those days. Afterwards, they'd gone for jerk chicken and jollof rice from a late-night market stall, and the rain caught by the street lamps had slanted silver and gold.

To avoid having to make conversation, and because the sudden nostalgia had made her sad, Eve went in search of the loo. The one on the ground floor was occupied, so she went upstairs, savouring the sense of trespass. She half-expected a red rope to have been placed across the stairs. There was a bathroom at the far end of the first-floor landing. But the door to the master bedroom was also open; an unfamiliar figure was rummaging through the dressing table. For a stunned moment, Eve thought she had interrupted a burglary – but then the woman looked up, laughing, and put her finger to her lips. With quick steps, she came over to the doorway, holding up a be-ribboned powder puff with an air of triumph.

'I was looking for the bathroom,' Eve blurted out, as if she'd been the one caught in the act of larceny.

'And *I* was looking for a beer trophy,' the strange woman said merrily. She dusted her nose with the powder puff, then dabbed it in Eve's direction. 'C'mon, aren't you curious as to what our oberführer keeps in her knicker drawer?'

Eve let out an appalled snort of laugher.

'I'm Fen, by the way,' said the stranger, stuffing her trophy into her pocket. 'Which one of them are you?'

The new wife had a deeply tanned face and unruly dark curls. She was younger than Eve had expected: the creases around her eyes, an arrestingly bright grey, looked to be from sun rather than age, though her hair had a few threads of silver. She was wearing a baggy fisherman's jumper over paint-spattered jeans and worn-down red leather ballet pumps. Everyone else had dressed up for the occasion. Even Eve had put on a silk blouse.

'I'm Eve. Eve Winslow. Known as Mrs Wyatt in these parts.'

'Is that so.' Fen put her head on one side to consider her better. Then she reached out and lightly touched the edge of Eve's right eye. The movement was so deft, Eve didn't flinch. 'What are you? No, don't tell me, I'm good at this – a little bit of Lebanese?'

Eve found she didn't want to disappoint her. 'Plain Midlands, as far as I know.'

'Oh. I'm Irish and French myself. Irish gypsy, Huguenot aristocrat. I'm afraid I take comfort there's not a drop of English blood in my veins. I think it's because the English haven't ever suffered true persecution – that's why they're such a phlegmatic race.' She spoke with absolute authority, and yet Eve didn't take her pronouncement seriously. This was someone, she felt, who was constantly improvising.

'Ladies? Hello?' Mrs Parish's voice floated up the stairs, a touch querulously. 'Can I help you with something?'

Eve and Fen exchanged guilty looks. 'Coming,' they chorused.

Off they went, giggling along the corridor. 'Fancy a smoke?' said Fen.

———————————

It was a joint. The first Eve had smoked in over five years, and even more deliciously illicit than her first, passed to her by a cute boy at a student house party. By the time she and Fen left the Mansion the sun had only just set, leaving a faint red smoulder in the horizon. Fen lit up even before they'd turned off the main footpath. The campus was illuminated by chains of Victorian style lamp-posts, and at this time of evening there were still plenty of people about. Eve looked around them nervously. 'I'm usually much more law-abiding, I promise,' Fen assured her, linking arms. 'But there was something about that soirée that made me think of condemned men and last breakfasts.' She exhaled luxuriantly. '*Ahhhhh.*'

Fen hadn't been resident at Cleeve long, but she'd clearly got her bearings. 'This way,' she said briskly. 'I'm an insomniac so I've done most of my recces at night.' She led the way to the thicket of beech near the service driveway at the back of the campus, behind the sports centre and the maintenance blocks. Here, the grass under the trees wasn't manicured lawn but dead leaves. The air was dank and chill, and the leaf mould gave off an earthy scent like ground coffee. Fen spread out her jacket on the ground, sank down on it gratefully and passed the joint to Eve. '*Santé.*'

Eve took a drag. 'Peter – he's my husband – would hate this.'

'Oops. I promised Gabriel I'd be on my best behaviour too. Still, I imagine the people most likely to snitch on us are all at that God-awful party.'

'They're not so bad,' said Eve, feeling an unexpected flash of loyalty.

'What about the mistress of ceremonies?'

'All *oblige* and no *noblesse*.'

It was the same line Eve had used on Peter, but Fen reacted much better. She laughed until she coughed. 'Oh,

I think I'm going to like you,' she said, wiping her eyes. 'Yes, I do.'

Eve's head was already swimming pleasantly from the pot. 'The boys call us beards,' she confided. 'Us wives, I mean.'

'Beards? Why?'

'It's some stupid joke about all their teachers being closeted homosexuals.'

Fen snorted. 'Well, there must be one or two. The senior common room at St Benedict's was awash with them.'

'Will you miss it? Cambridge, I mean.'

'Academic circles are terribly bitchy – I won't miss that. All the whining and one-upmanship! Gabriel thinks the schoolmaster life will leave him more time for his writing. And I'm an artist, so I can work anywhere.'

'But there must have been a lot of interesting people …' Fen didn't respond to this, just beckoned for the joint. She dragged deeply, frowning, and Eve wondered if she had unwittingly blundered in some way. 'Tell me about your art,' she said.

'I'll show you it to you sometime. When I'm feeling suitably brazen. It's – well. It's honestly rather a bore to talk about. How about you?'

'I—' Eve felt herself flush and was glad of the cover of darkness. 'I used to work in policy research. I liked it. But ever since Milo … Well. He's my son. He's nearly three.'

'Really? I assumed you were child-free.' Fen said this as if it were a compliment, and Eve was immediately pierced with remorse, thinking of Milo tucked up in bed under the watchful eye of the matron.

Someone was walking up the drive. As she passed through one of the pools of light cast by a lamp-post, Eve saw that it was Alice Gainsbury. She must have come from the pool – she was carrying a gym bag and her long mousy hair was dripping down her back. She stopped and frowned in their direction for a moment, but moved on.

Eve laughed guiltily.

'Who was that?' Fen asked.

'The chaplain's daughter. She's clever, I think, but a bit of a loner.' The girl had wide-set, rather staring eyes, and Eve had felt under her scrutiny on more than one occasion. For someone so on the fringe of things she was oddly self-possessed.

'Maybe we should have invited her to take a puff. Misfits need to stick together.'

'Is that what we are?'

'Oh, I do hope so,' said Fen, blowing smoke through her nose. 'Misfits are some of the most powerful people on this planet. Anarchy doesn't scare us and convention can't stifle us.'

Anarchy scared Eve. But just then, it seemed rather inviting.

———————

When Eve woke up just before seven the next day, to Milo's snuffles and squeals, there was a moment when she couldn't identify the optimism she felt as she hauled herself out of bed. Sundays were family days: the boys were occupied with homework or else watching videos and playing pool in the common room, under the supervision of the assistant housemaster. But today, Eve's usual feeling of Sunday release was compounded with a new and happy restiveness. The morning glowed blue, and the burst of crimson on the maple outside her window was like a shout of welcome.

The boys would be making the most of their weekly lie-in, and Eve usually took Milo so Peter could have one too. But Peter wasn't in bed and his running shoes were gone. When he arrived home for breakfast, smiling and flushed, his hair sticking up in sweaty tufts, Eve felt a gust of affection. However long the working day, however worried he was by a student's unhappiness or recalcitrance, Peter's Cleeve-bestowed gleam was a youthful one. Boyish, almost. But Eve liked that thought less. So she kissed him – a real, open-mouthed kiss – and tasted the salt above his lip and breathed in his animal tang, *mmm!*, and he looked at her with surprise and pleasure.

After breakfast, she bundled Milo into the buggy and went for a walk that took her past the cluster of faculty houses by the Lodge. She only half-admitted to herself that she was hoping to bump into Fen. But even at ten in the morning, the curtains of the Eastons' little cottage were firmly drawn.

Fen wasn't at chapel, either, though her husband was. Eve had slipped into the habit of going to the Sunday-evening service, leaving Milo and his father to have tea together. To her own surprise, she found she liked the old-fashioned, forthright hymns and the lulling of the prayers. Under a glaze of boredom, the students' faces were at rest and so seemed more open, more vulnerable to her assessing gaze: *spoiled, druggy, swot, slut, spoiled* ... And yet, for all this, her feelings in chapel were mostly mild.

Eve hadn't paid Gabriel Easton any attention before, but now he was one of those whom she watched covertly from across the aisle. It made sense that Fen's husband would be handsome: tall and lean with a sweep of salt-and-pepper hair and a darkly jutting face. He seemed to listen intently throughout the service, though he didn't join in any of the singing or responses. Eve considered introducing herself on the way out, but the First Lady button-holed him first. Perhaps she was enquiring as to the whereabouts of her powder puff.

Eve's optimism carried through to Monday morning, when she went to her job in the archivist's office. The archivist was a taciturn elderly man, who jealously guarded the more interesting records. As his assistant, Eve's main task was to create catalogue cards for the school magazine, which had been in publication in one form or another since 1870 and was mostly a dreary list of house reports and games results. Only the creative writing section provided fitful amusement. That morning, flicking through the December 1963 edition, her eye was caught by *On Seeing a Bowl of Freesias*, written by one James A. Pugh. *A bunch of golden freesias, what do they remind you of? To me, the green leaves are the essence of Old England. They remind me of the strong tranquillity of our countrymen, raised on our green, rolling hills. The flowers are golden like the many gifts we have given the world* ... Eve imagined this being read aloud in Fen's richly amused voice. Perhaps she should put it to one side to show her later.

I'll find you, Fen had said when they'd parted. *Leave it to me.* It had sounded like an instruction. But when it came to Tuesday evening and there was still no word, Eve snapped first at Peter and then Milo, whose look of bewilderment nearly undid her. She felt as if she was a teenager with an unrequited crush. It was humiliating, and it made the indistinct anger that had lately begun to thrum quietly away, somewhere deep inside her core, thrum all the louder.

Then on Wednesday morning, one of the squits scampered up to her with an envelope. 'It's from the new b– from Mrs Easton,' he said, blushing and gulping. Inside, there was a note.

Anarchy & cocktails?
Come to supper. Let's shake things up. x

Eve wondered afterwards if this was the moment when everything started to unravel. Generally, she felt that the disaster awaiting them had its own tragic inevitability. It was perhaps easier to think of it that way. But there were times when she thought no, that there was instead a series of tipping points, each one avoidable, and this was the first of several occasions when she could have pulled back. She could have stopped drinking after the second martini, talked more of Milo, less of her complaints. She could have been more reticent and less dazzled. As it was, she feared she unwittingly gave Fen all the encouragement she craved.

They each drew the other on.

ALICE

The new girl who'd said that Henry Zhang was fit, for an Asian, was called Bette Drummond, and I heard her name a fair amount, both from the faculty high-ups and the more lowly support staff, because almost from the first she was marked out as a leader. A leader of boys is seen as wholesome and heroic. A leader of girls is, of course, a more unsettling thing.

St Wilfred girls liked to sneer at the Cleeve girls' lack of style. Outdoorsy Cleevians favoured pastel polo shirts with the collars popped, gilets, low-slung jeans. The more bookish types were generally found in long plaid or floral skirts and sloppy knits. Bette stuck out because she was pretty much the only girl in the school with short hair, cut in a feathery pixie crop, à la Winona Ryder. And she dressed in dinky little tea-dresses worn with oversized granddad cardigans and black Chelsea boots. The boots were edgy, for Cleeve. All the other girls wore penny loafers.

There was, however, nothing unconventional about

Bette's prettiness. Her pixie crop was dark gold, and her features were pixie-like too: a droll little mouth, large hazel eyes and a tip-tilted nose. I'd see her sitting on the Lawn or strolling along the Avenue or lolling on the benches outside her dorm, and notice how the other girls always leaned in towards her, laughing at her jokes, looking at her for agreement, waiting for her to make their collective decisions.

Of course, there's a leader in every intake. I suppose I paid this one more attention than the others who'd come and gone because we were peers. And because I'd seen that Henry Zhang watched Bette Drummond, too.

What I hadn't anticipated was that Bette was watching *me*.

———————————

'Hello there. It's Alice, isn't it?'

I was on my way back from school. Four lower-sixth girls were dawdling by the Lodge. In their uniform of grey tweed skirts and pale blue blouses they looked like a cluster of Edwardian governesses.

'Yes?' I said cautiously. (How did she know my name?)

'I'm Bette.' Her voice was low for a girl's, and unexpectedly husky, but the chime of confidence came through loud and clear. 'I was wondering if you could help us with something. Because you know everything about this place, don't you? You grew up here?'

'Mm,' I said, non-committally. (Again, how did Bette know this? She'd only been at Cleeve five minutes.)

'Well, here it is. There's a repulsive lie going around about a friend of ours. Julius Simmonds and Tom Astley are saying that she blew them both at the social last Saturday. It's disgusting, and it's not true.'

'Simmonds and Astley are dicks,' I said matter-of-factly. 'Everyone knows it. Nobody with any sense will believe them.'

Bette's eyebrows flew up. 'That's hardly the point.'

She was right to be outraged. But I sensed that she was also savouring the drama of the situation and the way that the other girls were hanging on her words. One of them had her arms tightly folded across her chest. I looked at her, and she looked away. Her eyes were puffy.

'And that's why they need to be shamed in turn,' Bette continued, husky voice throbbing, eyes wide. 'We know what we want to do. We just need some help. We need to be *united*.'

She'd assumed I'd be flattered to be involved, or at least eager to show solidarity. I didn't see why she needed me, though. A girl like her – clever and popular – could plot any kind of revenge without having to recruit outsiders to the sisterhood. So I kept my expression neutral. 'I see.'

I found Bette Drummond interesting because I found all the big personalities on campus interesting. The benign dictators and the tyrannical ones. The lions and pirates.

The kittens who purred and the kittens who clawed. But I wasn't going to kid myself that I would ever be a part of their world, any more than they would ever venture into mine. I wasn't sure I wanted this to change, however worthy the cause. And this, I now saw, interested Bette.

She passed me a sheet of paper. 'Take a look. How would you feel about helping us access a photocopier?'

I looked at the flyer. It had the school crest at the top with a photograph taken from the school magazine of the boys in question – grinning, arms around shoulders, after a rugby match – stuck in the middle and a printed caption below: CLEEVE COLLEGE WELCOMES PERVERTS & LIARS.

I hesitated, just as I'd hesitated when those townie skanks were tormenting the squits. I hadn't wanted to be forced into an alliance with Cleeve boys, and I didn't particularly want an alliance with Cleeve girls either. But, as it happened, Julius Simmonds had been the genius to come up with 'Fishface', way back in his own squit days.

So I smiled a little as I handed the flyer back. '*Discere, Docere, Seminare.*'

Bette frowned and the other girls looked confused.

'Learn, Teach, Spread,' I translated.

'I know what it means,' Bette said impatiently. 'But—'

'It's the school motto.'

'Oh, that's *good*. Yes. Let's write it in ... Does this mean you'll help?'

'I suppose so.'

'It's very much appreciated,' said one of the sidekicks. As if she was thanking one of the hall servers for fetching an extra water jug. Bette shot her a scathing look.

'I know the code for the print room,' I continued, as if the other girl hadn't spoken, 'but staff are in and out of there a lot, even outside of school hours. A few of the head-of-department offices have copiers but they're hard to access. I think your best bet is the one in Archives, in in the basement of the Library. Nobody goes there once the archivist leaves at four, and I can get you the key. But I'll need it back as soon as you're done.'

Eve Winslow had a key. I'd seen it, neatly labelled and hanging on a peg behind her kitchen door, when I'd gone over to babysit. I couldn't see her or the doddery old archivist turning detective if their copier unexpectedly ran low on toner or paper. Plus, I hadn't liked the way she and the new beard had laughed at me the other night when I spied them smoking weed in the back drive, like a couple of townie kids on a dare.

'Thank you, Alice,' said Bette. She was queenly, but she wasn't condescending – I'll give her that. 'I owe you one.'

The flyers caused a minor sensation. A thousand of them were scattered throughout the school on the morning of an open day. I felt sorry for the cleaners and Facilities staff who had the job of clearing them all up. I don't think the student body took them seriously – the boys viewed it as a scandalous prank rather than a *J'Accuse* – but the faculty were almost as flustered as they were furious. They weren't used to this kind of defiance, especially from girls.

Simmonds and Astley adopted a pose of wounded dignity. Official talk of investigations and reprisals made the female intake 'practically ungovernable', according to their housemistress. Rumours of further insurrection swirled. Still, in a week or so the fuss had died down. I heard Pa tell Peter Winslow that he'd been asked to preach the virtues of reconciliation and forgiveness at Sunday chapel.

Pa being Pa, he didn't – instead, he gave the sermon on a particularly obscure aspect of Jesus's relationship with Jewish law. It was dense even for him. Bette gave the reading. Her husky voice carried surprisingly well; as soon as she began, I saw Pa's head snap upwards. This wasn't the piece of scripture he'd selected. Bette had gone for the Apocrypha, and the tale of Susanna and the Elders, in which a couple of Old Testament sex pests get their comeuppance. Henry Zhang was one of the congregants who got it ahead of the rest – I heard a delighted guffaw from the row behind me and knew it was him.

He was still laughing to himself when I fell in with him on the way out. 'Your dad should watch his back. It seems he's got competition in the fire and brimstone business.'

'Do you think the new gospel will have any effect?'

'Who knows. There's a certain species of creep who thinks that being branded a pervert is a badge of honour.'

Henry looked over to where Bette was receiving tributes from a ring of excitable girls. Her face wore the glow of heroism. 'But maybe times are changing,' he said. 'A female insurgency could be fun.' I didn't like the way he said this: it was flirtatious, but it was belittling too. And I knew the flirtatiousness wasn't for me. When Bette looked back at the two of us and waved, I ducked my head and moved on.

The next time, Bette didn't just wave: she called me over, leaning out of her common-room window to shout. Her throaty summons was unmistakeable.

I walked over slowly. 'Yes?'

'I said, I've got cake, and aren't you coming in?'

I hadn't been in the girls' boarding house before, and I'd only been in one of the boys' dorms when they were emptied out over the holidays and I was running some errand or other. This was the first Cleeve common room I'd entered when it was actually in use. Although the block was practically new, it still felt drab and utilitarian, despite the colourful bean bags and slouchy sofas. The floor was scattered with biscuit crumbs and empty crisp packets. Girls lounged with each other's heads in their laps, braiding hair or vacantly picking at their lips and nails. Ricki Lake was on the small TV set high in the wall. When I stood in the doorway it was like that classic saloon-bar scene from a corny old western. The stranger enters, and silence falls.

'This is Alice,' said Bette regally. 'Alice, this is everyone.' She twirled her fingers at the room. The girls looked perplexed. Wasn't I a townie? Or some kind of junior staff? 'Pass me my bag, would you?' she instructed a minion. Then, to me: 'Come on up.'

Sixth formers had their own bedrooms, though there wasn't room for much more than a bed and a desk and a narrow wardrobe. Bette flopped onto the bed and indicated I should take the chair. 'Sorry for the unsisterly welcome. The three girls you met the other day are the only ones who know about your role with the flyers, and they're sworn to secrecy. So the others don't know what to make of you.'

I looked around the small room. There was a silver-framed photograph of what were presumably Bette's parents on the desk and multiple Polaroids of Bette larking about with assorted photogenic friends. A colourful cotton sarong was draped over the window. The wall was plastered with magazine covers from *The Face* and *SKY*, and a poster of River Phoenix brooded above the bed. A shirtless Andre Agassi adorned the opposite wall.

'And what do *you* make of me?'

'I'm still working on it.' Bette reached down to pull a box out from under the bed. 'And, lo, a tuck delivery from the parentals. I wanted to say thank you for the photocopier, so dig deep.'

'Thanks.' I wasn't hungry, but it seemed churlish to refuse. Bette was unwrapping a package of brownies with a childish enthusiasm that was as unexpected as it was disarming.

'In my last school, we always pooled tuck,' she said, licking cocoa powder off her fingers. I saw her nails were bitten down, which also surprised me. 'People would lose their shit if they thought you'd been hoarding. Half of them were bulimics, which may have had something to do with it … I'm an army brat, you see, so I've been boarding since I was seven. All-girl gulags, up till now.'

'So what changed?'

'Daddy went to Cleeve. He always wanted a boy, so sending his only daughter here was the next best thing. What about you? How'd you end up at the local sin-bin instead of joining the sixth form here?'

'It wasn't a good fit.'

'And the townie comp is?'

'Not particularly. But I like the reasons for not fitting in there better.'

'You probably made the right call,' Bette conceded, wrinkling her tiny nose. 'Because the Cleeve natives are *definitely* restless. Underneath the polo-shirted airs and Latin graces – well, it's all a bit *Heart of Darkness*, don't you think? Heavy breathing and grunting. Eyes glittering in the undergrowth. Maybe even a shaken spear or two … I'm assuming that's why you dress the way you do.'

I blinked. 'Excuse me?'

'Well, you've obviously cultivated becoming part of the furniture because you think being sexless will keep you safe.' She did that finger-twirling thing again, this time in the direction of my clothes. 'All that weird baggy crap won't disguise you forever.'

I looked down at my outfit. Jeans, a boy's red plaid flannel shirt I'd found in one of the lost property bins, my school gym plimsolls. Come to think of it, I might have found the jeans in the lost property bins too.

'Look, you'll be gone from here in a year or two. You've spent so much time trying to stay invisible, what's going to happen when it's time to be noticed? You won't know where to start. I'm serious. This place has institutionalised you – neutered you – without you even realising it.'

I frowned. 'Why do you care?'

'I don't *care*. Or not particularly.' She rolled her eyes. 'I suppose I'm bored.'

I knew I should be offended. But it wasn't as if Bette was my first would-be meddler. Would this latest busybody succeed where all the others had failed? I pictured Bette in earnest consultation with the likes of Mrs Riley and, in spite of myself, I laughed.

Bette ignored the laughter. She scooted closer and reached for my hair, sweeping its drab curtains back from my face and piling it on my head. 'Look at you,' she instructed, indicating the mirror on the back of the door.

'What's that Hans Andersen story, the one about the magic tinderbox and the dogs? They had eyes the size of teacups. No, the size of towers. You have eyes like towers.'

I stared into my own eyes. My pale hair was piled high on my head. Bette moved my hand to hold it in place, then began pulling things out of the overflowing wardrobe.

'You're a swimmer, right? You've got the figure for it. Long and lean. Here, this has always drowned me.' She threw a black velvet jacket into my lap. 'And something fitted underneath. A plain boat-neck T-shirt or vest top. Actually, those jeans aren't hopeless. Slouchy's good. You just need some killer boots.'

Then she flopped back on the bed, sighing, eyes closed, as if suddenly overcome by boredom or the impossibility of the task. I got up to leave, trying to find the words to say thanks without sounding as if I'd been convinced of anything. 'I think—' I started.

Bette's eyes opened again. 'So tell me about Henry Zhang.'

EVE

Having made little or no attempt at redecoration in her four years at Cleeve, Eve was abashed to find the Eastons' cottage smelling of fresh paint. The kitchen was a buttery yellow, the living room an earthy terracotta. The standard-issue sofa and chairs had been replaced with a velvet sofa and worn leather wing-backs. The walls were crowded with interesting prints and paintings, lit by the glow of antique lamps.

'It's lovely in here,' she said, hugging her bottle of wine to her chest and breathing in the scents from the kitchen.

'One does what one can,' said Fen, grimacing. 'I rather feel as if I've been plonked down in a Lego house. The bricks are so *shiny* ... Mind you, our college digs were appropriately picturesque, but leaked heat like a sieve. I won't miss those East Anglian draughts.'

She told Eve that Gabriel had found the local pub – 'an absolute flea-pit, but he isn't picky' – and that she'd made a cassoulet. 'I adore peasant food, don't you?'

Eve wasn't a cook. Lunch was mostly Milo's leftovers; supper was often cheese and crackers. Peter usually ate the school meals, which were too stodgy for Eve's taste. The cassoulet wasn't to her usual taste either – pungent and animal, punchy with garlic. Yet as the wine flowed, she felt as if her wan Cleeve self was absorbing the colour of her new surroundings along with the richness of the meal.

It was almost like being back in London, in the world of grown-ups. Or college students, perhaps, except that the artisanal carelessness of the place wasn't the makeshift kind. Eve was reminded that when she'd lived on her own, or even in flat-shares, she had always put effort into her surroundings. She, too, used to paint her walls, finding quiet satisfaction in pale colours and clean lines, a lack of clutter. The trouble was, she was still treating her life at Cleeve as temporary, allowing the silt and scuffings of domestic life to layer themselves around her as if at any point she could simply shrug them off. Whereas Fen … Fen obviously had no such commitment issues.

And it seemed she'd decided to commit to Eve, too.

'Actually,' she confessed, sucking the last of her martini from the olive, 'we were bloody lucky to end up here. Headmaster Parish is a family friend of Gabriel's from back in the day. Strictly between us – even Parish doesn't know the particulars – Gabriel left St Ben's under a bit of a cloud.'

'Oh?'

'It's a tale as clichéd as time. The rapaciousness of youth, the vanity of middle age ... the insecurity of both. Inevitably – and messily – it all ended in tears.'

'Shit. I'm sorry.'

'It happens. We're working through it. Cleeve is meant to be a fresh start.'

Emboldened by the gin, Eve ventured, 'The, er, female sixth formers ...?'

'Good Lord, Gabriel's not *rampant*.'

Eve blushed, realising she'd overstepped the mark. But then, much to her relief, Fen laughed. 'Besides, my husband's weakness is for fragile hot-house blooms, all a-quiver with the singularity of their intellect. Not much danger of those here.'

'I know we should feel sorry for the Cleeve girls.' Eve rubbed the frosty rim of her glass. 'The school's still adjusting to a female intake. But these girls ... they're so *pleased* with themselves. And the way they look straight through you ...'

'Posh girls don't do diffidence. Or ambition. You'll get the odd mad and bad outlier, but most of them are as dull as tinned mince.'

Nearly all the bohemian types that Eve had met came from some kind of privilege, and despite Fen's mention of youthful sojourns in artists' squats and on the picket line for the miners' strike, she suspected Fen was the same. But she didn't pursue the subject. They'd moved into the living

64

room and she wandered around, looking at the pictures on the wall. 'Are any of these yours?'

'No. I'm having a bout of artist's block just at the moment. Right now it's easier to think of myself as a painter-decorator.'

'Didn't the school send someone to do the job?'

'I'm sure they would have, but I couldn't be arsed with the inevitable wrangling and delay. And I quite like painting walls – it's soothing. Whereas being boxed in by beige was not.'

'You should see the Laura Ashley nightmare at mine.'

'Ah. Well, if you really can't bear it I've got some paint pots I changed my mind about. How do you feel about Aegean Blue? Fuck it – if your living room's the same size as mine we could put on a first coat tonight! It's not even late.'

They opened up a tin and brought it under the light. A soft greenish-blue slop glistened within. Giddy with wine and bonhomie, Eve agreed. She suddenly couldn't think of anything worse than another morning waking up to those smug roses. When they got to Wyatt's, loaded with brushes, trays and paint, they found the place was silent. Milo was sound asleep and Peter had turned in for an early night, since it was the assistant housemaster's turn on duty. Eve and Fen put the stereo on low, found another bottle of wine and set to work. 'I never bother with masking tape and all that, however liquored up I am,' Fen informed her. 'I've got impeccable fine-motor skills.'

65

She was good as her word. Eve, however, struggled to keep her hand steady. She didn't care, feeling an almost primal joy as the flowers and trellises disappeared under a wash of mermaid blue. About half an hour in, Peter came down in his pyjamas and robe, squinting through the sleep in his eyes. When he saw Fen he apologised, flustered, and attempted to smooth down his hair.

'We're transforming ourselves,' Eve told him grandly, waving her brush aloft. Paint speckled the coffee table she was standing on. She could feel a blob stiffening on her cheek.

'Lovely,' he said doubtfully. 'Would you mind turning the music down a notch?'

'You missed a bit,' Fen called out as, re-smoothing his hair, Peter went back up the stairs.

The scene which greeted Eve the next morning – a painfully early one, thanks to Milo and her hangover – was not the triumph she was expecting. It seemed they should have used some kind of primer on the wallpaper, for the roses had re-emerged, lurking like malignant jellyfish under the blue. The coverage was patchy, to say the least, and the colour greener than she remembered. Eve surveyed the streaks and blobs, the crooked edgings, and felt distinctly seasick.

'I'll have a word with Joe Allen,' said Peter, and although he was being helpful (Joe was head of Facilities) Eve sensed his reproach. Unfairly or not, she had decided Peter was also to blame. They should have painted the house together, ages ago, with wine and music and mutual silliness. Why had she had to wait for Fen?

Peter duly organised for the room to be repapered and then painted magnolia. Eve said she'd go with whatever he liked: she'd moved on. The important thing was that life was changing. She'd dipped her toe into foreign waters and, one way or another, the dreary roses were gone.

———————————

From there on, Eve Winslow and Fen Easton's friendship was an established thing. They soon slipped into the habit of meeting in one or the other's house for coffee or cocktails every other day of the week. Or else they'd go for late evening strolls around the campus, arm-in-arm. Eve abandoned her lacklustre membership of the campus book group and events committee. She speeded up her walk, zipping past the likes of Nancy Riley with a cheery wave. She had more patience with Milo. The boys at Wyatt's said to each other that Winslow's beard must be getting some on the side.

Peter's relief at Eve's raised spirits was plain to see. 'I remember making my first friend at Cleeve,' he told her over the washing-up one Sunday evening. 'Harry Buller. I'd thought him horribly bumptious, at first. But he had a big heart to go with that braying voice. He looked out for me. That's when Cleeve started to feel like home.'

Harry had been Peter's best man but Eve had only met him a handful of times. Peter's contact with his fellow Old Boys was surprisingly sparse, but then Peter's devotion to his time at Cleeve was as much to the institution as the people. He got along with everyone, wherever he was and whoever they were, but he had no close friendships of the type Eve was used to forming with other women. It was, she supposed, a male thing and a public school thing combined.

'Fen's brightened you up no end, and I'm sure you're a good influence on her too.'

'How so?'

'Well, you're quite different people, aren't you? You're more of an introvert and that might well calm Fen down a bit.' He smiled. 'I think Gabriel finds her rather a handful.'

Eve raised her brows. 'Rather a handful' was how you talked about a disruptive child, not someone's wife. And she didn't much like being described as a 'good influence', either. As if she were a senior prefect, urged to set an example for the squits.

'How's Gabriel settling in?' she asked carefully. 'Is he … popular with the students, do you think?'

Peter rinsed the suds from the last of the dishes. He was being careful in choosing his words too, trying – as always – to be fair. 'I get the impression he intimidates them. Which isn't necessarily a bad thing. But he's got a very dry manner. He's used to teaching undergraduates, of course, and the brightest and best undergraduates at that. No doubt the adjustment is a touch bumpy.'

Eve herself was intimidated by Gabriel. Their paths crossed only fleetingly, as when she was at Fen's, he was usually working in the school library or else at the pub. When they did meet, he was unfailingly courteous, but wary-seeming too. Eve put this down to the fact he probably knew Fen had confided his infidelity to her. She pictured some ardent Cambridge undergrad – a bluestocking, as Nancy would say – winding a lock of hair around a finger and biting her ripe lip, as she hung on to the Hot Prof's every word. And, yes, it would be something, Eve thought, to kindle a spark in those chilly dark eyes.

It was several weeks before Fen showed Eve her work. Eve had expected something large scale and exuberant, in keeping with the flavours of Fen's cooking and the colours on her walls. But her canvases were generally small, layered in scratches of black ink – dense scribbles that were somehow both laborious and deft. Several depicted scenes from the darker edges of folk tales, of women suckling hedgehog-babies or girls vomiting frogs. Metamorphosis was a recurring motif. There was a series of nudes in flagrantly sexual poses, birthing their myth from between splayed legs. And so laurel branches thrust out from the forest of Daphne's pubic hair, and a monstrous spider crawled out from Arachne's. Blodeuwedd, the Welsh girl spun from flowers who was changed into an owl, trailed petals from her vagina that turned into a whirl of feathers, with sharp slashing talons and a cruel beak.

'They're incredibly striking,' said Eve. She'd crossed paths with quite a few creatives over the years, but she always felt inadequate responding to art, especially the art of someone she knew. Here, her fear of exposure was particularly ironic, given the images on display. The naked bodies represented all stages of womanhood, from the lithe curves of adolescence to the stringy or lumpen flesh of later life. But their faces – whether sly or vacant, ecstatic, enraged – were all, unmistakeably, Fen's.

'Nancy Riley is on at me to lead a wifely art class,' Fen remarked, shrugging off Eve's attempted tribute. 'No doubt she's hoping for some nice watercolours of the Lake.'

'Then I think you should do it. Give them all a shock. Didn't you say you wanted to shake things up around here?'

'Careful what you wish for, darling.' Fen's expression was unexpectedly serious. 'I mean it. I never start what I can't finish.'

ALICE

'Tell me about Henry Zhang,' Bette said, and then it all made sense. Bette wasn't the impulsive type. Before making any kind of move, she liked to do her research and be sure of her ground. I found out later that she'd been at three different schools before Cleeve, as the family had moved about according to her father's career. She was used to having to establish herself in new places and among strangers, and had developed strategies to make this work. I, with my insider knowledge and watchful eye, was to be one of these strategies.

So I told her what she wanted to know. Although Henry Zhang was a long way from being poor, money was tight, due in part to his parents' ugly divorce. He was a good student, if not an exceptional one, and planned to study Engineering at Leeds. He didn't lack for attention at the socials, and had dated a girl from one of the neighbouring boarding schools for a while, but she had been Asian too. So although Henry was quietly popular, he wasn't among the established big names on campus – boys like Rupert von Aldstine, who was rumoured to be dating a minor royal, or Toby Belling-Blythe, who'd grown up in a stately home in Cornwall, or Niko Diamandis, son of a Greek shipping magnate.

Bette must have already known most of this, but she listened to me thoughtfully all the same.

'Do you like him?' she asked me at the end.

My heart seemed to be noisily beating everywhere – in my head, in my feet, in my belly and my groin.

But I held her gaze. 'Would it make a difference if I did?'

Bette smiled appreciatively. 'A difference to me or to him?'

'Henry wouldn't ever date me.' *And the truth shall set you free.* 'Whatever clothes I wore. However … visible … I became.' I was still God's daughter at best. Fishface at worst. Henry's position in the Cleeve hierarchy wasn't so established he could afford to take chances, let alone risk being the punchline to a school joke. To claim his seat at the top table, he needed a girl like Bette on his arm. Bette understood this too.

I marched home that evening and told Pa I needed some money to buy clothes. He looked at me quizzically over his pile of marking. 'And what of the lilies of the field?'

'It turns out the lost property box is running low on useless proverbs.'

'I see. Hm.' He blinked a little. 'Buy what you need, then. There's some cash in the biscuit tin. Yes?' Then he waved me away and turned back to the fifth-form theology essays on the nature of the Trinity.

That night, I had a dream about Bette. I dreamed of finding her with her head bashed in, of seeing her pixie hair matted with blood and her pretty dress all filthy and torn. Henry was in the dream, crying, and I put my arms around him to comfort him. *Don't worry*, I told him, *we'll get through this together*.

I don't believe in premonitions. But even now, remembering the dream still turns me clammy with guilt.

The morning after, however, I shrugged it off easily enough – I had a shopping trip to distract me. The first thing I bought was boots. Not Chelsea boots, because that was Bette's look. I bought black Doc Martens, the real thing, with proper yellow stitching, unlike the knock-offs worn by the kids at my school. Their sturdy clump made me walk taller. After the boots, there wasn't much cash left, but I had just enough for some fitted T-shirts from Gap to go underneath Bette's velvet blazer, as well a long black slip-dress with a lace hem that I found marked-down in the weird goth shop in town. I decided I liked the plaid shirt from lost property. I wore it over the dress like a jacket. I piled up my hair and bought some eyeliner. Bette was right: invisibility needn't be my default after all.

The fact was, Bette needed me to look presentable if she was going to spend time with me. And she could afford to be generous: all the eyeliner and velvet in the world wasn't going to make a girl like me eclipse a girl like Bette. We both knew that. It's why I relinquished all my vain hopes of Henry for her. It was part of the unspoken contract between us.

A contract of mutual convenience, I suppose you might say. I got into the habit of swinging past the girls' common room after school on the days I knew Bette to be there. She'd shrug off her usual acolytes and we'd go to her room to eat tuck. Bette's tastes were defiantly lowbrow: she scorned Hall meals in favour of a diet of instant noodles, strawberry bootlaces, squeezable cheese and whatever cake her parents sent, all of which she kept under her bed, flouting the no-food-in-dorms rule. She even had her own (illegal) electric kettle so as to avoid the faff of using the kitchen. Even on sunny afternoons, she liked to keep her room dark. She'd put one of her gauzy drapes over the lamp, and in the noodle-scented shadows we'd talk and talk.

Bette was the first person I'd ever met who asked me questions I was actually interested in answering. *How would your life be different if your mother was alive? Why did you lose your faith? Do you want to be a lawyer because your dad was, and you think it'll please him? Or is it more likely to piss him off?* And she'd gift me things – a lace choker I'd admired on her once, a paisley scarf to tie up my hair. A cinnamon-scented lip balm.

In return, I spilled Cleeve's secrets. The two fifth formers who'd been caught by the PE master snogging in the gym

74

cupboard. The love triangle between Tracy in Catering, Ian in Facilities and John in Accounts. The squit princeling from Dubai whose father had telephoned the headmaster at the start of term to request accommodation for the boy's manservants. Mrs Easton smoking dope with Mrs Winslow. And so on. Bette found this tittle-tattle endlessly amusing and loved nothing better than being sworn to secrecy. '*No!*' she'd say, lips parted, cheeks flushed. 'You're *kidding*.' That was the thing about Bette: so cool and contained one minute, so unabashedly childish the next. She'd called me institutionalised, but for all her worldliness, I think she was too.

And so we'd play endless games of Would You Rather. *Would you rather be beautiful or clever? Poor or unlovable? Have a lifetime of bad breath or BO? Who'd you rather screw/marry/kill?*

Would you rather know how you're going to die, or when?

I worried this intimacy would end once Bette and Henry were together – which was unavoidable, yet took a little longer than I expected. 'He's difficult to read.' Bette was frowning and picking at her nails. 'Maybe there's something to be said for that whole inscrutable-oriental trope.'

I winced. 'Or he's playing hard to get.'

Bette lifted her brows and I could tell she was displeased by this idea. 'That's not how boys work. Sound him out, why don't you?'

I had perhaps slightly oversold my friendship with Henry to Bette, but I had the excuse of returning the book he'd lent me to waylay him the next day after dining hall. Our encounters were getting easier; now that I accepted he was destined for Bette, my heart had stopped its acrobatics.

'Thanks,' he said, as I passed him the book. Again, I was very conscious that our hands touched. 'Is it any good?'

'Sure. If gods and demons and Buddhism's your thing.'

'Well, it seems they're Mrs Easton's. She's doing some artwork inspired by it – she was talking about it at Art Soc.'

'I didn't know you're into art.'

'I'm not especially. But all the girls are, so Art Soc's suddenly got a lot more popular.' He grinned. 'You'd have liked Mrs Easton's talk. Lots of tub-thumping about the male gaze.'

'Why do you think I care about the male gaze?' Nonetheless, I recognised my own duplicity. I was wearing Bette's lace choker, after all.

Henry had noticed it too. 'You and Bette …' he began, then trailed off and looked at me sidelong. He was blushing slightly. 'You know, I liked it that you didn't give a fuck. In a place like this, that's a kind of superpower.'

Liked. Yes, that stung. 'Easy for you to say.'

'What does that mean?'

'I mean that you haven't got where you are by being unconventional.'

He looked displeased, the same as Bette had. I was abruptly tired of him. Or perhaps I was just tired of postponing the inevitable. 'But never mind that,' I said. 'Isn't it time you asked Bette to the social?'

So he did, and once he had, everyone at Cleeve pronounced them the perfect match. Her so pixie-ish and droll. Him so tall and laconic. And Bette didn't ditch me once they got together, keeping to our unspoken pact.

Now, when people noticed me, it wasn't because of my perceived oddness: it was because I was a friend of Henry and Bette's. Their wider social circle would say hi in passing. The squits no longer sniggered and stared. I'd come to some of the extracurriculars – lectures, concerts – and sit alongside the sixth-form girls. Sure, I still kept to myself, but this was more than ever by choice. I was grateful.

That's why I helped them. Leaving the school grounds without permission meant instant suspension, but it was a large campus, and I knew every one of its neglected storage lockers and basement passageways and other hidey-holes. The most infamous of these was a cabin in Cleeve Woods that had originally been used for the outward-bound club but had long since fallen into disrepair. Occasionally the maintenance team would be dispatched to put a new padlock on the door and another board on the windows, although enterprising adventurers always seemed to find a way in.

But I found somewhere better for Henry and Bette: the Chapel basement. I passed Pa's key to Bette, and one or other of them had a copy made in town. It wasn't without risk, of course, and it was hardly romantic either, since the place was a glorified cupboard crowded with old hymnals and broken chairs. It smelled of mould, with a single overhead bulb to light it. Still, perhaps the dilapidation was part of the appeal.

I was in the lower sixth, and I'd still not so much as kissed a boy. That didn't make me a total innocent. The Cleeve boys boasted, endlessly, of the fingerings and rubbings and suckings that went on at the socials, behind hedges, around corners, against walls. I'd overheard snatches of this my whole life, even if the stories weren't as blatant as the porno-magazine centrefolds found clinging to my school's chain-link fence or stuffed into the girls' lockers. Tales of advanced debauchery were as common as new haircuts after the holidays at Cleeve – most of them fantasy, I'd bet, but all described in terms of conquest and capture.

I remembered what Bette had said about Cleeve's heart of darkness. Panting and grunts, the glint of savage eyes. *Spears*. Was that Henry, with her? And did Bette like it?

Even now, part of me can't comprehend why I ever gave Bette the key. It made me go hot and cold with shame and envy, and it made me something far grubbier than a mere go-between.

I know what the tipping point was, though.

After meeting with Henry, to give him the book and tell him about Bette, I had happened to bump into my father. He had given me a long look. 'That boy. And that girl – the pretty one. Neither of them are going to do you any good.'

He was right, of course, and I suppose I knew it. It was inevitable my relationship with Henry and Bette was a hopelessly lopsided one. And in any case, the three of us were too young and, in our different ways, too insecure to manage ourselves better. But my father's warning didn't feel like a warning – it felt like a dismissal. What's more, the timing of it enraged me. *Now* he was taking an interest? *Now?* My father had left me to Cleeve for my entire life. Most of my meals were dining-hall leftovers. Most of my clothes came from the lost property bin. It was the cleaners and groundsmen who'd kept a protective eye on me around campus, and it was the housemasters' wives who found me things to do over the holidays. I'd taken myself to the matrons whenever I'd got sick. It was the school rowing coach who'd taught me to swim.

And *now* my father was telling me who I should or shouldn't be spending time with?

So, yeah, I guess that's what I had in mind when I invited Henry and Bette to despoil the sanctity of his chapel.

EVE

Fen and Gabriel came to dinner at Eve and Peter's, but it wasn't a success. Eve had been too ambitious with the food, attempting trout with a herb butter and breadcrumb stuffing. Slitting the raw, jellied flesh and packing it with the greasy crumbs made her feel clumsy and inadequate; fatalistically, she wasn't even particularly surprised when the fish turned out dry and needled with bones. The potatoes were undercooked.

She'd asked Peter to tidy up, but as ever, he'd been delayed or distracted, and when their guests arrived the place was still littered with Milo's clutter. Fen was wearing a low-cut black velvet tunic – though, being her usual slapdash self, the hem was coming down. Her easy voluptuousness made Eve – harried by the greasy fish and raw potatoes and all the Lego underfoot – feel narrow and crabbed. At once she regretted involving the husbands. Gabriel Easton already made her nervous and now Peter did too, because she sensed he didn't entirely approve of Fen, and Fen was in her most provocative mood.

A list had been found, behind the gymnasium, of all the wives and female teachers rated in terms of attractiveness. Whoever was responsible, the markings suggested it had been put to a wide-scale vote. To her shame, Eve's first thought was to wonder where she ranked. She had never been particularly insecure about her looks, but the way Gabriel Easton looked at her – *past* her – without even a flicker of interest, piqued her more than she liked to admit. It was not that she craved his attention, but it was crushingly obvious that he thought of her as being the same as all the other beards: just another under-educated, bored housewife.

Meanwhile, Fen was raging.

'Cleeve College,' she declared, 'represents everything that's wrong with this miserable island. It's a battery farm for the entitled, misogynistic little shits who end up running it.'

'Come now,' murmured Peter. 'That's hardly fair.'

'Indeed so,' said Gabriel dryly. 'Cleeve alumni are far more likely to end up estate agents and stockbrokers than government ministers or captains of industry.'

'Oh, pardon me,' said Fen, with dangerous sweetness. 'Objectively speaking, I should have made it clear that Oxbridge is awash with entitled shits too. But at least *they* have the decency to know their Latin declensions. Isn't that right, darling?'

Eve studiously avoided Peter's eye.

To change the subject, Peter asked Fen about her work, even though Eve had pre-warned him it was a sensitive subject. Peter, however, was well-used to drawing out information from the reluctant or recalcitrant. And so Fen was prevailed upon to explain her research into Chinese folklore and Buddhism, the writings of Wu Cheng'en, and the role of she-demons in Chinese mythology.

'The scorpion-goddess is my new muse. I'm planning a painting inspired by her.'

'The First Lady's portrait?' Eve inquired.

Fen laughed uproariously. Gabriel gave a wintry smile. Peter frowned and pushed his plate away. Soon afterwards he disappeared, summoned by the matron on house duty. This was typical. Last Saturday night, somebody had deliberately blocked the toilets with pages torn from a biology textbook. The week before somebody had eaten soap as a dare. This time, Peter told them on his weary return, one of the first years had allegedly put a curse on another. Pentangles had been drawn in red ink all over the victim's school handbook; hysterics had ensued.

'There must be something in the air,' said Gabriel. 'I interrupted a séance the other evening, in the cricket pavilion of all places. A group of second formers were scaring themselves silly by trying the raise the dead.'

'Who were they trying to summon?' asked Eve, intrigued.

'The Cleeve ghost. Some unhappy spinster who threw herself off the Clock Tower.'

'No, the school ghost is a girl who hanged herself in the Laundry twenty years ago,' said Fen. 'Joe Allen told me when he came to fix to the boiler.'

Gabriel shrugged. 'According to my second formers, she was a Victorian jilted bride.'

'Peter will know,' Eve said.

He had been staring down at his plate and looked pained at being asked to adjudicate. 'The school ghost is Lady Lilian,' he said reluctantly. 'A nineteenth-century daughter of the house who jumped off the tower in her wedding dress. AKA "the White Lady".'

'I told you so,' said Gabriel.

'That was the story doing the rounds in my day, anyway. Her papa was supposedly so broken-hearted he sold up and turned the family home into a school. I'm pretty sure the whole thing is an invention of some pint-sized Baron Munchausen.'

'No, I can believe it,' said Fen. 'The spirit of a woman scorned. The air here must be lousy with them.' She flicked a crumb of bread at Eve. 'What do you think, Eve? Shall the two of us haunt these hallowed halls once we're gone?'

In a transparent effort to change the subject, Gabriel asked Peter about discipline at Wyatt's. 'I suppose tonight's high jinks must be pretty typical. Von Aldstine's one of yours, isn't he? Reining him and his pals in must have been quite a challenge over the years.'

Peter looked uncomfortable. 'I gather things at home have been rather tricky for Rupert so, yes, there's been a bit of acting out. But he's more sensitive than people give him credit for.'

Fen snorted into her wine glass.

'Your house prefect's always inspired confidence,' said Eve hastily. 'And he's popular. I'm sure he helps keeps things in hand.'

'Zhang? Yes. Mind you, he's been a bit distracted this term. A new girlfriend and all that. But I'm lucky with the mix at Wyatt's, on the whole. They're a good bunch.'

'And don't they know it,' said Fen.

Peter excused himself and went to bed early. Gabriel said he had to get back to do some marking. The two women stayed on in the kitchen, drinking wine. Peter had left the pentangle-adorned handbook on one of the countertops and Fen picked it up idly. It was a slim blue volume entitled *The Cleeve Companion*. The leatherette cover was stamped with the school's crest in gold, and it contained a short history of the school, a map of the campus, a list of the clubs and other useful information, as well as a selection of prayers designed to address everything from homesickness to exam worries. It was the prayer section that had been most heavily graffitied with pseudo-demonic scribblings.

The first page after the headmaster's welcome letter was grandly titled 'Expectations'.

Cleeve College expects

- that a student will never mispresent the work of others as their own
- that a student will never take or deface the property of others, nor the property of the school
- that a student will never use intoxicants of any kind

And so on.

Fen read the list aloud in richly rolling, sardonic tones, exactly as Eve had imagined her reading out the creative writing piece about freesias from the school magazine. Because of the wine, it all struck her as incredibly funny.

'You do realise that we broke most of these "expectations" the first evening we met? Trespass! Theft! Intoxication!'

'Then maybe we should have another go,' said Fen. 'But work our way through the whole list this time. With a little luck and application, we could cross everything off by Easter.'

'You're not serious.'

'Plagiarising, cheating, drinking 'n' drug-taking, lying, stealing, trespassing, failing to report a violation ...' She ticked them off her fingers. 'Any one of those activities is a hundred per cent more fun than another round of watery coffee with the beards.'

'You missed out sexual delinquency.'

'Right! What would it take for you and Peter to have a quickie in the cricket pavilion?'

'As long as we don't have to combine it with a séance ...'

'So you're in?'

Eve hesitated. The idea seemed, in the moment, impossible to take seriously. A little bit of mischief. Some harmless fun. 'I'm in.'

They linked pinkies, laughing at their own ridiculousness.

'Where shall we start?' Eve asked. 'At the top of the list?'

Fen moved off to open another bottle of wine. 'Trespass is the perfect gateway crime. How would you feel about a midnight swim?'

———————————————

On the night of their break-in, Eve lay in bed next to Peter as wide-eyed as a kid on Christmas Eve. Just before one, she bundled some clothes on over her swimsuit and slipped out of the house, where the cold November air met her face like a slap. Eve had never been much of a rule-breaker at school, and her time at university had been overshadowed by the loss of her parents. True, her twenties had been enlivened with the usual amount of disreputable bars and the men she found there, impromptu travel, a spontaneous adventure or two. But during those years, the idea of a husband, and a house and a child, had seemed a mysterious, almost exotic, prize. They were something to be won after a series of challenges – not the challenge itself. *That* was what she had unaccountably failed to grasp. She thought of the Cleeve girls, slinking about and tossing their hair, so ignorant and self-satisfied, and she felt an angry kind of pity. Doubtless, they assumed it would be different for them. But they had no idea. No idea at all.

And now here she was, the teenage rebel she'd never been, running wild through the elite institution she'd never attended. The campus was deeply asleep, the amber pools cast by the pathway lamps the only light source other than the moon, which was sailing high in a sky studded with stars. Fen had swiped a copy of the night-time security guard's schedule from the Lodge, but even so, any faint movement in the shadows made Eve start, guilty laughter bubbling in her chest.

Fen was waiting for her at the side entrance to the pool. She had the code to the door scrawled on the back of her hand and was brandishing a thermos. 'Martinis,' she said. She put her hand to her mouth and belched gently. 'You can't have a pool party without martinis.'

They went in without turning on the lights. The north end of the pool hall was a sheet of clear glass looking onto the wood, and was generally covered by blinds. Fen opened them so that moonlight streamed in. They undressed quickly, shivering slightly despite the fuggy warmth of the place. Eve was wearing a plain black one-piece and so was Fen, who looked both fleshy and unexpectedly muscular in hers. The two women waded down the steps into the water, exclaiming at the chill.

Fen reached for the Thermos and poured Eve a measure into the cap, swigging from the cannister herself. 'All that's missing is music.' Her voice was already slurred and seemed too loud in the oddly underground acoustic of the hall. Eve realised she must already be quite drunk.

Eve winced as the alcohol hit the back of her throat. Although she was not much of a swimmer, she splashed around, partly to keep warm and partly to persuade herself that this was as fun as she was expecting. Her natural cautiousness had begun to reassert herself. She peered out at the night and the black tangle of trees outside the glass.

'Shit.'

'What?'

'I don't know ... I thought ... for a moment ... I thought I saw somebody out there.'

Fen just laughed.

'The security guard's not due for another forty minutes, right?' Eve asked.

'Maybe he changed his schedule.'

'If it wasn't the guard, then what if it's somebody else up to no good?'

'Then they're hardly likely to sound the alarm on us, are they?'

Fen hauled herself out of the water. Eve thought she was going to close the blinds. Instead, very leisurely, she pulled down the straps of her swimsuit, smoothly easing it off her body and then kicking it aside. It lay in a sleek black puddle on the tiles. Eve thought of discarded sealskins, selkies, as – half-mesmerised – she watched Fen, entirely naked, stand before the glass, with her arms raised in a kind of triumph or else challenge. Then she turned and dived into the pool.

It felt like a very long moment before Fen came back up. Her curls had straightened, hanging around her face in long black snakes and rippling over her heavy breasts. In the semi-darkness, her eyes were the same silvery colour as the moonlit glass.

'What the fuck?' Eve hissed, splashing over. 'What if they saw you?'

'Relax. There's nobody out there. You were imagining things.'

Fen's underwater flesh was greenish white, apart from the dark triangle between her legs. A selkie. A siren. The water rocked in its tiled prison.

'You should get naked too.' Fen looked at her, as if she knew exactly what Eve was thinking. Her voice grew low and her mouth curved. 'Maybe we should throw in sexual delinquency while we're at it. Cross another expectation off the list. Hey – what if we got blind drunk and fooled around in the pool and ended up drowning by accident? Imagine if our naked corpses were discovered floating here in the morning! Would *that* shake things up enough?'

Eve just stared. There was a long moment. Then Fen flung back her head and laughed – too loudly. The sound was an explosion. Eve could almost feel its reverberations shudder through the water. 'I'm joking, obviously. Nobody has to drown.' Fen lifted up her arms again and then smacked them down, sending an arc of water shooting upwards. 'Whooo-*hooo*. Let's have another drink.'

For a moment, Eve hesitated. Then she too crashed her arms down, again and again, so that the water struck her flesh and the chlorine stung her eyes and she was surrounded by a dazzle of spray. She threw back her head and cried out – her own primitive ululation.

Whooo hooo, whooo hooo, whooo hooo.

ALICE

Cleeve has pretentious names for the school year, along with everything else. The autumn term is Advent, spring term is Lent and summer term is Trinity. By the second week of Lent, there was trouble in paradise.

Bette was clever. She was one of only two girls taking Latin for A-level, alongside History and English, and was set on reading English at one of the grandest Oxford colleges. She approved of my plan to study Law: 'There's something very precise about you, Alice. Analytical. I find that reassuring.' Bette liked to be in control, and she liked to be prepared. But as I got to know her better, I came to realise that her need for due diligence on everything from prospective boyfriends to brands of soap was a defensive measure, because her imagination was constantly running away with her. 'I can't trust my intuition,' she said. 'It gets me into mad panics and terrible scrapes. That's why I need you. You're so much more grounded. You're like Henry that way.'

One of the ways Bette's imagination got the better of her was over Henry. She was constantly second-guessing him. I found this insecurity surprising, especially given it was Henry who most obviously benefitted from their relationship. Since dating Bette, Toby Belling-Blythe had asked to be his study-partner and Rupert von Aldstine – who was in the year above – invited him down over Christmas. I saw Henry in fist-bumping huddles with these and other lions and pirates, or else in brotherly cahoots with Bette's hangers-on. The skinny, uncertain boy who'd once stared at me in the swimming pool seemed a vision from another life.

Or maybe Henry wasn't quite so sure of himself after all.

'I don't always know where I am with Bette,' he said to me, out of nowhere, as we walked back from the bus stop together one Saturday afternoon. 'She blows hot and cold. It's intense.'

I could have said the same. I told myself this was because Bette was so busy, and not just with Henry. Cleeve students had packed schedules, what with all the prep and extracurriculars they had to fit around lessons and sports. Even for sixth formers, free time was doled out in small, stingy blocks, mostly between lessons and before meals. Saturday afternoons and Sundays were more leisured but Henry, being both sporty and a prefect, had even less free time than most. And Bette was having extra Latin coaching with Mr Easton on the weekends. Everyone was scared of Mr Easton.

That day, Henry and I met her outside the Humanities block. She was loaded down with textbooks and seemed distant and distracted. When Henry asked her how the extra studies were going, she answered him shortly.

'Easton's a slave-driver,' he said. 'Worst gog on campus.'

'I thought all you boys were eternally grateful to him on account of his trampy wife.' Bette furrowed her brow in mock innocence. 'Didn't she top that "most fuckable" list of beards and dinner ladies that was doing the rounds? I'd love to know who got your vote.'

'You know I didn't have anything to do with that.'

'Seems to me there's a lot of things I don't know about you.'

Henry caught my eye over her head. *You see?*

He moved on, out of patience. The moment he was out of hearing, Bette clutched my arm. 'Henry's up to something. Something bad. Now he's got in with the von Aldstine set, everything's changed. They're always in a huddle, you know? It's fucking *sinister*.'

I looked at her hand, at the bitten-down nails. The skin around them looked sore. 'Boys will be boys, pigs will be pigs. Henry's just playing along.'

'No, this is different. There's something *up*. Plotting and whispering, and Henry's mixed up in it somehow. And he won't talk to me.' Her eyes were a little too wide, her breath a little too hot. She seemed feverish. 'You can find out, can't you, Alice? For me?' I started to object but she carried on talking over me. 'Because there's something fixed up for Saturday night. After hours, on campus. Hetty overheard Niko talking about it with one of the Rolfe twins.'

'OK, so they're sneaking out to drink or smoke or whatever. Big deal.'

'They could be meeting girls.'

I stared. 'From where? The town? Doesn't seem that crowd's style, let alone Henry's.'

'Then follow them, see what they're up to. Go on. I'd get into hideous trouble if I was caught sneaking out – the housemistress already has me down as an agitator. But *you* can come and go as you please.' Bette was calmer now. Her fingers curled around my arm again, but their pressure was more affectionate than urgent. Her eyelashes quivered and her head was tip-tilted in a way that any boy must find irresistible. I softened too, despite myself. 'I know I'm sounding paranoid. But I don't like being in the dark. And you always know everything that goes on around here.'

I was well aware Bette was flattering me. Still, it felt good to be confided in again. And it was true Pa had never needed to set a curfew so I had near total freedom to roam. I knew the security guard's timetable, too. *That* didn't require much insider knowledge, mind you. It hadn't changed in years.

Most of the boarding houses had their own tried and tested escape routes. Bolts had been screwed into the frame of ground-floor sash windows to prevent them being raised more than eight inches or so, but these could always be worked loose with time and effort. Skylights were also popular. If you could get from them onto the roof, you could make your way down via a fire escape or, in the case of Hawkins House, a helpfully positioned tree. Then there was the trick of sticking gum or Blu-Tack onto the motion sensors. So although break-outs weren't frequent, I'd witnessed more than a couple during my night-time excursions over the years. And then there was Hazard Night, of course, when boarding-house doors were left deliberately unlocked for an hour of sanctioned mischief-making. But I always stayed safely shut away at home for that.

That afternoon with Bette, I was feeling restless anyway. Although I didn't like being drawn into her and Henry's soap opera, an espionage mission had its appeal. Nobody could challenge me on campus at midnight; here, at least, my freedom would be absolute.

According to Bette's eavesdropping source, Henry and his cronies were meeting by the Clock Tower just after midnight. So I simply got there ahead of time and stayed out of sight, waiting. Sure enough, at the appointed hour dark figures began to sidle into view: first two, then three, then five. Their faces were hidden by scarfs and caps and their movements were purposeful. No giggling or high-fiving. Henry was easy to spot; I'd know his rangy frame anywhere. Rupert von A was marked out by the gleam of blond hair ruffling out from under his beanie. After checking watches and briefly conferring, they set off in the direction of Cleeve Woods, making sure to avoid the CCTV cameras that were fixed to the more high-prestige buildings. I was much more sure-footed than they were in the dark. After all, however familiar this place was to them, it was pretty much the whole world to me. One way or another, I'd spent most of my life in its shadows.

It wasn't hard to work out where they were going: the derelict cabin that had once been HQ for the outward-bound club was less than ten minutes' walk along the footpath. I watched from a safe distance as the boys spent a minute or so fussing with the boarded-up windows before shifting a plank of plywood aside and squeezing through. Someone had gone ahead, for there was a faint glow coming through the cracks. A burst of laughter met the final arrival, who got his leg stuck on the rotting window frame. Then someone repositioned the plywood and it fell quiet again. I could hear talking, but it was muted, and I wasn't close enough to make anything out.

It was all just as I'd thought: a few mates downing shots together and calling themselves an elite drinking society. I decided to peek inside. Perhaps there would be some weird homoerotic hazing ritual. Smirking to myself, I stepped into the little glade where the cabin was situated. But I was stopped from going any further by a hand on my arm.

I almost screamed. I'd been so sure I was undetected, I'd forgotten to be on guard for late arrivals. But it wasn't one of the boys. It was a unknown girl. 'Oh no you don't,' she said, with soft but unmistakeable menace. 'This here's invite only.'

I peered at her. There was just enough moonlight filtering into the glade to see her face. She was about my age, with thick make-up layered over tan skin and eyebrows as skinny as Bette's but not plucked so well. Big bold brown eyes, big gold hooped earrings. No Cleeve girl, that was obvious, but she was attractive, and that was obvious too. Her black puffa jacket didn't wholly disguise her curves. I began to think that Bette had been right, after all, and I was in the process of interrupting some townie hook-up. I took a step back.

The girl laughed a little. 'You don't remember me? Cos I remember *you*. You was there the first time I met the chink.'

Henry. I remembered her, then. In the skank v. squit face-off behind the shopping centre over two years ago. She'd been the girl who kept her counsel. Flicking ash on the squit's head with languid grace. Her sleepy cat's smile. She was smiling now. This time I noticed she had a chipped front tooth.

I looked past her to the cabin. I didn't feel threatened, exactly, but I was far from comfortable. The woods rustled.

'So you know the ... you know Henry?'

'Yeah, I know Henry. I know all of yous, really. All you Cleeve twats.' She put her head to one side. 'You're not the only one who likes to keep watch, Alice.'

I shivered. How the hell did she know my name? 'What are you doing out here, then – birdwatching?'

'It's a public footpath. I got as much right to be here as anyone.'

'So it's a public footpath … but a private party. And you're the bouncer.'

I meant it sarcastically but she gave a shrug of agreement.

Jesus. What the hell was going on in that cabin – sex? Drugs? Both? I tried to picture Henry in the thick of all this, and failed. But how well did I know him, really?

'All right then, Alice,' said the girl coolly. 'Time to fuck off.'

She obviously wasn't worried I was going to raise the alarm. I wondered exactly how much she knew about me.

I hesitated.

'Fuck off,' she said again, and this time it was almost kindly. 'Swear to God, there's nothing for you here.'

I didn't sleep well once I got home. I kept going over the encounter with the strange girl, and each time I came to a different conclusion. None of them were good. The prospect of facing Bette, and having to tell her that her worst fears were probably realised, made my stomach churn. It looked as if Henry wasn't the person either of us thought he was. This should have made things easier for me. Instead, it filled my head with ugliness and sharp edges.

It felt as if I'd only fallen asleep for five minutes before my father rapped on the door. 'You have a visitor,' he announced. Blearily, I squinted at my clock. Pa is an early riser, but seven o'clock on a Sunday morning is definitely not my chosen wake-up call. Bette must be even more desperate than I thought. Slowly and resentfully, I pulled on my dressing-gown and went downstairs. In the chilly morning light it seemed even more ridiculous that I'd got myself mixed up in all this. Whatever *this* was.

But the person waiting impatiently on our doorstep was Henry.

Startled, I pulled my tatty dressing-gown more tightly around me. I wondered if my nose was shiny. I regretted not brushing my hair.

'Hello,' I said warily.

'Sorry to disturb your morning like this. I know it's early. I just really needed to talk to you.'

Henry didn't look his best either, to be fair. It was the first time I'd seen him wearing glasses in a long time, and they were unfashionable wire-rimmed ones. He looked tired and drawn. Should I invite him in, I wondered. But no. Pa would be there, padding around with his coffee pot and with his eyebrows all quizzical. I shut the door and joined Henry on the step.

'Lindsey told me you followed us to the cabin last night,' he said abruptly. 'I'm guessing Bette put you up to it.'

Lindsey. 'Bette's worried about you.' I adjusted my robe again. 'And after last night, it seems to me she was right to be.'

His face tightened. 'I wouldn't take Bette's concern at face value. This obsession about what I'm up to every minute of the day and night – it's suffocating.'

I rubbed my eyes. I felt very tired. 'Does it never occur to either of you that I might not want to talk, endlessly, about your relationship drama?'

'All right,' Henry said slowly, rocking on his heels. 'All right, yes, maybe it's unfair to burden you with our issues. But it's a bit late to claim you don't want to get involved. You've been involved from the start. And now you've gone all Special Ops just because Bette's got one of her mystery hunches. You're the same as me in that respect. Bette clicks her fingers and we both come running … Why *are* you so invested in her – this – us?'

Shit. Was I blushing? I remembered what Bette had said when I'd asked her why she cared about my need for a makeover. I decided to copy her insouciance too. 'At the start, I suppose I was bored.'

'And now?'

'Now …' *Now I feel stupid and wretched, and mad at you.* 'Now I'm getting pissed off. But I'm also curious. Who *was* that girl? Lindsey. She says she knows you. What was she doing there last night?'

'It was a drinking game. A night of drinking games, OK. Stupid and childish but that's all. You can leave Lindsey out of it.'

'So you want me to lie to Bette by omission.'

Henry sighed. 'I'm asking you not to stir the pot, that's all. I'm going to talk to her. I promise. You can trust me. After all, the two of us were friends before Bette came on the scene. Weren't we?'

Were we? I felt my cheeks go warm again.

In the grey light, his skin looked sickly. 'I just need to work some stuff out. That way nobody gets hurt.'

Bette appeared satisfied by the account I gave her of my reconnaissance mission. 'I can see I was overreacting now. I always do,' she said. 'My head fills with static, blackness – it's like I can't make sense of anything else.' Then, rousing herself: 'You were a total hero to track them through the woods like that. I would have been scared shitless and spoiled everything. God. Boys are *silly*, aren't they? If they want to be all macho and mysterious about some lame piss-up, then more fool them.'

More fool me, perhaps, but I wasn't ready to let this go. Henry's obvious agitation had got under my skin. I started wondering about the others who were involved – I'd spotted Rupert von A's white-blond hair in the dark, and I'd recognised Niko Diamandis too, because he was famously short. I assumed the Rolfe twins were the other two of the five, because Bette's friend had overheard them conferring with Niko about the meet-up.

Of the five boys, Rupert had the biggest following and the lordliest manner. Niko liked to party and dabbled in drugs; the Rolfe twins were known for pranks and mild insubordination. Rupert and Niko were in the upper sixth, the others in the lower. Henry and George Rolfe were the only ones of the set to have steady girlfriends, and Henry was the only one who didn't come from serious money. He also had a lower profile than the others – at least until he started dating Bette. I didn't know what all this added up to, if anything, and I suppose I would have done as Henry asked and let it go if there hadn't been an almighty bust-up between him and Niko two days later, in which Niko got a black eye.

'… and he was lucky the damage wasn't worse. If Henry Zhang hadn't been pulled off in time, there would have been a bloody nose, too.'

I heard this from Tina, who ran the tuck shop and was married to Phil, the groundsman who'd broken up the fight. Then I got another second-hand version from Bette, whose account was even more dramatic.

'I had no idea Henry has a violent streak,' she told me. She was pink-cheeked, excited, almost triumphant. 'He's usually mild-mannered to a fault.'

'So what was the fight about?'

The official line, which both boys stubbornly stuck to, was that it was a disagreement over match-fixing in cricket that had got out of hand. Nobody believed this for a second, but since neither were known trouble-makers, they had their sixth-form privileges docked for a week or two and were otherwise let off with a warning.

'Henry told me that Niko was spouting all this bullshit about the Chinese takeover of Hong Kong. And then he somehow brought Henry's mother into it, and Henry *lost* it. Honestly. Defending the honour of one's womenfolk with one's fists! So primal, isn't it?'

Again, Bette sounded admiring. At that point, she couldn't ever have imagined all that righteous masculine rage being turned on her.

Niko was known to be a bit of an arse, but I didn't find this explanation any more credible than the cricket dispute. It only made me more determined to find out more about the mysterious Lindsey. She'd made a shooing motion when she'd sent me off, as if I was an actual child, and the memory of it still stung. *Swear to God, there's nothing for you here.*

I judged her to be maybe a year or two older than me, but I'd never seen her at St Wilfred's, which meant she must have gone to the bigger comprehensive in the neighbouring town. St Wilf's was oversubscribed so it was still likely she lived in the area. In which case, there must be someone working at Cleeve who knew of her.

So I went to give Moira a hand with laying tables in Hall for the Friday formal. Moira's worked in the kitchens for years and likes to chat. Her daughter's a QC in London, married to a fund manager, and the two of them are always on at Moira to take early retirement and put her feet up in the nice little house they've bought her. Moira, however, intends to carry on working alongside her mates at Cleeve 'until they carry me out'. No doubt the likes of Mrs Easton would say that Moira's in the grip of some kind of workplace Stockholm Syndrome. But I've noticed they have a lot more laughs in the school kitchens than they do in the teaching staff's common room.

Anyway. As Moira put out the posh placemats and I went along behind with the napkins, I asked her if she knew a girl called Lindsey, about my age, with a chip in her front tooth.

'Sounds like Lindsey Bates,' she said. 'Why d'you ask?'

'I bumped into her the other day and she seemed to know a lot about the school. I was curious, I guess.'

'Well, Lindsey had a Saturday job here last term. In the Laundry, I think it was – one of her aunties used to work there, back in the day. And when I say back in the day, it was before my time, so twenty years ago at least. Hey, luvvie,' she said to Janet, who was sorting cutlery at one of the sideboards, 'it was Lindsey Bates, wasn't it, that worked in the Laundry with Helen? Our Alice was asking about her.'

'It was.' Janet came over to join us with the knives. 'But I'd be careful if I was you,' she told me. 'Bateses are trouble.'

'What kind of trouble?' I thought I might already know, however. I'd heard the Bates name before. Whenever people at my school traded tales of a neighbourhood bust-up, there was often a Bates involved.

Janet sucked her teeth. 'My sister lives on the same estate and she says police and social services come knocking on the Bateses' doors two days out of three. One of Lindsey's uncles went and got a smart new house in the Grove and folk say it's best not to ask where the money came from, because at least two of her cousins have done time. Proper villains, they are. And there was a Bates kid that hanged themselves and another one that ran off and another one that ended up in a nuthouse.'

Moira looked uncomfortable. 'Almost makes you believe in a family curse. But I never heard a bad word about Lindsey. A smart girl, Helen said, and a hard worker.'

Janet nodded. 'That may well be true.' Then she patted me on the arm. 'Still. Keep your wits about you, won't you, love? When it comes to a Bates, it's better safe than sorry.'

I tried my best to follow Janet's advice. I really did. In the end, it turned out that some of us were safer than others. All of us, though, were sorry.

EVE

The swimming pool break-in made Eve feel faintly uneasy whenever she thought of it. True, she had felt like a teenager again, but she had also remembered why she'd disliked those years of affectation and blunder. Fen liked to test boundaries, that was clear. The trouble was, Eve couldn't decide what her own boundaries were or how far she'd go to maintain them.

Certainly, Fen was nothing but gleeful when she rang Eve the next day. 'Wasn't it fun? There's a lot to be said for the healing power of water. And nakedness! It was like being back in the womb, but better, on account of the martinis ... You know, I'm starting to actually think we can *own* this place. Remake it in our own image, expectation by expectation! What do you think? Which one shall we try next?' Then, as if she sensed Eve's hesitation, her tone turned coaxing. 'It's your turn to choose.'

So Eve did. She went for cheating, because it was one of the more straightforward ones, and Nancy Riley's latest project was a cake-decorating competition in aid of the local fire station. Eve and Fen submitted a joint entry, which Fen commissioned from a baker friend whom she said owed her a favour. The result was a sponge replica of Cleeve's Clock Tower that looked more like an architectural model than a cake, complete with the marzipan figure of Lady Lilian in her wedding dress tumbling down the side. Since the theme of the competition was 'Heroes', their entry was not deemed eligible, though it still got an honourable mention from the judge. Eyes were collectively narrowed and lips pursed, but nobody was brave enough to call them out on it.

They celebrated by crossing 'intoxication' off the list. Strictly speaking, this had already been achieved several times over, but for ceremonial purposes they shared a bottle of vintage champagne in the Chapel, drinking out of the chalice used for communion wine.

Fen had swiped the champagne from the bursar's office where some grateful or ingratiating parent had left it for the headmaster. 'So that's thievery done too,' she said, stretching out luxuriously in her pew. Eve smiled to herself. Fen had a shoebox stuffed with her so-called beer trophies, for swiping the First Lady's powder puff had only been the first of Fen's petty thefts. One day, she said, she was going to make an art installation out of them all. Eve assumed she was joking, but you could never be sure with Fen.

'You know,' Fen mused, 'I think God might have the hots for me. When I said I'd like to use the Chapel this evening for private prayer, I'm pretty sure he winked.'

'I don't believe you.'

'All right. But he *definitely* smirked.'

'Only because he's working out the terms of your damnation.'

'Well, cheers to that,' said Fen, raising the chalice. 'Hell's where all the fun happens.'

That same week, two people had warned Eve off Fen in the course of one day. The first, inevitably, was Peter. The provocation arose from a marital spat over an old school friend of Peter's who was coming to visit. Eve had assumed they'd all go out together, or else eat informally at home, but Peter announced he would be meeting his friend that evening in the pub down the road from Cleeve. Alone.

'Didn't it occur to you I might want to go for a drink too?' It was lunchtime, always a fraught occasion, and Eve was trying to stop Milo throwing his spaghetti hoops on the floor. 'Monkey, please do *stop.*'

'But you don't know Anthony.'

'Exactly – *No*, Milo! – Your school pals are a mystery to me.'

Since being at Cleeve, Eve felt a renewed interest in the people from Peter's school days. She was curious to see if she could match them to the types she lived among now, or if they'd evolved past recognition.

'That's not true. You've met Harry plenty of times.'

The Winslows' wedding had been a quiet civil ceremony with only three friends apiece, given the awkwardness of Peter's warring parents being in attendance. Harry had performed his best-man duties with aplomb, keeping the peace and officiating at the lunch afterwards; his speech had recounted assorted Hazard Night high jinks in which he and Peter had painted the pillars at Cleeve's entrance gates pink and filled the headmaster's office with balloons. Harry was, to Eve's mind, perfectly pleasant and perfectly forgettable.

'You should have invited Anthony to spend the night.'

'He's staying with friends locally. In all honesty, I don't think the two of you would get along. Anthony and I weren't ever close. We're only meeting up because I was distracted when he phoned and couldn't think of an excuse to get out of it.'

Eve knew she was being childish but she couldn't stop herself. 'I'd still have liked to be included in your plans. We hardly do anything together.'

'But you're out all the time with Fen.' Peter's voice had a rare edge. 'The two of you are practically inseparable. In fact, I assumed you'd be seeing her tonight.'

'Are you jealous?'

'Maybe a little.'

Peter scooped Milo out of his high chair and gave him a sloppy kiss on his tummy. Milo screeched with joy and grabbed at his father with tomato-sauce-slick hands. 'Bad Daddy! Bad Daddy!' Peter never seemed to mind if Milo was covered in filth. He actively revelled in goopy fingers being stuck in his ear.

'I'm sorry,' said Eve, trying to mean it. She reached for the baby wipes. 'I still find this place quite lonely, you know.'

'There are other interesting people on campus apart from Fen. Gabriel showed me her artwork the other day.'

'Did he? I'm not sure Fen would have liked that. She can be very protective of it.'

'Perhaps she's afraid of what it might reveal.'

'What's that supposed to mean?'

'Well, you have to admit her work is very ... dark. Chaotic. Sexual.'

'And you object to that, do you?' Playfully, Eve tugged at his ear. They'd started having regular sex again, more or less for the first time since Milo's birth, and it annoyed her that Peter couldn't see that the renewed lightness, the *buzz*, that Fen had brought into her life had a lot to do with it.

'I found her vision disturbing. It's hard to explain. I'm not ...'

'Not an art critic, certainly.'

'No.' He was frowning. 'It's more that I don't ... I don't believe that Fen means well.'

Eve attempted a laugh. 'There's more to life than being well-meaning.' There were spaghetti hoops on her sweater and she went to change, Milo in tow. When she came back, Peter was still standing there motionless, hands in his pockets, his face troubled.

───────────

The second warning came from the First Lady, of all people, and was delivered only an hour or so after Peter's, when Eve was ambushed on her way back from depositing Milo at a birthday party for Penny Hammond's youngest.

'Coo-ee, Mrs Wyatt! Do you have a minute?'

Eve took a breath. 'I prefer Eve, actually. Or Mrs Winslow.' *You patronising cow,* supplemented Fen's voice in her head.

The First Lady twinkled rosily. 'Of course. Just my little joke. Join me, won't you?'

The last time Eve had been into the Parishes' private residence it had been at the drinks party where she had met Fen. In the early spring sunshine, the drawing room looked less glittering and more chintzy than Eve remembered. Mrs Parish arranged herself among the sofa cushions with a happy smile. '*Now* we're comfy! Tea?' A tray was laid out ready. 'Milk?' Her teeth were as shiny as her pearls.

Eve waited.

'I'm so glad we can do this, just the two of us. I was hoping to pick your brains about your friend Fenella, you see.'

'Oh?' Eve kept her tone cool.

'Mm. We're a little concerned.' *We?* 'She was seen picnicking the other day in the fields behind the tennis courts. Drinking a bottle of wine at half-past eleven in the morning, in sight of students. It wasn't the first occasion, either.'

Eve took a measured sip from her cup. 'Then shouldn't you be talking to Fen about it?'

'That would be the next step, certainly. However, I never like to cause undue fuss, not if there's a way of keeping things *pally*. Because it seems to me that you have Fenella's ear to a degree that even poor Gabriel does not. I would *hate* to put you in an awkward position, but a friendly word at the right moment could do a world of good, no?'

'Fen is hardly in need of an intervention, least of all from me.'

'There's no need to be defensive, dear – I'm not here to judge.' Mrs Parish laughed her pretty laugh. 'Let's face it, this place is enough to drive anyone to drink.'

Eve was so surprised her mouth actually fell open.

The First Lady put down her cup. 'Come now. You're not one of the paying customers. That means we can speak frankly to each other, yes? Because you've always been an odd fit here too; I could see that from the start. Though, in your case, that's not necessarily a bad thing.' She smiled. 'Tell me. What does Peter think of your friend?'

Eve was struggling to keep up. 'He, uh, likes Fen well enough. But he's ... he's not used to creative types.'

'You mean he's not used to strong women. That's what being brought up in a place like Cleeve will do to you.'

Eve's colour rose. 'That's absolutely not true of Peter. He's liberal. Enlightened. And I'm hardly a shrinking violet —'

'Yes, yes.' A dismissive flap of her hand. 'You're a modern woman and Peter's a wonderful man. But although I'm sure he likes women well enough, at some fundamental level we're bound to make him slightly uncomfortable. That's why he'll only *truly* be at ease in male company. He's like my husband that way. As I said, it's the inevitable result of a traditional public school education. It's why introducing girls into the sixth form here was absolutely the right thing to do.'

Headmaster Parish had bulging pale eyes and broken-veined cheeks and a pompous manner. The idea of he and Peter having anything significant in common was abhorrent. All the same, Peter's reluctance for Eve to join him and Anthony wasn't exactly new. Was this a pattern she had only just started to notice?

Meanwhile, the First Lady mused on. 'Of course, the introduction of girls has not been without its risks. In a place like this, it doesn't take much to upset the balance. All of our rules and niceties – they're not as entrenched as they look. Cleeve is not as safe as it seems.'

Safe was an odd choice of word, Eve thought.

'And by that I mean that our ecosystem at Cleeve is perhaps more fragile than you imagine. Hundreds of disparate people, the majority of whom are in a hormonal maelstrom of one sort or the other, cooped up together in a wholly artificial environment and governed by a mix of convention and ritual alone! You disrupt something like this at your peril. Perhaps you should tell that to your friend.'

'That almost sounds like a threat.'

'Oh no. The *gentlest* of warnings, I assure you. I have some experience in these matters, as it happens. I've known women like Fenella before.'

Eve believed her. The smile she gave made Eve think that she'd ground them to bone-paste beneath her heel.

After this encounter, Eve was more determined than ever to join Peter and his school friend for a drink, if only to disprove the First Lady's point about her husband preferring male company.

However, it was clear by the time she'd had her first gin in the grotty pub that Peter had been right. She and Anthony weren't going to get along. He was a portly, balding banker who made jokes along the lines of 'Those who can, teach. Those who can't, go private. Isn't that right, Winslow? Haw, haw!' He made a big deal of what a dweeb Peter had been until his long-awaited growth spurt and how he'd been one of the so-called Leftovers, which Eve already knew was the nickname given to a handful of boys who, like Peter, were thrown together on exeat weekends when everyone else had gone home to their families. Then

Anthony boasted about the hard liquor he and his fellow cool kids used to smuggle into their tuck boxes, whereas the 'sissies and squares' were reduced to playing something called the Fainting Game. 'They'd try and hold their breaths until they'd keel over with piss in their pants, because that was the closest thing they could find to getting high. Haw, haw!'

'Whereas real men get their jollies from snorting coke off call girls,' said Eve. 'Or at least that's what I read in *The Cleeve Companion*.'

'Haw, haw! You've got a live one here, haven't you?' said Anthony, nudging Peter so hard he spilled his drink.

Peter met Eve's eyes over the rim of his glass. *I told you so*, his look said. *I'm sorry*, she mouthed.

Eve made her excuses as soon as she could. She wanted to go vent to Fen, but it was Gabriel who opened the door.

'Ah,' he said, frowning from under his formidable brows. 'Fen's not here at the moment. She's working late in the studio.' There was a pause. He cleared his throat, as if bracing himself. 'You could come in and wait for her. I'm sure she'll be back soon.'

Gabriel's obvious reluctance to invite Eve in goaded her into accepting the invitation. She was surprised when he joined her in the sitting room; as an awkward silence settled over them, she realised they hadn't ever been alone together before. Eve thought of Bette Drummond, whom she'd spied talking to Gabriel just yesterday afternoon under one of the cherry trees by the Chapel. Bette's attitude had definitely been flirtatious – peeping out at him from under her lashes, then tilting her head back to laugh as one hand idly twirled a strand of hair. But Gabriel had had his back to Eve, and so she had no way of knowing his response.

Perhaps Mrs Parish's intervention had unsettled her more than she realised. Her suspicions were based on little or nothing. Certainly, it seemed wholly perverse that a girl like Bette would be dazzled by a man like Gabriel, surrounded as she was by Gilded Youth and that handsome boyfriend of hers. Although Eve knew Gabriel was only a couple of years older than Fen, he had the kind of deeply chiselled bone structure that age would turn to gauntness; she saw, even now, how the lamplight cast unflattering hollows.

'Do you think Fen is happy here?' she asked abruptly. The gin she'd drunk at the pub had emboldened her, but Gabriel didn't seem particularly disconcerted by the question.

'Why do you think I would know?'

'You're her husband.'

He gave a crooked smile. 'My wife believes intimacy is contingent on an element of mystery.'

'Poor Gabriel', that's what the First Lady had called him. Eve thought of Bette Drummond again. 'Are *you* happy here?'

'Well, I'm finding a new appreciation for *The Tristia*.'

Eve did not follow. Gabriel gave another oblique half-smile. 'Ovid. That was a joke, by the way.' His fingers drummed on the arm of his chair. Silence resumed.

It was a relief when Fen burst in. Her curls were wild and her hands were ink-stained. She was exuberant, lit from within. 'Sorry. Sorry! I got carried away with my goddess. Those bastard scorpions are cooperating at last.' She gave Gabriel a lingering open-mouthed kiss, then turned to Eve and winked. 'You look bored rigid. He hasn't been quoting Latin poets at you, has he?'

Gabriel's face was grave. He caught at his wife's hand. *'Da mihi, si quid ea est, hebetantem pectora Lethen, oblitus potero non tamen esse tui.'* Then he got out of his chair, and nodded stiffly at Eve. 'I think that's my cue to leave.'

Eve had initially decided against telling Fen about her conversation with Mrs Parish. The only possible way to relate her warning was to make it funny, and although there had indeed been a black sort of comedy about the encounter, Eve hadn't found it much of a laughing matter. Now she'd changed her mind. She would talk to Fen about the First Lady's warning, and she would also mention Bette Drummond and her crush. As soon as they were alone, she cleared her throat in preparation. But Fen got there first. 'Gabriel's a pompous arse, but I do love him,' she said gaily. 'Isn't that funny?' She put her head to one side, eyes closed, considering. 'Or is it just *sad*?'

'What was he saying back there? In Latin?'

'Ah, alas for Ovid. "Give me the waters of the Lethe that numb the heart, if they exist, I will still not have the power to forget you."'

'Lethe ... that's one of the rivers of the underworld, isn't it?'

'Love blooms in Hades as well as Heaven, you know. God, Eve. Stop looking so droopy. Forget those miserable dead Romans – we've got martinis to drink and mischief to make.' She went to fetch the gin, followed by the list of Expectations, which she kept between two catalogues on the bookcase. 'Hm. We've done most of the fun ones, which makes the challenge trickier. How can plagiarising be made amusing, do you think?'

Eve was growing bored of the game. She tried to distract Fen by telling her about Peter's terrible school friend and his *haw, haw, haw*-ing. However, she could see that Fen was only listening out of politeness.

'Let's stick to plagiarism for now,' said Eve, knowing she was beaten. 'I've been asked to write "A Day in the Life of a Housemaster's Wife" for the school magazine. I was thinking we could have a look in the archives and pull out an entry from 1920 or similar. The magazine has been recycling the same old crap for decades so it would probably only require a couple of tweaks for me to pass it off as my own.'

She didn't think it was much of an idea but Fen was pleased. 'I've been waiting for a chance to snoop around the archives. And I'm sure your predecessors came up with some gems. "This morning, I was honoured to attend a flower-arranging class with the Nonceshire Guild of Fragrant Lady Fascists."'

'"For luncheon,"' Eve supplied, '"I prepared the boys a nourishing repast of gruel sandwiches, salted with the tears of the local peasantry."'

Fen grinned appreciatively. '"As darkness fell, I listened to my darling husband administer a sound thrashing to Featherstonehaugh Minor. Had a wank."'

It was only nine so Fen proposed they head to the archives to make a start. The campus was busier than usual, as the school orchestra had given a concert that evening, followed by a reception for local worthies. Nobody gave them as second glance as they walked past the Mansion and towards the Library, a stern temple to Victorian gothic that housed the school archives in its depths.

The more precious documents, relating to the early history of the Cleeve estate and the founding of the school, were in display cabinets in the Mansion. Other records were organised according to provenance or theme and filed in the archive's two storage rooms. Copies of the school magazine were kept in the smaller room, next to a cupboard and a filing cabinet both labelled 'Misc.'. This was essentially junk that Eve hadn't yet got round to sorting. About half of it had been gathering dust for the last decade or more; the other was more recent donations from Old Boys. As she opened the door to her cramped basement office, she saw the latest delivery waiting for her on her desk. It would be just the same as all the others: boring photographs, tedious report cards and annotated scripts from end-of-term plays.

Fen, however, was enjoying the novelty. 'I feel like Indiana Jones,' she said, pulling out a random drawer from the Misc. cabinet and rifling through the contents. 'Can we go upstairs and raid the Library next?'

Eve went straight for the magazines and started efficiently flicking through. 'A Day in the Life' was a reliable means of padding the word count. *A Day in the Life of a Housemaster*, *A Day in the Life of the Matron*, *A Day in the Life of the Bursar*. She yawned. There was even *A Day in the Life of the Archivist*. She yawned some more.

Fen held up a battered blue manila folder. 'This here's a bunch of medical records. And detention reports! All at least twenty years old.' She bent to pick up a yellowing memo that had come loose. 'I thought you had to shred this kind of stuff.'

'I'd happily set the whole lot on fire if it were left to me.'

Fen flicked through further pages, her brow creased in thought. 'I don't know why you think your job is boring. Surely it's only a matter of time before you stumble upon an ancient treasure map or scandalous love letter.'

'Perhaps I'll fake one, just to liven things up for the archivist who comes after me.'

'Why don't we do that, then, instead of your magazine

article? Forgery is so much more creative than plagiarising.'

But Eve was already fed-up of the project. She spent more than enough time among dusty filing cabinets as it was. As soon as she found something she thought she could use, she stuck the magazine under her jacket and hustled Fen out of the room.

Fen had been serious about raiding the Library, or at least borrowing a book out-of-hours. The librarian locked up at six on Saturdays, so when they climbed the basement stairs and stepped into the foyer all was dark and quiet. Fen was just reaching for the light switch when some sound or movement in the room ahead made her freeze. Eve froze too. Then Fen turned towards her with the most extraordinary grimace and motioned violently for Eve to join her, a finger on her lips. She pointed.

Eve peered through the glass panels of the door. There, in the shadows of the bookshelves, a kneeling woman was giving head to a man. *She* was the First Lady, but *he* definitely wasn't Headmaster Parish.

Fen clapped her hands over her mouth. Eve, too, felt appalled laughter building explosively inside. Somehow, they managed to tiptoe back to the stairs down to the basement; somehow, they managed to maintain silence until they were safely out and away. At long last, in the shadows behind the tuck shop, they began to splutter and gasp, clutching at each other, temporarily speechless with hilarity.

'That,' Eve finally managed to get out, 'was Tristan von Aldstine.' It was the hair she recognised: it was as white-blond as his son's. An Old Cleevian himself, just like his father and grandfather before him, Tristan had even worked at the school as a rowing coach one summer, before marrying into money and disappearing into the world of wealth management. Since then, he'd graduated from rowing coach to school governor. 'If you cut my veins,' he'd told Eve once, when dropping Rupert off at Wyatt's, 'you'll find my blood runs claret and navy.'

'He must have come for the reception,' she said.

'I think he *came* after the reception, by the sounds of it,' said Fen gleefully. 'And, lo, that's another expectation we can cross off our list.'

'How do you mean?'

'"Cleeve expects every student to report a violation of its rules".'

'Is there a rule against adulterous blow-jobs?'

'Sexual delinquency should cover it.'

They collapsed again. 'Still,' said Fen, recovering slightly as she wiped her eyes, 'it makes me think more kindly of our gracious oberfüher.'

'I don't.' Eve was thinking of Mrs Parish's perfumed threats and pearly smile. She knew Peter was wary of Tristan von Aldstine and had as little as possible to do with him, preferring to discuss Rupert's progress with his wife. Von Aldstine Minor contrived to be both charming and boorish; she'd bet his father was the same. 'She's a vile hypocrite.'

'Oh, I can forgive her that. Shows she's human at least. And a red-blooded human at that! Who'd've thought?' She started laughing again. 'Honestly, the irony … it's too delicious for words.'

Fen, Eve saw, was speaking the truth. She was genuinely elated by the whole business. Not Eve. She wondered if Cleeve's sway was stronger than she realised, and she was growing more conventional, and censorious, in spite of herself. Is that what she was trying to disprove with her minor acts of rebellion?

'Madeleine Parish,' she said abruptly, 'thinks you're a bad influence on me. And the school in general.'

'Ha. So I should hope.'

'Peter said the same.'

'Well, they're right. I *do* want to influence you – but I want to influence the school even more. Do you know about the theory of creative destruction? How the creation of something new and different requires the death of the old?'

'It sounds rather chilling.'

'"And, whoever must be a creator in good and evil, verily, he must first be an annihilator and break values. Thus the highest evil belongs to the highest goodness: but this is creative."' Fen paused. *'Thus Spoke Zarathustra,'* she said, as if that cleared everything up.

'Let's leave Nietzsche out of it. I'm more of an e. e. cummings gal.'

To her annoyance, Fen took her at her word. 'Mm. It's true you *are* rather an innocent.'

'How so?'

'Well, you seem curiously uninterested in what's going on below the surface of campus life. The First Lady's blow-jobs are the least of it. I mean, do you even know what goes on in the outward-bound cabin past midnight? How about the sad little unrequited love story between the chaplain's daughter and your husband's house prefect? Or the flourishing drugs trade round the back of the Laundry? Or the beating that—?'

Eve put her hands over her ears. 'Stop it. I don't want to know this crap. It's just more petty teenage bullshit.'

'Ah, but that's where you're wrong. Sex! Intoxication! Thwarted longing! Crime and punishment!' Fen's eyes glittered. 'This stuff's the bedrock of life and art – think of the potential that could be unleashed. You don't know what these people are capable of. You don't know what *I'm* capable of. Embrace the madness, and we can be creative destroyers together, my friend.'

'Destroyers of what? Of who?'

But Fen just shook out her curls and laughed.

ALICE

The next time I saw Henry and Lindsey together was in town after school, when I was on my way for a swim at the municipal pool and stopped to get fries at the Burger King knock-off on the High Street. There was a smoking area for staff round the back, which also happened to be the shortcut to the leisure centre. I spotted Lindsey, in the burger joint's lurid orange uniform, talking to Henry alongside a thickset older man in a leather jacket. There was a dishevelled youngish guy hovering nearby, with greasy curtains of hair and a twitch. I recognised him because he'd been caught selling pills to kids outside my school. Crack-Head Kyle they called him.

What the fuck was Henry doing with these people?

I stayed behind the shelter of a well-placed skip.

The older man had a gold stud in one ear and an affable air. At least, he seemed to be joking about with Henry, who looked tense and uncomfortable. Then he gave Henry a thump on the back and went on his jaunty way, with a wink for Lindsey and a whistle for Kyle. Like a dog, Kyle shambled off obediently after him.

Henry and Lindsey exchanged a few more words, though I couldn't hear what they were saying. Lindsey took a final suck of her cigarette and ground the butt under her heel. Then she kissed him on the cheek and went back inside.

That kiss.

Friendly? Perfunctory?

Something more?

It enraged me, anyway. Not just on Bette's account – mine too. I wanted Henry to be better than this.

Henry stood there after she'd gone, staring onto the ground as if transfixed by its sprinkling of fag butts. He only moved away when one of Lindsey's co-workers came out to light up.

I intercepted him as he passed by the skip. 'Déjà vu,' I said.

Henry actually flinched. 'Wh–what?'

'You, me, a couple of scary townies. Lindsey Bates. Just like the first time you lovebirds met.'

'She's not my— Christ, Alice, are you full-on stalking me now?'

My turn to flinch. But I kept my anger in focus. 'I went for chips after school. As I occasionally do. *You're* the one out of context here.' I narrowed my eyes at him. 'Shouldn't you be in your cricket whites right now, busy thwacking willow on leather?'

He mumbled something about a sick note. 'I'm late. I need to get the bus.'

He quickened his pace. I caught up with him. 'OK,' I said cheerily. 'You say you're not having a fling with Lindsey. Why, then, are you hanging out with Crack-Head Kyle behind the bins at Burger Biz?'

'Please. If I was doing drugs I wouldn't be getting them from *that* leper.'

'Oh, I beg your pardon. I should have known you Cleevians would have a nice upper-crust dealer who makes his deliveries on an actual silver spoon.'

'As it happens,' said Henry defensively, 'Kyle says he sells dope to one of the Cleeve beards.'

Mrs Easton, I'd bet. Rumour had it she was on the edge of a breakdown or some other spectacular fall from grace. Only yesterday, I'd seen her having some sort of dispute with Mr von Aldstine in the car park after the governors' meeting. Jabbing fingers, raised voices, the lot.

But I wasn't going to let this distract me. I lowered my voice. 'Listen. I'm being serious here. Crack-Head Kyle's one thing, but the Bates family are another. Who was that man you were talking to? Lindsey's uncle, cousin, boyfriend …? You lot at Cleeve wouldn't know this, you're so insulated from the world outside the college, but the Bateses are notorious round here. They—'

'I know who the Bateses are,' Henry said roughly. 'I'm not as stupid as you think.' Then he gave a hollow laugh.

'No, maybe I am, actually. I've been an idiot. The least I can do is own it.'

'So tell me—'

But if there had been a moment when he was going to open up, it had passed. His face hardened. 'I don't owe you anything, Alice. Please stay out of it. It's for your own good, OK?'

EVE

Eve would never have imagined a Cleeve year could pass so quickly. Advent and Lent terms were done, and now the end of Trinity was fast approaching. In Fen's company, the usual markers of the school calendar had sped past and then blurred, folding into themselves. Over the breaks, when the Eastons were away travelling (not *holidaying* – Fen was very specific about that), Eve found that time dragged in the way it used to during term time. It was hard not to envy their escapes: Morocco for Christmas, Syria for Easter. ('It's almost as if they want to make a point about being among Pagans during Christian festivals,' Nancy Riley sniffed.) Meanwhile, Eve, encouraged to reconnect with old friends by Peter, found for the first time that she wanted to talk about Cleeve. The arcane rituals and mannered slang, the hierarchies and power-plays ... These had become more interesting to her, and important, than simply being the trappings of her confinement. But she tried to explain everything too quickly, tangling up her anecdotes and botching her punchlines. Behind their polite smiles, she could see her friends thinking, *What has become of her?* It was almost a relief to be back at school.

That June was an almost indecently abundant month at Cleeve. Heavy spring downpours followed by an early heatwave had produced a lushness that was almost tropical. The playing fields and lawns were a saturated green of improbable brightness. Trees were feathered, blossom foamed. Amidst all this fecundity, it seemed even more cruel than usual that the summer term was exam time. Anxious parents kept the housemasters' phone lines permanently busy while their offspring wilted over textbooks or tried to distract themselves with rowdiness and tumult. Peter knew the backstory of every student he'd ever taught at Cleeve as well as every boy in Wyatt's; he knew who would bounce back from disappointment and who would be badly knocked, who needed coddling and who needed, as he put it, 'a kick up the backside'. As a result, he could never really relax until August, when the A-level and GSCE results came in.

Eve, however, could sunbathe in the garden with impunity, unencumbered by the need to study or coach or fret over the declining Oxbridge admission rate. She used to feel an unkind pleasure in this particular freedom, because it was a rare moment of feeling she had the upper hand over Cleeve. Yet this year, she felt something of the summer term's giddiness too, as the studied nonchalance of the sixth formers fell away and they grew drunk on nostalgia, rediscovering their tribal loyalties as parting loomed. According to tradition, the upper sixth would only go home the Saturday after the last A-level exam was finished, a milestone that was celebrated by the revelries of Hazard Night on the Friday before. The rest of the school would break up a week later; the leavers would then return for the commemoration service and farewell ball. All these events required exhausting levels of both vigilance and forbearance from the staff, most of whom were counting down the days to the holidays even more keenly than their students.

Eve was looking forward to Fen's take on all of this. They would be wryly amused bystanders together. Now that their game had tailed off, she was hopeful their friendship would both settle and deepen. She'd had enough of pranks and plotting and swigging cheap wine in the woods; she wanted to be an adult again.

But during the exam weeks, Fen proved elusive. She said her work was taking her in a new direction, but there were several occasions when Eve passed by the art department (where Fen had use of a studio) expecting to see her, only to find she wasn't there. 'I've got a new project I'm researching,' Fen said by way of explanation, her gaze narrow and distant. 'But I don't want to talk about it.'

Still, the next time Eve encountered Fen carrying her sketchbook she decided to persist. 'How's the annihilation going?'

Fen looked at her strangely. 'What are you talking about?'

'Your theory of creation through destruction. *Thus Spoke Zarathustra.*'

Eve had spoken lightly, so she was surprised when Fen's face darkened. 'All right. Yes. Imagine I was an actual god, Eve. No, don't laugh. Imagine I had the power to bring all of this crashing down – with just one blast of fire and brimstone. Should I throw the thunderbolt?'

'Er, I don't much want to meet a fiery death, thanks.'

'Me neither. That's the trouble.' Fen was still frowning. 'Because I don't ever start something I can't finish. I have to see things through. You know?'

Eve did not. Trying to get her head around the conversation made her feel tired. Not only were Fen's conversations frustratingly cryptic, she was also much harder to pin down. When they planned a day trip to London to go to the theatre, Fen cancelled at the last moment – leaving Gabriel to telephone to apologise for her, just as Eve was going out of the door. 'She had to see a friend, I think,' he offered.

'A friend in a nursing home,' Fen said, when she returned. 'Don't ever get old, Eve. Fucking horrible business.' And that was all she would say on the matter.

'I'll be surprised if the Eastons are back next year,' Nancy observed to Eve, as they sat in her kitchen assembling the goodbye gifts for the Wyatt's leavers. (Eve was late to the

132

task, as usual. Nancy had 'popped by' to remind her, as usual.) 'Gabriel's not been what the headmaster hoped, or so Madeleine tells me. He's just not cut out for teaching young teenagers. They're frightened of him, poor loves. And you can hardly blame them. He's so cold! The sort that would slit your throat and not think twice of it.'

Eve was startled. 'Whatever you do mean?'

'It's in the eyes,' Nancy said darkly. 'I'd feel sorry for Fenella if I didn't think they were two of a kind. I'm sure *she* knows where the bodies are buried.'

'I really don't understand why you would say any of this.' Mechanically, Eve reached for another helping of chocolate bars and socks.

'Whoopsie – you left out the fountain pen. See? You need to tuck it in here.' Nancy gave herself a little shake. 'No. I'm sorry. Of course you know the Eastons much better than I do. Or any of us do, really. I know Peter gets along with Gabriel. And I'm sure Fenella has all sorts of wonderful qualities, once you get to know her.'

'Fen's been a good friend to me.'

'You have other friends here too, you know.' Nancy pursed her lips and set to fussing with the fountain pens. 'Or at least you could if you wanted to.'

Eve saw that Nancy was hurt, and she was sorry, and a little ashamed of herself. She resolved to do better. But that evening, she found out that Nancy had been tattle-taling to Peter, provoking one of their worst fights in a long while.

That afternoon, after the gift-bag packing, 'somebody' – so Peter said – had spied Fen smoking a joint on a bench by the Lake. Students were all safely inside doing lessons or taking exams at the time, but that hardly lessened the offence. Drug-taking meant on-the-spot dismissal for staff and expulsion for students, and even though Fen wasn't technically a Cleeve employee, the distinction, as Peter observed, hardly mattered. Fen was damn lucky the person who spotted her only told Peter about it because, as she explained, she was concerned for Eve as well. After all, everyone at Cleeve knew Mrs Easton and Mrs Winslow were joined at the hip. Partners in crime, people said, as if it were a joke. But if actual law-breaking was taking place, what did that make Eve – an accomplice?

Eve laughed bitterly. 'And you honestly believe Nancy Riley told you this purely out of concern for me and my reputation?'

'No, Eve,' Peter said evenly. 'She's mainly concerned about mine. Because if you are tainted by your association with Fen, then I'm even more so. It's *my* job – my professional reputation – at stake here, not yours.'

Eve knew this was true. Nonetheless, her husband's high-minded manner infuriated her. 'Yes, it's always been about you, hasn't it? *Your* job. *Your* school. *Your* dream. I'm just here to make up the numbers. Because, let's face it, nobody trusts a bachelor housemaster.'

'I came to Cleeve on your encouragement! We made the decision together – we're building a life here together. Or at least I thought we were. Until the Eastons came.'

'Then you weren't paying attention. Because *until* the Eastons came, I was pretty close to losing my fucking mind. And nobody, least of all you, seemed to notice.'

There was a long, fraught pause. 'All right, Eve,' Peter said quietly. 'You're right, the fault is mine. I've neglected you and let you down, and that makes me more sorry than I can say. I hope that if I say that from here on things will be different, you'll believe me. But you must see that if we're going to move past this – if we're going to have the life that we as a family want – then you're going to have to start to draw back from Fen. Or at the very least find some way of reining her in.'

'She's an adult, for Christ's sake! She's not my responsibility. I've done nothing wrong here.'

Peter gave her a long, knowing look. It was the same look he gave his boys when he interrupted them mid-prank, and she flushed guiltily. Her husband wasn't stupid. Or blind. He'd seen her go out at all hours; he'd have smelled the martinis on her breath. He'd have overheard her plotting on the telephone.

'I'm not trying to be a killjoy,' he said gently. 'I'm genuinely worried for Fen, and I know Gabriel is too. I

135

saw her talking to a man the other day by the bus stop – he was this incredibly down-at-heel, seedy-looking fellow. If that's who she's buying her drugs from … And then there's her drinking. I gather Madeleine's already had a word with you about it.'

Eve grimaced. 'So it's not just Nancy who's been tattling to teacher. I imagine Gabriel's in on it too. Are the four of you plotting an intervention? Are Fen and I about to be forcibly enrolled in a re-education programme for wayward wives?'

'This isn't a joke.'

'Well, I'm certainly not laughing.'

'Seriously, Eve. Madeleine's sharper than she looks. She can be a tremendous champion if she's got your back, but I wouldn't like her as my enemy.'

'My God! This is all such bullshit. Madeleine Parish is the biggest fraud on campus.'

There was a knock at the house-side door. They both ignored it.

'What do you mean by that?' Peter demanded.

Eve lifted her chin. Fen had called her an innocent. So what did that make Peter? Clueless, that's what. 'It's time you faced the fact that the fine upstanding citizens of Cleeve aren't nearly as pure of heart as you think they are. This place *reeks* with hypocrisy.'

'This is what I'm talking about! Fen's pouring poison in your ear. Don't you see it? She's not made you happier. She's only making you more cynical and dissatisfied and—'

The knocking at the door grew louder. 'Uh, Mr Winslow?' said a boy's voice. 'Are you there?'

'Don't answer that,' said Eve.

'I'm on duty.' Peter went to open the door. One of the year eleven students was there, a thin, freckled boy with a face like porridge. He was wringing his hands. 'I'm sorry to disturb you, sir,' he said, 'but when I went to my room just now I found someone's removed all the light bulbs. I know it's supposed to be a joke, but it's really not, because I've got Chemistry first thing tomorrow, and there's so much reading still to do and—'

'It's fine, Jacob. I'll come and sort it out,' said Peter.

'Don't go,' Eve told him. Then, in a furious undertone, 'Don't you *dare*.'

He went.

Later, she overheard some of the boys describing, in awestruck tones, how the perpetrators of the light-bulb prank had come in for such a tongue-lashing that the entire population of Wyatt's, from lofty leaver to lowly squit, were temporarily cowed into submission. Peter Winslow's outbursts were rare but explosive, and so accorded an almost reverential level of respect. Eve's own fury gave way to envy. Teenage boys were far more easily impressed than they knew. But in Cleeve, female rage had little currency.

ALICE

I quite like exam time, even if it's only mocks. I appreciate the condensing of time and sharpening of thought. It's a bit like intensive swimming, for me. You're pushing yourself to your limits, yet your propulsion needs to be relaxed as well as controlled. *Catch, pull. Flow. Breathe.*

The Friday of Hazard Night, I came home straight after my European history paper. (The Ascendency of the Ottoman Empire: 1453–1606. Piece of piss.) Cleeve's rosy bricks were basking in the afternoon sun. The lawns and playing fields were green lakes; the sky was a Club Med blue. It was a scene straight off the front cover of the '95 prospectus, in fact. Then I found Bette waiting for me.

She had only been inside the cottage once before. I didn't encourage visitors. It wasn't that I was ashamed of the place, exactly, but when I thought of the lengths Bette and her friends went to customise their cells – the windows draped with sarongs, the walls papered with posters, knick-knacks cramming every surface – our few plain rooms didn't seem simple so much as barren. Pa and I are both tidy people but that's no excuse. My bedroom is still papered in the pale pink stripes that my mother had picked out for my nursery.

As well as making few concessions towards home décor, we didn't usually bother locking up. Bette had walked right in. There was a public footpath through the woods and some of the estate meadows, and you'd occasionally see middle-aged dog walkers plodding by, but Cleeve had always been a safe place.

Bette didn't look safe, however. When I opened the door to the living room, she sprang round like a cornered animal. Her eyes were wild and red and her face was all mottled. 'You knew, and you didn't tell me,' she spat before I could so much as open my mouth. 'Traitor.'

'Knew what?' Then, stupidly: 'Is this about Henry?'

'Who else? Henry the lying, cheating man-whore Zhang.'

Uh-oh. Somehow, Bette must have found out about Lindsey. 'Are you ... are you sure about this? Because I confronted him about it, and he swore there was nothing going on.'

Confronted was perhaps too strong a word. So was *swore*. In any case, my words only further enraged her.

'So you *did* suspect! I *knew* it. Because you know everything that goes on at this school, don't you? All your spying and lurking and *worming* into things ... And then you *lied to my face* when I asked you if I had anything to worry about. My God. After everything I've done for you –' Her breath hissed. 'That key you gave me? To the Chapel? Henry kept hold of the copy we made and he used it with *her*.'

My mouth went very dry. 'Oh.'

'*Oh*,' Bette mimicked savagely. 'Hurts, doesn't it? You thought the two of you were friends and in fact he was playing you the whole time. Sniggering behind your back. Laughing at you, betraying me.'

'I don't know what he was thinking,' I said weakly. She was right: it did hurt. Like a punch to the gut. With a knuckle-duster.

'He was thinking with his dick. All that crap he spouted about respecting me too much to pressure me into anything ... my God. What a fool I've been.'

'I'm sorry—'

'So you fucking should be. I guess you were too busy drooling over my boyfriend to remember where your loyalties lie.'

'I never ... drooled.' I was struggling to keep my calm. I'm not used to rows, maybe because I'm not used to friendship. I couldn't even tell if Bette's reaction was extreme or not.

'Bullshit. You were always hoping the two of us would implode, weren't you? I bet you're *loving* this. Little Miss Nobody's chance to shine. So now you can go slithering off to that bastard, offer him a shoulder to cry—'

'Hello?'

We both froze. It was Pa. 'Oh dear,' he said mildly. 'I seem to be interrupting something.' He rubbed his beard thoughtfully, then turned to Bette. 'Perhaps you'd like a cup of tea? A glass of water?'

Bette ignored him. She thrust her head towards me. Her eyes were burning slits, her voice a furious rasp. 'Don't ever talk to me, don't so much as *look* at me again. If you see me coming, you'd better turn and walk away. Fast.'

The door slammed behind her.

The silence afterwards rang in my ears. After a while, Pa put his hand on my shoulder. 'I'm sorry, my dear. But perhaps it's for the best, hm?'

He went into the kitchen and brought me a glass of water. 'Here, it's a sunny day. You need to keep hydrated.' He sighed and said, almost as if to himself, 'Really, it's beginning to seem as if the old guard were right. Admitting girls into the school was a mistake.'

I hurled the water glass across the room. It exploded into shards against the door. Then I left.

———

I went to my bench. I walked quickly, mechanically, barely looking where I was going. There was a weird sort of low keening sound, and it took a while for me to realise it was coming from me. I came to a halt and clenched every muscle as hard as I could. *Get a grip of yourself.*

It was still warm, still sunny, still preternaturally quiet. Rain was due to come in overnight, but there was no hint of cloud. It would have been fitting, perhaps, if there'd been a menacing pressure in the air or a bank of darkness broiling at the horizon. But there wasn't. It was just a lovely June day.

I reached the Lavender Walk only to find that Margaret Mumford was already occupied. Even worse, it was Lindsey Bates who was in possession of it, her bare legs slung over the armrest and a jacket rolled up at the other end to make a cushion. She was smoking and sunning herself, apparently without a care in the world. An apple core and an empty crisp packet lay on the ground beside her.

I looked around. The path was deserted: most people would be in class. 'What the fuck are you doing here?'

'Nice to see you too, Alice. How're the mocks going? History this morning, wasn't it?'

She was trying to spook me, and it worked. I wasn't going to give her the satisfaction of letting her see it, though.

'History was fine, thanks. How's the security business?'

She blew a languid plume of smoke in my direction. 'Oh, the usual. Cracking heads, breaking hearts.'

I was used to this breezy confidence in Cleeve boys, not townie girls. And in a different girl, I might even have admired it. Her breasts strained against the thin cotton of her T-shirt. I stared at her chipped tooth, her spidery eyelashes, the pencil-thin arc of her over-plucked brows.

And yet, lounging on that bench, Lindsey didn't look out of place. She somehow managed to look as if she owned it, and the rest of Cleeve too.

'Don't get too comfy,' I told her. 'Henry's girlfriend knows about the two of you and she's raging.'

'Is that a fact.' Another lazy drag on the cigarette.

'I'd steer clear if I were you. She's got a lot of friends here.'

I knew how pathetic I sounded even before Lindsey laughed.

'I got friends too. But what about you, Alice? They're not as nice as they look, your Cleeve boys.' Her eyes narrowed. 'And right here's a case in point.'

I turned round. Rupert von Aldstine was strolling along the path, with the happy ease of a man with an unconditional offer to study Geography at Durham and a summer full of clubbing and yachting ahead.

Rupert was reckoned to be one of the best-looking boys in school but I'd never seen the appeal. He was ruddy and muscular, with white eyelashes and an overgrown thatch of baby-blond hair. Today, I thought he looked particularly unappealing, in baggy worn-down mustard cords and a grey hoodie, his bucket hat worn at a jaunty angle.

He looked straight through me but grinned at Lindsey. 'Greetings, oik. What are you doing up at the big house? Shouldn't you get out of here before they release the hounds?'

'The only dirty dog around here is you, Rupes.'

'*Woof! Woof!*' He laughed delightedly. 'Watch out for this one, Fishface.' It had been so long since anybody'd called me this it took a moment to realise he was talking to me. 'She'll have the coat off your back if you as much as turn it for a minute.'

Off he sauntered. I hadn't understood any of their exchange but, like Henry, Rupert seemed to know Lindsey surprisingly well.

Lindsey watched him go thoughtfully. 'Never bet against the house, Alice. First rule of the game.' Then she went to stub out her cigarette on the wrought-iron arm of the bench.

I put out my hand to stop her. 'Don't do that.'

'Why should you care?'

Why should I indeed? The cigarette wouldn't hurt the metal. All the same, the gesture infuriated me. 'It's disrespectful.'

She looked at me as if I was mad. 'To a *bench*? It's not your private property.'

'The bench is a memorial, though.' *Which I've adopted for my mother*, I added silently in my head.

'Yeah, I'm aware.' Lindsey flicked the carved lettering on the back. 'That's my cousin Peggy. So if anyone's got dibs on this thing, it's me.'

The wood was aged and weathered; the bench must be close to twenty years old. I didn't hide my scepticism. 'Why is there a memorial to your cousin at Cleeve?'

'My auntie worked here back in the day. I s'pose she or the people she worked with organised it.' Lindsey touched the name again, this time more gently. 'It was a suicide, poor kid. I never knew the girl, and my auntie's passed and all. But this here bench is a good place for thinking.'

'Also smoking and littering, apparently.'

'Hm.' Lindsey looked at me knowingly. 'Bugs you, don't it, that us Bateses have a stake in this place, just the same as your Ruperts or your Henrys or your God-bothering dad?'

I felt a twinge of guilt. 'I'm sorry about your cousin. And you're right – it's a nice spot for a memorial.'

'No better place to survey the crime scene.'

I was startled. 'What?'

'Never mind. I'm only messing with you.' The Clock Tower bell struck four, and Lindsey swung her legs off the bench. She kicked the apple core into a flower bed. 'Well, I'd best be off. Don't want to be late for my appointment.'

An appointment at Cleeve? With who?

She put on a pair of dark glasses, fluffed out her hair and smiled her sleepy smile. 'Tell Henry I said hi.'

It was Hazard Night that night. The last one in the long history of Cleeve, though of course nobody knew it at the time. The event took its name from an apocryphal saying by a nineteenth-century headmaster, who warned his boys not to be 'blind to the hazards of too much liberty'. Revelries began, as they always did, at 5 p.m., with the sixth formers' game of Fox and Hounds.

First, they drew the hound's name out of a hat. Then the foxes – i.e. everyone else – tucked coloured scarfs into the backs of their waistbands to make tails and ran off to hide themselves around the campus. The hound went running after them; as soon as he or she tagged a fox, the fox discarded their tail and became a hound. The last fox standing was the winner.

Playing was a privilege of the upper and lower sixth, but Bette had said I should join in too this year – 'You're practically one of us.' No chance of that now. I'd always secretly thought it looked fun, though I used to roll my eyes and huff if someone pushed me out of the way as part of the chase or – as on more than one occasion – tried to use me as a human shield.

The game was timed to end when senior supper was served. The boarding-house day ended, as it always did, with cocoa followed by quiet time. Then between ten and midnight the back doors were unlocked, and the soon-to-be leavers were let loose.

I spent the last Hazard Night just as I had spent the sixteen ones before: at home alone with the curtains drawn. I had spent most of the afternoon in my bedroom, too, lying in the semi-darkness, listening to the distant laughter and howls and barks from the hounds. Henry was probably running about and baying at the shadows without a care in the world. Laughing at both of us, like Bette said.

As night fell, I became increasingly jumpy. A couple of times in the past, our windows were egged. Another year a crucifix with a blow-up sex doll was planted outside the Chapel. Mostly, though, Pa and I were left alone. Each graduating year competed for the biggest and best prank, but they were pretty much all variations on the same theme. Classrooms covered in tin foil or filled with balloons. Hallways carpeted in bubble wrap. The rugby pitch stuck all over with plastic forks ... It was a major pain in the arse for the staff who had to clear all of it up in the morning, even though the Facilities department always brought in reinforcements. But at school reunions, years later, all the old buffers would tear up with pride at what comic geniuses they'd been. Even the ones who'd had a shit time at school, who never got picked for any teams or who were themselves pranked relentlessly ... even they used to raise a chuckle.

There were still rules, of course. The first – on pain of expulsion – was that no student who wasn't a school leaver was allowed to participate. The second was that all eligible students had to be back in their boarding houses and checked off by their housemaster by midnight. The final rule was three-fold: no booze, no sex, no criminal damage. If any of this was detected, or even suspected, then the leavers' commemoration service and ball would be cancelled. This

147

had only happened twice in my seventeen years: back in 1986, when someone threw a bottle of Bollinger through a Mansion window, and again in 1991, when two boys from Miles House were fifteen minutes late for check-in. Harsh, everyone agreed, but fair.

So, yeah, it was just another night of innocent fun.

Until they found the body.

EVE

The rain came in at about one in the morning, a good hour after the Hazard Night-ers were safely back in their dorms, though none were asleep. While the rest of the boarding houses snored, the soon-to-be leavers sprawled on the beds of their confederates and murmured together, first in torch light and then in the pale glow of dawn. Their exhilaration was mingled with solemnity, because this night together would be their last. True, they would spend one more night on campus, after the leavers' ball, but the rest of the school would be gone by then, along with most of the rites and sacraments that had bound them to the place, and each other, over the last seven years. And so they sprawled on their beds together, reminiscing like old men, laughing like children, as the warm summer rain drummed against the glass.

Eve also lay sleepless, listening to the rain. She had wanted to be alone – craved it – but she had also been sure that Peter would come knocking on the door, admitting his sins. It had been three days since their quarrel and he was still sleeping in the guest bedroom.

No doubt their estrangement was exacerbated by Hazard Night. It was always a testing event for housemasters, and Peter was more than usually on edge during the run-up to this one. Although some staff treated the event with fond tolerance, Peter found it less amusing than he used to. Eve suspected he was torn between his loyalty to the school's traditions and eccentricities and his own increasingly risk-averse nature. Then there was the fact that this year's leavers had several veteran trouble-makers among them. And so Peter and his colleagues were bracing themselves for an especial onslaught – students with a wild-child reputation always did their utmost to live up to it on Hazard Night, in the hope of pulling off a stunt that that would go down in the Cleeve annals of greatness.

(And so it proved. The crowning glory of the night was a recreation of Stonehenge, constructed out of benches on the Lawn, with Headmaster Parish's beloved Triumph parked in the middle. It would have been hailed as an epoch-defining prank had it not, of course, been for the murder.)

As yet ignorant of all of this, Eve lay in bed and tossed and turned and quietly seethed, not sure who she was most angry with: her husband, her friend or herself.

Eve and Fen had watched the game of Fox and Hounds from the bell-room of the Clock Tower. Eve had done everything by the book, arranging for someone from the Facilities team to let them in and signing some sort of health and safety form. She had brought ear-plugs, for when the mechanised bell rang, and bottled water, but no booze. Although the embrasures were covered in wire netting, presumably to stop any would-be Lady Lilians from jumping out, the view was undeniably impressive. Eve felt her spirits lift. Up here, high in the warm blue air, she and Fen could gain a much-needed sense of perspective. Everything was simpler when seen from a distance.

Certainly, from this God-like new vantage-point, it was possible to view Cleeve as Peter did: as its own small harmonious world, thriving and thrumming with purpose. A green and pleasant land, where everything was in its rightful place and everyone was doing his or her rightful best.

The First Lady had described this ecosystem as fragile. Unsafe, even. As the evening light grew low and honeyed and the shadow of ancient trees washed along the grass, Mrs Parish's words seemed even more absurd. Love it or hate it, Cleeve was impregnable. Eve watched the foxes and hounds dash about below, letting out whoops of triumph or dismay, yapping and bellowing as they darted between shelters or sprang after prey, and the ridiculousness of the game didn't annoy her like it had before. After all, despite the privilege and the posturing, they were just kids, and most of them fairly ordinary ones at that. Just overgrown, excitable kids, running about in the sun.

Fen, however, seemed in a less charitable frame of mind. She'd come late, saying she'd had someone to see, but without sharing further details. Eve had half-expected her to complain about the lack of alcohol or to suggest they sabotage the clockwork. Instead, Fen looked out at the view with unseeing eyes and silently picked at a patch of loose mortar in the brickwork. Perhaps she was merely tired. She'd mentioned that her insomnia was back. But the fidgeting was new.

'Are you nervous?' Eve asked.

Fen drew back. 'Why would you say that?'

'Because of Hazard Night. In theory, everyone's a target. How do you think the Classics department will fare?'

Eve worried Gabriel Easton might come off badly. Peter hadn't ever suffered anything worse than butter on a doorhandle, but less popular gogs didn't do so well.

'They'll leave Gabriel alone if they've got any sense,' said Fen shortly. 'I learned that the hard way.' And she went back to picking at the brickwork.

As a distraction, Eve pointed towards the Lawn. 'Looks like we have a winner.'

The last fox standing was the von Aldstine boy. He donned an orange-plastic fox mask and was born aloft on the shoulders of cheering hounds. The rest of the players streamed after them towards the Hall, yapping and yodelling, arms slung around waists and shoulders in happy camaraderie. Colourful ribbons of polyester – the discarded fox tails – littered the ground in their wake. Fen watched dispassionately.

'In a real hunt, the fox ends up dead,' she said.

'That would certainly up the stakes. But I don't think it would do much for admissions.'

'Oh, I don't know. Maybe a death match could be incorporated into the selection process. See which of the little darlings has the necessary killer instinct.'

This sounded more like the old Fen. Eve smiled. 'Do you think any of the students ever guessed what we were up to, with our list of expectations?'

'If they did, they would have despised us for it. Perhaps they would've been right to. Whatever were we thinking, with our silly games? I've been the worst. All that empty artistic posturing – what a *clown*.'

Fen wasn't saying anything that Eve hadn't thought herself on occasion. But Fen's self-abasement was so out of character as to be alarming. And there was more.

'"It'll all end in tears." That's what everyone's mother used to say. And everyone's mother was right.' Fen laughed sourly to herself. 'Here's another one: "It's all fun and games until somebody loses an eye."'

'We both know you can't take Cleeve too seriously, else you'd go mad,' said Eve lightly. 'Or turn into Nancy Riley.'

'But you *should* take this place seriously, Eve. I didn't. I'm beginning to see that was a mistake.'

Her sudden intensity was unnerving. 'Fen … What's going on? Is everything all right?'

'Not exactly.'

But Fen didn't continue. She was frowning a little to herself. She didn't look visibly upset, more as if she was trying to weigh something up.

Then the bell began to toll. They should have been ready for it – it was why Eve had been advised to bring the ear-plugs – but it made them start. Six o'clock.

The noise was much louder than Eve would have imagined. The boom of bronze seemed to reverberate through her bones. They both put their hands over their ears, grimacing.

Afterwards, the silence rang.

'Great. Now I've got a headache,' said Fen, abruptly turning to go.

'Wait, let's take a moment. You said there was something wrong …?'

'Forget it.'

'You've not been yourself lately. I'm worried.'

'That's very touching. But I don't need you, or anyone else, turning me into their special project.'

'That's not what I'm doing. Friends look out for each other—'

154

'Fuck's sake, Eve! If you want to look after someone, then maybe you should stop hiding away with me and go spend time with your actual kid.'

And then she was gone, leaving Eve alone in the dusty tower and the throbbing air.

ALICE

When I heard there had been a death, my first mad thought was that it was Bette. A vision flashed before me of her and Henry in some kind of murder–suicide situation, though which of them had committed which was a little fuzzy. I suppose it was because of the wildness of her the last time we'd met. I remembered my dream of finding Bette with her head bashed in; it was a nightmare precisely because the scene had a whisper of wish-fulfilment.

The body wasn't found until ten. The rain that had come in overnight had persisted, so the usual Saturday-morning dog walkers hadn't been out in force. But one hardy local had set out along the woodland path, spied the open door to the cabin and thought they might take shelter there – presumably just as Mrs Easton had. They had immediately run to the school lodge to raise the alarm. It was the porter on duty who phoned the police.

I'd spent a sleepless night and was still wallowing in bed when I heard my father talking to someone in the hall. Even though I couldn't make out any of the words, something about the tone of the conversation brought me out of my room as soon as I heard the front door close. I stood at the top of the stairs, looking at my father's pale face below.

'There's been a terrible accident. Incident. A death, in fact.' He was as formal as a stranger. 'I'm very sorry to tell you that Mrs Easton has been … Mrs Easton has been found dead.'

'Shit. Sorry! Sorry. What happened? Was she … ill?'

But Pa wouldn't have looked like that if it had been a mere heart attack.

'It's not immediately clear. She was found in the outward-bound cabin, in the woods. I'm told that a man – a person of interest – has been found nearby. The police have taken him in for questioning.' He cleared his throat. He was still speaking very stiffly, like a bad actor reading from a script. 'However, we don't know what we are dealing with and it would be reckless to speculate. Obviously, I don't have to tell you to not to discuss this with anyone before the headmaster has had an opportunity to address the school. The staff are being notified as we speak.'

On normal Saturday mornings students were in class until lunchtime, but the morning after Hazard Night was a holiday. I checked my watch: the upper sixth would be being collected by their parents right about now. I could just imagine the hysteria that would set in once they saw the emergency services swarming around campus.

My father was obviously thinking the same thing. He said, almost as if to himself, 'It's only a week until the end of term. We can send everybody home early. But in the meantime – the shock, the dismay – there will be much … work to be done.' He blinked. His stiffness was softening, but into something faltering and unsure. 'I should – they'll want me to … People will expect …' He moved his hand blindly over his face. 'The expectation …'

A crisis like this was what a chaplain was supposed to be for. To comfort the bereaved; to provide hope and counsel and make sense of the senseless. To lead his frightened flock out of the darkness and towards the light.

I realised my father didn't know what to do.

'Maybe you should pray,' I said tentatively. 'It might, you know, centre you a little.'

'That's a good idea. Yes. The trouble is … the funny thing is … I seem to have forgotten how to.' And he gave a small shamed smile that I'd never seen on him before.

I suppose I'd known, deep down, that my father had lost his faith a while ago. It was still a shock to have this confirmed. When I'd announced, with typical twelve-year-old stroppiness, after chapel one Sunday, that God Is Dead, Pa had just laughed a little into his beard and said, 'Maybe, maybe, but his spirit lives on to torment us.'

Where was Mrs Easton's spirit now? And was it a tormented or tormenting one?

Crack-Head Kyle was picked up shortly after the police arrived on the scene. He was found lying insensible in a makeshift tent about a quarter of a mile from the cabin, his clothes covered in blood. He claimed to have no recollection of the last few hours, on account of having taken an industrial amount of drugs. That was the story he stuck to throughout his police interview. He couldn't remember. Yes, he might have gone to shelter in the cabin when his tent began to leak. Yes, it was possible he might have surprised Mrs Easton there. Had they got into an argument? He couldn't say. Had he lashed out, shoving her against the cabin's rusty storage locker, so that she fell to the floor with her head cracked open? *I'm not a violent person*, said Kyle. And then he began to cry. *I'm sorry*, he said. *I'm sorry. I don't remember. Only the blood. I'll remember the blood for ever.*

Now, I can't swear to the accuracy of this. It's what Jean in Catering told me, who got it from Kath in Accounts, who got it from Ian in Facilities, whose brother-in-law was one of the police officers involved in Kyle's arrest.

But what is indisputably true is this: with prompt medical attention, Fenella Easton would have survived. Instead, she bled to death on the cabin floor.

And what was she doing wandering the woods at one o'clock in the morning? Her husband testified that she suffered from insomnia and often roamed the campus late at night. Her torch was found in the cabin. There were no toxins in her body other than alcohol, no drugs on her

159

person. Her wallet had been left at home. The only money found on Kyle had been a grubby five-pound note and a handful of loose change.

If Kyle had ever sold Mrs Easton dope, his lawyer must have advised against him admitting it – and the Cleeve authorities must have heaved a sigh of relief. For as long as Fenella Easton's little weaknesses stayed a secret, then her – and by default the school's – reputation was safe. She had been tragically unlucky to stumble into the path of a vagrant in the grip of a drug-induced psychosis. But, as I heard Headmaster Parish tell my father and his colleagues, such a crime, though thankfully very rare, could have happened anywhere. Such was the lamentable state of the modern world.

The concerned parents of Cleeve weren't, of course, satisfied by this particular take on things. The murder had been committed on school grounds, after all. An unsuccessful campaign was mounted to revoke the public right of way through the woods. CCTV was installed on every building and wall on campus; the grizzled night-time security guard was let go and two young toughs hired in his place. However, it was the news that Hazard Night was cancelled indefinitely that caused the greatest uproar in the school. 'There's *no way* Easton's beard would've wanted this,' I heard several boys say aggrievedly. And, 'She would *hate* this to be her legacy.' As if Mrs Easton had been the glad-eyed champion of pranksters everywhere.

I thought of her skulking and bitching with Mrs Winslow, smoking weed and necking booze in the shadows. I remembered her scathing laugh and her glittering stare. She had been anarchic, all right. But I don't think Fenella Easton ever gave a crap about anyone's desires except her own.

EVE

Eve's first thought, monstrously, was that Gabriel Easton must have done it. All of a sudden Nancy Riley's dire words seemed self-evidently true. He *did* have the cold eyes of a killer! He *would* know where the bodies were buried! White noise filled her head; she barely heard the rest of what Peter was telling her, though his face was so pinched, his speech so clipped and agonised, that each word seemed to come out in splinters. Later, when it was established that Gabriel had in fact been with Peter when Fen was killed, Eve felt a rush of disgust at her imaginings. But she was also conscious – yes, she had to admit it – of a trace of disappointment. There was a logic, however twisted and horrifying, to a domineering husband murdering his high-spirited wife. There was, however, no sense to the way Fen died. She hadn't fallen victim to a crime of passion. She had died in a squalid accident – a bloody, drug-addled blunder.

After Peter told her what had happened, Eve groped her way towards the bedroom and curled up on the bed in the foetal position. Milo padded after her and she drew him up to nestle against her, and so that she could rest her chin and drip her tears onto his soft head. She whimpered softly as her son pressed his warmth against hers, his chubby hands occasionally pulling and patting at her with uncharacteristic softness. 'Mummy,' he said gravely. 'Sad Mummy is sad.' He was trying to comfort her, and this only made her cry more. 'I'm sorry,' she whispered into his hair. 'I'm sorry.'

Peter had been the one to break the news to Gabriel Easton, too. Headmaster Parish had tasked him with it as soon as the porter phoned from the lodge with the news of the body. He had been with Gabriel when the police arrived and accompanied him when he went to formally identify his dead wife. Peter was his usual stoic, supportive self throughout – or so Eve was told. For as soon as he told her what had happened, he left. He and the rest of the school administration were plunged into a maelstrom of crisis management and she didn't see him for the rest of the day.

That night, by which time the majority of students had been tearfully taken home, Eve dried her eyes, strapped a sleepy Milo into the buggy and went to find her husband. She wasn't the only person still looking for Peter; to go AWOL at such a time was so out of character that she began to worry. She finally tracked him down at the back of the Lodge, scrubbing off the giant cock-and-balls some wag had spray-painted on the wall.

Peter had begun the clean-up operation the previous night. Some of the Wyatt's boys had shamefacedly told him about the graffiti, which went against both the rules and spirit of Hazard Night, and, Peter being Peter, he hadn't liked the idea of the leavers potentially having their ball and graduation ceremony cancelled because one idiot had gone rogue. So once the dorm was quiet, he'd left his deputy, Steve, in charge, grabbed a bucket of soapy water and a scrubbing brush, and set off to remove the evidence. Gabriel Easton, as sleepless as his doomed wife, had seen Peter from his window and gone to help. An uncharacteristic gesture, Eve would have thought, except the truth was – and it was high time she admitted it – she hardly knew the man at all.

By the time she found Peter, he was scouring off the last flakes of paint, panting slightly from the effort.

'They're good kids,' he said by way of explanation. 'I didn't want them to get in trouble.'

'It's all right. They've all gone home. Nobody cares about a bit of graffiti, not now.' Eve spoke gently, but she was angry. Whatever the demands on Peter, however dreadful his day, it was *her* friend who had died.

Milo looked between his parents, confused by the unexpected outing. 'Snack time?' he asked hopefully.

Peter rubbed his eyes, still holding the scrubbing brush. Dirty suds dribbled down his arm. 'I'm so sorry about your friend. You know that, don't you?'

'Yes. It's …' Her throat closed. 'It's horrible beyond words. Beyond everything.'

'They're saying – people here are saying – not aloud – it's a whisper, really – that Fen went to buy drugs. That's why she was in the cabin with that man who the police took away.' Peter turned and looked at her searchingly. 'Does that make sense to you? Do you think it could be true?'

'I don't know.' Eve felt herself begin to tremble. She picked Milo out of the buggy and held him close, hoping his warmth would steady her. 'Maybe. Yesterday … the last time I saw her … Fen was agitated, upset. I didn't really understand what was going on.' She swallowed. 'We argued. Hurtful things were said. I felt, for the first time, that maybe I didn't know her like I thought I did.'

Peter was silent for a long while. Eve waited for him to be generous, to be kindly. She buried her face in their son's silky hair, breathing in his warm biscuity smell, and anticipated the moment things between them would be put right.

'I'm really sorry, Eve,' Peter said at last. 'But as I said before, I don't believe Fenella Easton meant well. You can't say you weren't warned.'

Eve had never thought of herself as an especially good person. She tried to be nice and useful; she wanted to be a supportive wife, mother and friend. Yet she recognised her own selfishness and impatience would always get in the way of this to some degree. She had always taken comfort

– pride, even – in the fact that Peter was the better person. It was one of the few things in her life that she felt was rock-solid.

But that night, watching her husband stand before her, dripping with dirty water and moral judgement, Eve felt certain of nothing. Because suddenly Fen was there too, shaking out her curls, lasciviously sucking the last of her martini from an olive. 'Have you ever thought,' this ghost-Fen drawled, 'that maybe, just maybe, your husband is a prick?'

ALICE

It was a strange summer. If I'd known it was to be my last at Cleeve, I suppose I might have made more of it. As things were, it was just a long hot period of blankness that needed to be got through – not that I was much looking forward to whatever was waiting on the other side.

In the aftermath of the death, two of the regular commercial hires pulled out, leaving the campus emptier than it had ever been over the holidays. In previous years, I would have revelled in my undisturbed ownership of the place. But although it was now easier than ever to pretend to be Queen of the Castle, my favourite childhood game had lost much of its appeal. Turns out it's not so much fun presiding over a kingdom without any people in it.

Without the summer camps in residence, I didn't have my usual holiday job of manning the desk in the Facilities office. This left the days even more empty. For a few years when I was small, we'd visit my maternal grandmother during the holidays, but she died when I was six. Then we used to go to the seaside with the family of one of my mother's schoolfriends. But for the last few years, Pa and I had got used to spending the whole summer at Cleeve, and though I'd sometimes be invited by the beards to tag along on their family activities or expeditions, I used to find this rather a chore. I thought I was the same as Pa: that I must be better off with my own company.

The Sunday night after Mrs Easton's body was found, and once all the students had left, everyone still living or working on campus joined Pa for prayers and a candlelit vigil. He didn't hold it in the Chapel, but by the Lake. He kept his words simple and people strained to hear his voice at times; he didn't look or sound at all like his nickname: he was just a sad, tired old man.

Poor Pa. I knew he'd have to dial everything up once the school returned. I also knew how bogus the full-on Cleeve production of a memorial would be. Here, without the pressure of our paying guests, people could be honest, and I think it made their grief more sincere. Mrs Winslow spent the whole vigil looking as if she was about to faint or throw up. The porters and caretakers and groundsmen, with whom Mrs Easton had always been effortlessly matey, loudly blew their noses and wiped their eyes. The headmaster and his First Lady kept glancing at their watches. Mr Easton didn't attend. He remained shut up in his cottage and wasn't answering the door to anyone except the police.

A couple of people muttered it was lucky Mr Winslow could provide Mr Easton with an alibi, because 'it's almost always the husband, isn't it?' Meanwhile, Kyle Thomas Henderson, of no fixed abode, was safely in police custody, set to plead guilty to manslaughter by reason of diminished responsibility.

I know this probably makes me a terrible person, but even during the vigil I found my thoughts drifting towards Henry and Bette. Henry sent me a postcard in August, which I stuck to the wall above my bed. It was a picture of the Hong Kong skyline and simply read *I hope you're having a good summer. HZ.* I didn't hear from anyone else and I knew perfectly well that this wouldn't change once school resumed. Bette would see to that.

I went to Burger Biz a few times, wondering if I would run into Lindsey. She would probably only have jeered at me, but the idea of her was an itch I needed to scratch. Lindsey and Henry. Lindsey and Rupert. Lindsey and the Bates family. Lindsey and Crack-Head Kyle. Lindsey and the boys I'd followed … to the cabin in the woods. Yes, the thought of all this was more than a mild itch. It was something ugly and aggravating that I wanted to scrape out of my head.

The Cleeve administration didn't know who could have forced open the padlock to the cabin door or moved the boards over the windows, but somebody in Facilities lost their job over the failure to keep the place secured. The police said the cabin had likely been used by vagrants for a while, citing the empty beer bottles and food wrappers and cigarette butts they found there. If the school suspected the litter came from another source, they kept quiet about it. Over the summer, several parents informed the headmaster's office that they were withdrawing their children from the school, and admissions enquiries were noticeably down. The last thing Cleeve needed was more bad press.

Oh well. With Lindsey absent, at least my favourite bench was restored to me. But now whenever I sat on the Margaret Mumford memorial, I wondered about the girl who had committed suicide and Lindsey's cryptic talk of crime scenes. There were lots of ghoulish stories floating around Cleeve. Some were cautionary tales, others unvarnished tragedies. The six boys who died in the Spanish flu outbreak of 1918. A groundsman who lost his hand in a wood chipper. Three local kids who smashed their car into a lamp-post and died in a fireball, not three miles from the school … I had, now I came to think of it, heard a rumour about a girl from the Laundry who killed herself, though I was fairly sure the suicide had taken place on a farm.

From Lady Lilian to Fenella Easton, Cleeve had a plentiful supply of ghosts.

So I abandoned the bench and took refuge in the pool. I'd thrash up and down until my fingertips turned greenish white and wrinkled, every breath burned and my legs were limp as string cheese. Occasionally, I'd look up through the fog in my goggles, and for an absurd half-moment I would see a boy looking down at me from the side. A skinny dark-haired boy with an uncertain smile.

Catch, pull. Flow. Breathe.

EVE

Eve didn't leave her husband over the holidays, but she thought about it.

Peter always booked himself on an array of training courses and conferences over the summer. That year Eve pushed him to sign up for as many last-minute places on last-minute courses as he could find. She and Milo went to house-sit for an old university friend while Peter was away, and when he came back she shocked everyone by agreeing to spend their holiday time with Nancy Riley and family in a seaside rental. 'Are you sure?' Peter kept asking, doubtfully. 'Are you *sure*?' Nancy Riley asked, pink with pleasure, but her voice betraying an undercurrent of suspicion all the same.

Eve was sure. Surrounded by the busybodying Riley brood, she and Peter would be shielded from each other. And it would be good not to have the quiet and space to think. None of her thoughts were happy ones.

Back in Cleeve, in the week before the students returned for Advent term, Peter quietly moved his belongings into the guest bedroom. He was trying to be tactful, to give Eve the space she needed. Two months after Fen's death, at completely unpredictable moments she would find herself bursting, violently, into tears. Once she even hurled a wine glass at the door.

'It's only natural. You'll feel better with time. You'll get through this,' Peter kept saying, but the more he said it the more meaningless it sounded. Sometimes Eve worried it was not she who was withdrawing from Peter, but that he was withdrawing from her. His patience with her had become more professional, she thought; it was the kind of care-taking he employed with his boys. The distance between them started to frighten her, but she was unable, somehow, to close the gap. She no longer even knew which of them was maintaining it.

She found herself seeking refuge in Milo's company as well as his needs. Motherhood was becoming less of a condition and more of a job, with her child's growing self-sufficiency providing her with breaks and formalised child-care supplying holidays. The true liberation for Eve was the discovery that some of her time with Milo could feel like a holiday too.

But even if Eve was to leave, where were she and Milo to go? Her unhappiness with her life at Cleeve had changed with Fen's arrival, and even with Fen gone, Eve realised she had come to feel differently about the place. Liberated from her awe of Cleeve, she was able to let go of some of her resentments and rediscover some of its beauty.

Things got to the point where she found herself confiding to Nancy about Peter. 'I worry a part of him must be scared I'm turning into his mother. His dad's a drunk – I think that's one of the reasons he was wary of Fen. But his mother's actually *mad*. Always jeering or shrieking and throwing things. And when I'm having an outburst I can sense the shutters come down: it's like he retreats into a kind of defensive blankness. It's as if he's not really there.'

'Come now! You haven't been endlessly "outbursting".'

'Well, no. But I've been crying a lot. And one time I threw a glass.'

'I threw a tin of beans at Richard's head once.'

'Really?' Eve perked up a little, despite herself. 'Why on earth?'

'Well, I know I'm not especially clever, but I *am* very organised. A doer, not a thinker, that's what my teachers said.'

Eve nodded, unsure as to where this was going.

'So I didn't go to university. I went on a secretarial course instead. I quite liked the idea of becoming an "executive PA" – being the right-hand woman to some City bigshot, working in a smart London office, wearing a smart little suit.' Nancy rolled her eyes humorously. 'Then I met Richard, when I was temping at one of the private girls' schools, and one thing led to another, and now I'm *his* right-hand woman instead. And I *love* it, don't get me wrong. I love how he and my boys depend on me. But sometimes … just now and then … I think that, actually, I might have enjoyed a more official job? And one afternoon, I was in the kitchen peeling spuds or something, and Richard came in in a bit of a bother about writing some article for the prospectus, and I offered to help, and he laughed and said, "With what, your O-level in Home Economics?"' Nancy paused. 'And I picked up a tin of beans and just *hurled* it at him. I didn't even say a word. It's lucky I'm such a rotten shot, else it could have done some proper damage. As it was, the tin whistled past his head and crashed into the clock on the wall.'

'Good for you,' said Eve.

'We laugh about it now, of course. It's become just another of those funny family stories – "The time Mum threw the beans at Dad's head". But I can't tell you how angry I was at the time. I don't know what got into me, to be honest.'

Eve squeezed her hand, and Nancy squeezed it back.

———————

Gabriel Easton was on compassionate leave, with no date fixed for his return. Nancy said she'd heard he was staying with a friend from Cambridge. 'I do feel guilty for thinking so badly of him,' she confessed to Eve the next time they met. 'I popped round to drop off a frozen lasagne a day or two after Fen's, you know, *passing*, but he didn't answer the door. The awful thing is, I could hear him crying inside. It was so loud, it was more like a howl. An animal howl.'

Now it was Eve's turn to feel guilty. All she'd done was post an incoherent note of condolence through the door. Since she knew some of the complications of the Eastons' marriage, and could guess at the rest, it was her own squeamishness that had stopped her from attempting more.

Eve wondered if Fen had been as evasive and elliptical with her husband as she had been with her in the days leading up to the death. All that talk of destruction, thunderbolts, games gone dangerously awry … looking back, it was almost as if Fen had sensed the impending horror. Could Gabriel have sensed it too?

'People are still whispering about him,' Nancy continued. 'It's criminal, really. The actual killer is already locked up and Gabriel's been completely exonerated. I mean, he was with Peter when it happened, for goodness' sake! Mike – the security guard – told me he'd seen the two of them trying to clear the graffiti on his rounds, and that Gabriel was scrubbing at the paint like a man possessed.'

'Perhaps that's part of the problem,' said Eve. 'Gabriel always seems so intense. It unsettles people.'

'Well, *I* for one am resolving to be *much* less judgemental in future,' said Nancy righteously. 'Everyone puts on a brave face around here, but you never know what goes on behind closed doors.'

Eve thought of Nancy's words on her way back to Wyatt's that same afternoon, when she passed Tristan von Aldstine getting out of his Range Rover. Rupert might have left the school, but his father was still a governor and, thanks to the PR crisis of Mrs Easton's death, the school board were meeting practically every week. Most of the governors had attended the official memorial service, held two days previously on the first Saturday of term, but Eve hadn't spotted von Aldstine there.

Tristan's ruddy cheeks were considerably more weather-beaten and his pale hair more silvery than Rupert's but, like his son, he was very much cock-of-the-walk. Today he was wearing the posh gent's off-duty uniform of corduroy trousers and a sloppy-looking shirt. However, there was nothing off-duty about his expression, which was grimly preoccupied. Where would he and the First Lady contrive their next tryst, Eve wondered. Perhaps they had a local love nest somewhere for when the thrill of their Library hook-ups wore off.

So it was all the more unexpected to bump into von Aldstine's mistress coming out of Wyatt's just as Eve was going in.

'Eve! What a *surprise.'*

But it's my house, Eve thought. 'Were you looking for me?'

The First Lady let out a tinkling laugh. 'No, no. I wanted to check on dear Peter. He hasn't seemed himself lately and I wanted to see how he was doing. Of course he always puts a brave face on for his boys, but in times like these, friends need to be there for each other.'

Since when were Peter and Madeleine Parish friends? But then, Eve admonished herself, Peter was friendly with everyone. Except her, these days.

Mrs Parish pushed her dark glasses to the top of her head and put a confiding hand on Eve's arm. 'Peter's the *soul* of discretion, but I did wonder if the strain of the recent tragedy is taking its toll.'

'I'm the one who was close to Fen.'

'Well, *exactly*. No doubt you're feeling terribly blue. I'm sure Peter's support is *boundless*. But even boundless support needs a little encouragement along the way, hm?'

Mrs Parish looked so small and soft, with her bright eyes and rosy mouth, her crown of shiny hair. Still, she was the sort who'd be dumpy in a couple of years, thought Eve with satisfaction. The pearly teeth would start to yellow. She'd grow matronly. The girlish laughter would come to sound incongruous, and the likes of von Aldstine wouldn't look twice.

'Peter and I have perfect faith in each other,' she said. 'Don't think I don't appreciate how rare that is.'

The ice in the First Lady's eyes glinted. 'I'm very happy to hear that. I found the memorial service immensely comforting, myself. Such a sad, but necessary, way to begin the new school year. Our dear chaplain can be a little *dusty* at times, but I think he really hit his stride, didn't he? Hardly a dry eye in the house! Such a pity poor Gabriel didn't feel strong enough to attend. I really think it would have done him good.'

'To see how beloved and respected his wife was by the Cleeve community?' Eve asked drily.

'Tragedy can be something of a makeover artist, I've found.' This time, the glint was humorous. 'Now, I'd love to stay and natter, but I have someone waiting for me.' She repositioned her dark glasses. 'You be sure to take care of yourself, Eve. You and Peter. After everything we've gone through, we don't want any more trouble. Mm?'

The day was as sunny as the First Lady's smile. Nonetheless, a tremor of foreboding ran down Eve's spine.

ALICE

I might have lost my summer job, but I still slipped into the old habit of helping out and running errands as the start of Advent term approached. The morning of Arrivals Day, I went into Wyatt's to distribute a stack of *The Cleeve Companion* onto the new squits' desks. I heard a noise from near the senior common room and realised someone was on the payphone in the corridor.

It was Henry, and he must have been talking to a family member because he was speaking Cantonese. Despite myself, I stopped to listen. I had never heard Henry speak in his mother tongue before. He seemed to be talking very fast and loud, and the words sounded choppy and rough to my ignorant ear – or maybe it was just the contrast to Henry's more usual public school tones. The conversation ended on a placating note; I guessed he was most likely talking to his mother.

Henry put the phone back in the cradle with the universal huff of adolescent exasperation. Then he turned and saw me before I could move on. He looked discomfited, almost furtive, as if he had been caught out at something. 'Oh. Alice. Hi.'

'Hi.' I kept my distance at the end of the corridor. 'Sorry. I wasn't actually eavesdropping. And, you know, I wouldn't have been able to understand anything if I was.'

'Well, no.' He gave a little cough. Mutual embarrassment clouded the air: I suppose we were both thinking of our last encounter, when he'd basically told me to fuck off. Since then, I'd learned how he'd betrayed Bette, who had taken out her fury on me. I knew I should be angry with Henry, and I was, but I was also painfully conscious of how trivial this all was. There had been a violent death. It was something the school would be talking about for months, years, to come. Should Henry and I be talking about it too? Was this the moment when I should ask Henry whether the chain of events that led Kyle to the cabin on Hazard Night was in any way connected to whatever he and Lindsey and the rest had been doing there?

Since I'm a coward, I settled for the most banal opener possible. 'Thanks for the postcard,' I said, at the same time as Henry said, 'I owe you an apology.'

'I mean it,' Henry continued. 'I was an absolute arse to you that day outside Burger Biz. I was in a bad place and I took it out on you. I know you were only trying to help, and to be a good friend to Bette. And to me, of course.' He tugged distractedly at his hair, such a familiar gesture that I felt my throat ache. 'Not that I deserve it.'

181

'Have you talked to Bette since … uh…?'

'No. Not since she tore strips off me outside the Clit. She sent me this weird cryptic note over the holidays but then she wouldn't return any of my calls. Have you heard from her?'

I shook my head.

'Well then,' said Henry ruefully. 'I suppose we'll have to be outcasts together.'

But it turned out Bette had other ideas.

Once the rest of the school had returned, I was careful to avoid Bette's regular hangouts and gave the girls' boarding house a wide berth. So the first time I came face to face with her was in chapel, at the memorial service for Mrs Easton. (Pa did his best, but it was still dreadful. The choir sang *Panis Angelicus*, and the boys coughed and adjusted their collars, and all the girls lavishly cried.) Anyway, I was conscious of Bette turning to stare at me as she walked in, and staring at me even harder as she walked out. She'd lost weight over holidays, so with the new sharpness of her cheekbones and the increased shortness of her hair, she looked more hard-edged and yet more fragile at the same time. I supposed the burning stare was meant to make me feel intimidated.

A couple of days later she ran me to ground after school. 'I've come to warn you,' she said. Her voice, always husky, was hoarse and trembling. I noticed her nails were bitten down to the quick. 'You need to stay away from Henry.'

Oh, Jesus. 'Let's not get into all this again.' Pointedly, I returned to my book.

I had been reading on a bench (not Margaret Mumford's – another, less haunted one) but now Bette snatched the book out of my hands. 'This is for your own good. I swear it.'

She didn't sound threatening, however. Not like in our last encounter – there, she'd had a savage energy and heat. This time she was almost pleading.

'Look, Bette, this is our last year at Cleeve. There's no need for us—'

'I didn't want to come back. I *begged* Daddy to find me somewhere else to take the exams. Mummy was on my side. She said the school had failed in its safeguarding duties, and that we were all traumatised, and no wonder, because it could have been any one of *us* lying dead in that cabin. But in the end I caved. I suppose a part of me always knew there was no escaping it, and that I *had* to come back. To face *him*. To face everything. If this is fate – well – there's no point running away.'

I looked at her blankly. 'I don't understand you.'

'Christ, Alice!' A flash of her old queenliness. 'Just *listen*, will you? What I'm trying to say … that is, what I'm trying to tell you … is that I'm part responsible.'

'For what?'

She closed her eyes. 'For Fenella Easton's death.'

183

EVE

The second weekend of term, Eve went to see Gabriel Easton. She felt she couldn't put it off any longer. For one thing, people kept asking if she and Peter had heard from him, assuming a closeness between the two couples that hadn't strictly been there, and which Eve felt too embarrassed to deny.

Peter himself didn't think she should go. 'There's a reason Gabriel hasn't been in contact with anyone here. He needs time and space. You should wait for him to reach out, when he's ready.'

'It's been months. Fen would want me to check on him,' said Eve stubbornly. 'I'm sure of it.'

And Peter just looked at her, with the too-calm, too-distant expression he wore more and more these days. 'I think you'll regret it,' he said.

Nancy found her the address; Gabriel was staying in a friend's holiday cottage in a seaside town near Hastings. It would be a long journey for Eve, who was a somewhat nervous driver at the best of times, but Nancy bolstered her resolve. 'It's a marvellous thing you're doing – poor Gabriel needs to know he has friends at Cleeve and that we're *all* rooting for him.' She had volunteered to take care of Milo for the day and even packed Eve a picnic lunch, bundling up a fresh stack of condolence cards and a homemade fruitcake for her to take with her.

Despite everything, Eve felt a thrill of freedom as Cleeve's entrance posts receded in her wing mirror. Leaving campus while unencumbered by husband or child still had some novelty value and it was one of those September days that feel like summer. She rolled down the window and turned up the radio, indulging the fantasy that she was on some adventurous road-trip, footloose and fancy-free. Then the pop jingle changed to a ballad, and a plaintive one at that, and she remembered she was going to visit a grieving widower to … what, exactly? Offer comfort? Apologise?

Ask questions?

Something had been wrong with Fen before she died. Now that the fog of grief had begun to lift, Eve was more certain than ever that Fen wasn't simply acting capriciously. She was troubled by something, maybe even a little frightened. Gabriel might not be responsible for his wife's death, but Eve still wanted to know if he was to blame for her distress. It was becoming all she could think about.

There was a risk, of course, that the whole trip would be for nothing. Although Eve had tried Gabriel's telephone number at various times of the day, nobody ever picked up. It was very likely that she might arrive at the house only to find that Gabriel was out or had moved elsewhere without notifying the school. She did not admit to herself that this would be a relief, and by the time she reached her destination, she was feeling increasingly confident that it would be a wasted trip. What's more, the cottage was named Mermaid's Nook and had wind-chimes in the garden and a trio of jolly ceramic mermaids on the door – it was impossible to imagine Gabriel Easton in such a place. Eve could hardly contain her surprise, therefore, when he opened the door mere moments after she knocked on it.

Part of her shock was at how much grief had aged him. His striking gauntness was now closer to skeletal, and his skin looked stretched thin with exhaustion. A tall man, he was now oddly stooped. She hoped her dismay wasn't too obvious on her face. 'Eve,' he said, even more startled than she was. 'My goodness.'

'I tried to phone ahead,' she said, more defensively than she meant to.

'Ah. Yes, I'm afraid I keep unplugging the damn thing from the wall. I'm finding it hard to sleep and so …' He trailed off. 'I'm sorry. Won't you come inside?'

'Thank you, yes. I'm sorry for the intrusion. It's just that I … we … your friends – the people at Cleeve – thought somebody should, ah, come and see how you were.'

Gabriel blinked at her dazedly. The interior of the cottage had the scuffed, unloved feel of a holiday rental out of season. Beyond the tiny hallway, Eve glimpsed a kitchen stacked with dirty plates.

'Sorry about the state of the place. A friend lent it to me. They've been very kind. As have you, of course, coming all this way. Can I make you some tea?'

Eve asked for a glass of water and clumsily handed over the fruitcake and the cards. She was horribly conscious of how much Gabriel wanted her gone and how much she herself longed to escape. Both of them were grimly going through the motions nonetheless. While Gabriel fetched the water, she went to wait in the sitting room. She expected more kitsch mermaids and nautical-themed bric-a-brac. Instead, she found that the walls were covered from top to bottom with Fen's art. Everywhere she looked were prints and etchings and paintings, many of which she hadn't seen before, but all of which were unmistakeably – grotesquely – familiar. Because Fen's face was everywhere – as she-beasts and she-demons, queens and enchantresses, nymphs and crones. Laughing, snarling, pouting, sighing, weeping … old and young, ugly and beautiful, blessed and damned.

One drawing caught her eye because it was a rare scene of violence. A young girl-Fen swung from a noose, her eyes bulging and hands clawing at her throat as her breath was choked out of her. Fen hadn't portrayed herself as dying in any of her other works, and for this reason the sketch

187

particularly unsettled Eve. On an easel in the centre of the room, and taking up much of the limited floor space, was Fen's last and unfinished painting: the scorpion-demoness inspired by *Journey to the West*.

It was much larger than any of her other pieces, almost life-sized, and though some of the details were yet to be filled in, the visceral power of it took Eve's breath away. The creature's vicious pincers and bristling sting looked ready to leap off the canvas; rising up from between the claws was the head and torso of a naked woman. This version of Fen was wanton and seductive, her mouth lasciviously open, her cheeks rampantly flushed. Her hair writhed around her head in snaky tendrils.

'I need to have her by me,' said Gabriel, coming in quietly through the door. 'I know it must seem strange, or possibly distasteful.'

'No, not at all. I'm sure she'd be glad you were taking comfort from her art.' Eve averted her eyes from the scorpion-Fen. 'Everything must be so incredibly raw.'

'It is,' he said slowly. 'Mostly, it's unbearable to me that I wasn't there for her, at the end.'

Eve swallowed. 'The last time I saw Fen, she seemed rather … upset. Jittery. In fact, in those last couple of weeks, she didn't really seem herself. I don't know if it's something you noticed.'

'Ah. Yes. Now and again, Fen would get very low. If her work was going badly, she'd have the most awful black slumps. But then if her work was going well, she'd sometimes become almost manic – high as a kite.' Gabriel smiled faintly. 'The artistic temperament is not to be trifled with.'

Eve wondered if this could explain the ramblings about Nietzsche and the notion of being a god with a thunderbolt. The more she thought about it, the more unhinged it seemed. 'She said a new project was giving her trouble.'

'Yes, that's what she told me. But I don't know what she was referring to. All of her work is here. Every last half-scribble. If she was starting something new, it must have been at the purely conceptual stage. It's a special kind of torment, accepting I'll never know what it was.'

They were both silent.

'I'm glad you came,' Gabriel said at last, rousing himself a little. 'I was going through some of Fen's things a while back and I found something addressed to you. I meant to drop it off before coming here, but what with one thing or another ...'

He handed Eve an envelope. There was an undeniable frisson to the idea of a message from beyond the grave; Eve had a strong feeling that she should only read it once she was alone.

'You weren't tempted to open it?' she asked.

'Why would I do that? I've always respected my wife's privacy. Even after death.'

Eve nodded. 'I know how much she loved you.' It was the sort of empty platitude one was expected to say in these situations. But in Fen's case, Eve felt it maybe wasn't such a straightforward declaration. *I do love him. Isn't that funny? Or is it just sad?* Fen had said. And then that line about love blooming in Hell.

'Do you? How curious,' said Gabriel, with a touch of his former acerbity. 'I wasn't always so convinced.'

'Well, she wouldn't want you to feel guilty, I'm sure of that.'

'Guilt?' He was startled. 'Why guilt, of all things?'

'I just meant … because of Cambridge. Because of why you had to leave.' Eve was flustered. 'I'm sorry. I should never have brought it up. It's not that I—'

To her surprise, Gabriel began to laugh. 'So Fen blamed our Cambridge exit on me, did she? My God, the front of her.' He shook his head admiringly. 'As it happens, Eve, I've never broken my marriage vows. Fen, on the other hand …'

'She said there was a student,' Eve said weakly.

'Yes. One of my postgraduates. He and Fen had something of an *amour fou*. The student dropped out, and there was subsequently a lot of … recrimination. Fen was usually much more discreet. But on this occasion it wasn't something we could clear up, or not entirely. The whispers were starting to become deafening. Cleeve was meant to be a fresh start – for both of us, I suppose.'

'Oh.' Eve felt incredibly foolish. And betrayed. But mostly foolish. *The rapaciousness of youth, the vanity of middle age … the insecurity of both.* Fen's bitterness had been very convincing. But of course, there she had been talking about herself. And the rest had been lies. Lies as arresting and as irresistible as her art.

Gabriel was looking at her kindly. 'Don't be upset. Fen was Fen; I knew what I was getting into. It may seem now that perhaps you did not. But I do know how fond she was of you. Most of the time, she meant well.'

This was the exact opposite of what Peter had said. Which of them was right? The Fen-faces thronged all around in their competing guises; for a moment it was as if all the pictures seemed to move and speak and Eve's head filled with a cacophony of Fen-laughter and Fen-sobs and Fen-whispers and Fen-shouts. Her breath came fast and light; she had a panicked sense of being surrounded, besieged. She gulped down her water and told herself to get a grip.

Meanwhile, Gabriel got up stiffly from his chair and went to inspect another of the drawings. 'You know, when you said I shouldn't feel guilty my paranoid mind immediately went to what the rest of Cleeve must be saying. I know some of them feel it's a little *too* convenient that Kyle Henderson was found by the cabin in the state he was.'

'He's confessed.'

'Yes, and that is a comfort of sorts. But if I didn't have an alibi I know what the whispers would be, Kyle Henderson or no.'

'You mustn't waste your energy worrying about the odd conspiracy theorist.'

He didn't seem to have heard her. 'I wouldn't have changed Fen for the world. But Peter's a good man. Generous as well as decent. You're very lucky there.'

Eve tried to smile. 'I know.'

'He went out on a limb for me. So please thank him from me again. For all his kindness.'

It seemed the right place to end the conversation. As they said their stilted farewells, Eve wasn't really listening to her own words and neither was Gabriel. His eyes were fixed on the scorpion-demoness.

Back in the car, Eve finally opened the envelope.

There was a Post-it stuck to a folded piece of paper. *Sorry to have been such a bitch this p.m.*, went the confident, looping scrawl. *I know there are some lines that shouldn't be crossed. But let's celebrate the ones that can, eh?! xx*

The paper was their list of expectations. Eve had copied them down from *The Cleeve Companion* herself. She cast her eye down the page, seeing her own neat tick-mark alongside each completed challenge. *Plagiarising, cheating, intoxication, lying, stealing, trespassing, failing to report a violation.* However, the final expectation had acquired a new tick since she'd seen it last, done in Fen's unmistakeable large and vigorous hand.

Sexual delinquency. Tick!

Eve caught her breath. The only reason Fen would have sent her incriminating tick to Eve was because it was something she wanted to be asked about. She had, perhaps, been ready to confess the reason for her strangeness and abruptness on the last day of her life.

ALICE

In the immediate aftermath of the death, there had been hardly any chance for the student body to react before they had been swept up by their concerned parents and borne off home. But press interest in the case revived with the start of the autumn term, and the gaggle of reporters who'd been staking out the school gates returned to their post. Cleeve issued stern warnings against talking to the press, backed up by threats of expulsion or dismissal, but this only added to everyone's sense of self-importance. The girls in particular were determined not to let the summer hiatus rob them of the chance to parade their trauma.

Even the new intake of lower-sixth girls, who didn't know Mrs Easton from Adam, were getting in on the act. There was a lot of sighing and hugging and staring into the middle-distance and weepy collapses in the middle of class. The boys, too, weren't above talking up the significance of every fleeting encounter they may or may not have had with Easton's beard. Nothing had higher social currency than some kind of connection to the deceased.

I'm being unfair. In spite of all the posturing, everyone – from lowly squit to lofty leaver – was sincerely and deeply shocked. Even the kids at my school were obsessively talking about Mrs Easton, and asked for my insider's view with a kind of respectful awe that, I'll admit, was uncomfortably close to flattering. To be a girl at Cleeve was a constant performance in any case, and in the aftermath of the killing, the sixth-form girls' minority status was cast in even sharper relief. Perhaps it was the first time they – we – truly understood that to be female is to always carry with you, at some level, the fear of a lonely cabin in a dark wood.

Anyway. I didn't for one moment believe in Bette's latest proclamation. Bette, I'd come to realise, thrived on drama. Her stand against the sex pests Astley and Simmonds, admirable as it was, had been as much about self-promotion as social justice. Claiming to have some sort of proximity to Mrs Easton's death was surely no different.

So after Bette's admission of responsibility, I continued to slouch idly on the bench and said in the same unimpressed tones of our first encounter: 'Oh, really. Why do you say that?'

'Because Henry killed her,' she hissed.

I sat up so fast it made my neck crick. 'You've gone mad,' I said flatly. Bette's new brittle manner was only a cover, I realised. Any minute now the hysteria boiling away beneath it would erupt. I looked around, hoping somebody else would come round the corner or emerge from the bushes to rescue me.

'I wish I had,' she said, slumping down beside me and worrying at a hangnail with her teeth. 'My God, I certainly *feel* mad. I've been living with this knowledge all summer. I can't eat, I can't sleep. I'm losing my fucking mind. But I'm also totally sane. *That's* what's crazy.'

I tried to collect my scattered wits. 'Listen. We know who killed Mrs Easton.' I was talking slowly and carefully, as if to a child. 'It was Crack-Head Kyle. And even though nobody's saying it out loud, Mrs Easton most likely went to buy weed off him and the guy lost it. He's *confessed*, Bette.'

'That doesn't mean anything,' she said impatiently. 'The man was off his head on drugs. How the hell would he even know whether he'd done it or not? And the police could have put all sorts of pressure on him. God – Headmaster Parish probably charged into the interview room wielding a cricket bat.'

I snort-laughed at this image, I'm ashamed to say.

Bette, however, was deadly serious. 'You know the school would do anything to avoid a scandal. For all we know, they offered this man hush-money to admit to the crime. They've got more than enough funds to buy him off.'

'This is batshit –' I stopped myself. 'Conspiracy theories aside, I don't see what any of this has got to do with Henry. Henry Zhang! Of *all people*.'

'Why? You don't think he's capable of such a thing? Because they all are. Or most of them. Don't forget how Henry smashed Niko Diamandis's face in last term. If he hadn't been dragged off him Niko would've ended up in hospital. He was left *black and blue*.'

'No, he wasn't. Niko got a black eye, that's all. They were mates again by teatime. That's what boys—'

'Don't you *dare* tell me "boys will be boys". Don't you see how this place has indoctrinated you?' Bette was blazing again. 'You think you're so special and different, this supercilious outsider, but you don't see the truth of what goes on here, not really. Because you're too close to it. So close you can't even see what's right in front of your nose.'

'Fine.' I folded my arms across the chest. 'Please enlighten me, then, as to why the hell Henry Zhang would murder Fenella Easton.'

'Are you actually retarded, Alice, or are you just fucking with me? We both know *exactly* what the motive was. They were sleeping together, of course. You already knew that.'

This time I had to grip the arm of the bench to steady myself. Because even as I opened my mouth to explain that no, Bette had got it wrong, I realised the full extent of my error. For when Bette had confronted me with Henry's betrayal, she'd never actually named her love rival. Henry, I remembered with blistering clarity, had denied anything was going on with Lindsey when I'd asked him, and Lindsey hadn't ever confirmed a relationship either. She'd just smirked. I had leapt to the obvious conclusion, and it was the wrong one.

I remembered when the Eastons had first arrived at Cleeve and how I'd bumped into Henry just after he'd helped Fenella carry in her easel. I'd asked him what she was like. Different, he'd said, and laughed. It struck me now that his laughter must have already had a covetous edge.

Mrs Easton had given him that book, the Chinese fable about the demon and the monks. He'd gone to her Art History classes. I'd overheard the Art master say that Mrs Easton was painting a character from Chinese mythology – perhaps one of those fiends in female form I remembered reading about. That would be fitting. She'd probably asked for Henry's help. The unique insight of his heritage ... I felt a shudder of revulsion.

I realised Bette was waiting for my response. Her whole body was vibrating with tension.

'Yes, you're right,' I somehow managed to say. 'It's just that ... even now ... it seems so unlikely. So wrong.' I couldn't even find the words to explain my mistake. Mortification had struck me dumb.

'Exactly. I know this makes me a wicked, terrible person, because nobody deserves to die like that, but I still can't get past the idea that Henry chose her over me. She had actual *grey hair*. It's *disgusting*. She must have been twenty years older than us at least.'

Despite myself, I couldn't help thinking of all the sixth-form girls who'd made eyes at Mr Easton, at least until they learned what a despot he was. Fenella Easton might not have been conventionally pretty like Bette or even conventionally sexy like Lindsey but even I, the virginial chaplain's daughter, recognised the heat she gave out.

'I'm still so humiliated whenever I think of it,' Bette went on, dragging her knuckles over her face. 'Do you know how I found out?'

'You said, uh, something about the key for the Chapel storeroom ...'

'Yes. I was suspicious in any case. Henry had become so damn furtive. I knew he was hiding *something*, and I was worried because I'd made this big deal about wanting to wait before sleeping with him. That's why I gave him the key, all tied up in a purple ribbon. It's pathetic – I'm pathetic – God, the whole thing is *mortifying* – but I told him it was my pledge to him. That I'd meet him there, on his birthday.'

Her face burned white and red. 'And then ... then ... I was walking back to the dorm on Thursday evening, the Thursday before Hazard Night, and I saw Mrs Easton on the path ahead. She'd dropped her bag and her things had spilled out. I was going to help her pick them up, actually. But then I saw one of the things she was putting back in the bag was my key. *Our* key. It was unmistakeable. The shiny-new copy of the rusty old key you'd given to me and

I'd solemnly presented to Henry, all tied up with my purple ribbon. He'd given it to *her*.'

'Jesus.'

'But you knew this already.'

'Yes,' I said, trying to recover myself. 'Right. But even so … I'm still struggling … you say Henry killed her but also that you're responsible?'

'Well, after I saw the key and realised what was going on, I had to confront him. I'd been sobbing and sobbing all night long, but by the morning I was mostly furious. Because I'd done *everything* for Henry. Before he was with me, people liked him, sure, but he wasn't brothers-in-arms with Rupert von Aldstine, was he? He wasn't fucking *prom king* material. So when I saw him outside the Clit, I was so angry – I started shouting – I don't even know if half of what I said made any sense – but I do know I told him I would make it my mission to destroy him. Him and his slut.'

'And then …?' I prompted. Bette had lapsed into silence and was biting frantically at her nails.

'Then I got a sick note from Matron and holed up in my room for the rest of the day. But before class the next morning I heard from Georgina – her boyfriend's in Wyatt's – that Henry somehow managed to sneak out at night with the people who were doing Hazard Night. He wasn't involved in any of the pranks. They wouldn't have let him – it's strictly a leaver's thing. So what was he doing? Where was he going, if it wasn't to see Mrs Easton?'

I rubbed my neck. 'You think the two of them met in the cabin on Hazard Night.'

'Exactly. They must have rowed – probably about me – and then he pushed her over, and she cracked her head open. And he left.' She drew a deep, shaky breath. 'So you see that, even if Henry killed her, I'm also to blame. I pushed him to the edge.'

'OK, it's a, um, theory,' I said cautiously. 'But I've seen Henry since. He seems … well, he seems pretty normal.' Certainly not like somebody who'd murdered his secret lover only a couple of months previously. 'Wouldn't you have to be a complete psychopath to do something like that and then go home to your family and back to school and act like nothing's happened? Look at you. You're living with just the, you know, *suspicion* of a crime and you're a wreck.'

'Henry can be very cold, Alice. Cold and controlled. Remember, you don't know him like I do.'

'So what are you going to do?'

Bette looked surprised. 'Protect him, of course.' She seemed more her old self again. 'Because he's a victim too, isn't he? You know how predatory Fenella Easton was. She was always sniffing around the good-looking boys – she was shameless about it. Did you hear about that picture she was working on in the art studios? The spider-woman thing? Apparently it was practically pornographic.'

'Uh … that doesn't mean she deserved to die.'

'*Obviously* that's not what I'm saying. You're missing the point. I'm simply explaining why I've decided that Henry's freedom is my cross to bear. My silence, and the guilt I'll always feel about it, is the price I have to pay for my part in this.' This time, I couldn't help thinking the tremble in her voice was for effect. 'Henry knows. I sent him a note over the holidays saying that I'd always protect his secret, but he had to understand that we couldn't ever speak to each other again.'

'And ... and what about Kyle?'

'Who?'

'The man who's going on trial for the murder.'

Bette shrugged. 'He was already a criminal. It's very sad, obviously, but a man like that was bound to end up in prison one way or another. At least this way Henry has the chance to put his life to good use. To atone. It could even be the making of him.'

Her eyes glistened. Heroically.

I didn't really know what, if anything, to believe, but I felt like crying too.

EVE

After her visit to Gabriel Easton, Eve kept returning to her last encounter with Fen. She re-examined it obsessively, trying to look at it from all angles, in different lights. Eve wasn't satisfied by the explanation that Fen was having artistic difficulties, because she'd spoken of Cleeve in a way she never had before: not mockingly or contemptuously, but almost as if it frightened her. She'd talked of games ending in tears, of dead foxes and blinded eyes. But the strangeness – the wrongness – hadn't been confined to that afternoon in the tower.

On the last day of her life, Fen had talked as if she felt under threat.

But on other occasions, it was Fen who positioned herself as the destroyer.

Imagine I had the power to bring all of this crashing down.

You don't know what I'm capable of.

After a couple of sleepless nights, Eve decided the only thing for it was to break into the Eastons' cottage and see what she could find. She had no idea what she was looking for, and it was possible she was simply struggling to accept that Fen had been consistently dishonest with her. But she couldn't get away from the thought of Fen's final note and what it might signify. *There are some lines that shouldn't be crossed. But let's celebrate the ones that can ...* Eve was increasingly sure the note was the prelude to some kind of confession.

Getting into the cottage was easy. Eve knew which plant pot hid the spare key, and if anyone saw her going in or out she could always say Gabriel had asked her to find some item to post to him. All the same, she had a superstitious urge to lock the door behind her. She didn't want to be caught by surprise.

She was unprepared for how strange and sad the Eastons' home looked without its occupants. The curtains were all drawn and every surface was fuzzy with dust. All Fen's things were there just as she had left them; it looked as if Gabriel hadn't moved a thing. Her denim jacket was on the back of the kitchen chair. Her 'Queen of All She Surveys' mug, with a residual scum of tea staining the bottom, sat on the coffee table next to her sketch-pad. Her Moroccan slippers, with the sole coming away and half the beads missing, were still lying where they'd been kicked off at the bottom of the stairs. Yet Eve couldn't entertain the fantasy that at any moment Fen would burst through the door to reclaim her life.

The shadowy, dusty silence of the place had the feel of a mausoleum.

Eve felt a surging of grief for Gabriel, and also for herself, as the memories crowded around. Old stains on the farmhouse kitchen table brought back the generous spices and savour of Fen's cooking. Her hand tingled as she stroked the faded green-velvet cushion that Fen had liked to hug to her chest when talking on serious matters; her eyes filled when she saw a flyer for a concert the two of them had been going to attend pinned to the noticeboard, alongside a photograph of her and Fen gurning beside their infamous Clock Tower cake.

Gabriel had taken all of Fen's art with him, but there wasn't anything missing from the walls because Fen had preferred to store most of her pictures out of sight. This was one of Fen's most intriguing paradoxes: a confident extrovert who repeatedly and nakedly exposed herself on canvas … yet hid most of her creations away. It struck Eve that she had no idea how successful an artist Fen was. Her talent seemed obvious, at least to Eve's untrained eye, but Fen had never mentioned exhibitions or galleries, and Eve hadn't known how seriously she should take her occasional references to 'my patrons and panderers'.

No wonder Gabriel had surrounded himself with Fen's self-portraits and all the contradictions they embodied. He wasn't just trying to be close to his dead wife: he was still trying to work out the truth of her. The kindest interpretation of Fen's work was that she had been attempting this too. Creating multiple versions of herself on canvas wasn't simple narcissism, but an attempt to find and interrogate her real self.

Eve saved the marital bedroom for last. She knew that being there was a violation, but the pull was nonetheless irresistible. When she pushed open the door, she was met with a disorder of rumpled bed-sheets; the air smelled musty and animal. The purplish-brown colour of the walls had a fleshy warmth, and bosomy nymphs frolicked on the bed's antique painted headboard – Fen had told her once, laughing, that the décor of the master bedroom was 'bordello-chic'. Eve would have thought it hideous, once. Now she thought of her own prim, pale bedroom and sighed.

The wardrobe was another antique, a walnut hulk that was too big for the room and was scuffed and scratched in the same way the headboard was. Eve, feeling more and more of a voyeur but less and less able to resist, rummaged through Gabriel's tweedy Cambridge-don suits and Fen's jumble of clothes, some of which looked like they might have been expensive and others which could have come from the school's lost property box. At the bottom of the wardrobe was a shoebox that Eve recognised, because it was where Fen stored her so-called beer trophies.

Fen, completely unabashed, used to say that she was planning to use her petty thefts for an art project, or else that they were talismans for witchcraft ('my gypsy blood has started to itch'). The collection had increased since Fen had first shown it to her, and the lid no longer fit. Eve pulled out the box and rifled through. There was the powder puff Fen had stolen from the First Lady's dressing table, the day she and Eve first met. There was Peter's 'Super Coach' engraved whistle, on a ribbon in the school colours. He'd spent ages looking for it last term, Eve remembered guiltily. Then there was one of Nancy Riley's floral Alice bands. One of the black eye-masks Eve used for sleeping was there too, which gave her pause. Each trophy was meant, in some way, to be a signifier of its owner, so what did Eve's represent? Was this meant to be her distinguishing feature – blindness?

Among the jumble of bits and bobs, a bright-green polyester scarf caught Eve's eye. It took a moment or two before she remembered where she had seen it before: in the game of Fox and Hounds. The foxes had all worn scarfs like this tucked into the backs of their waistbands. Eve tried to remember whose colour had been green. She couldn't think of any good reason why it would have been stashed away here.

The scarf's lurid green took on a sinister hue. Hurriedly, Eve stuffed it back in the box, which she wedged back in the wardrobe before taking a final look around the room. It was only then she noticed Fen's pocket diary on the bedside table, lying next to an Iris Murdoch novel and a smudgy wine glass. It caught her eye because she'd given it to Fen for Christmas;

it was turquoise suede, an expensive, impulse purchase that she'd rather regretted – 'Oh, OK,' Fen had said, looking taken aback. 'I didn't know that we did gifts.' Eve hadn't seen the diary since, and was unexpectedly moved to find that it had been put to use. She had just begun to flick through it when a sudden noise from down below stopped her in her tracks. Somebody else was in the cottage.

Gabriel, she thought instantly, and was flooded with the clammy sweat of shame. He would think her ghoulish at best, a crazed pervert at worst. She was frozen to the spot with embarrassment and indecision. But listening to the movements below, she started to think that there was something furtive about them. Somebody was moving about with the same anxious care as she had when she'd first entered the house. And Eve had locked the door behind her: she remembered distinctly.

Eve knew it was absurd to be frightened. It was most likely someone from Housekeeping or Facilities come to read the meter or check on a dripping tap. Still, she was jumpier than she used to be these days, more aware of moments of isolation and vulnerability. All the women were.

She stuffed the diary into her back pocket and went to the top of the stairs, listening. Whoever was in the house had grown bolder: their movements sounded less hushed and more confident. Very quietly, Eve descended the stairs. Her heart was banging against her ribs when she pushed open the door to the living room and found

Madeleine Parish going through the little writing bureau by the window. When she saw Eve, she started violently.

'My goodness!' she exclaimed, clutching her chest and laughing. 'What a fright you gave me.'

'Sorry if I startled you.'

There had been no denying the expression that had flashed across Madeleine's face. It was cold fury. A blink-and-you'll-miss-it moment. But Eve hadn't blinked.

The First Lady smoothed down her shiny hair. 'Gabriel telephoned to ask if I could send him some paperwork. So what are you doing here?'

She'd taken Eve's line. But Eve could be insouciant too.

'He mentioned Fen left a note for me when I last saw him. He wasn't sure where it had got to so I thought I'd better look for it myself.'

'Ah, yes. Your mercy mission to the grieving widower. I'm sure Fenella would be very grateful you're taking such good care of him.'

'Did you find it?'

'What?'

'The paperwork you were looking for.'

'Not so far, no.' Madeleine pushed a wodge of folders and notepads to one side, only for them to start to slip off the desk. She caught and righted them with an unsteady hand. 'I fear everything's in a bit of muddle … You?'

'Yes,' said Eve, very slowly. 'Yes, I found what I was looking for.' Then she smiled. It was smile that was designed to be both mysterious and laden with significance. And although she didn't have an exact strategy in mind, and was operating on pure instinct, she was rewarded when she saw the other woman's gaze falter.

Neither of them had turned on any lights, and the sunshine seeping through the drawn curtains had faded. It was not just gloomy but claustrophobic inside the cluttered, abandoned house that seemed so infused with a dead woman's presence. Someone's breath was coming fast and shallow; it took a moment for Eve to realise it wasn't hers. Mrs Parish took a step closer to Eve.

'Be very careful,' she said, 'be *very* careful that you don't make the same mistake your friend did.'

'Why? What's going to happen to me – is someone going to find me with my head bashed in?'

She meant to sound scathing but perhaps she merely came across as histrionic. The First Lady's lip curled. 'That's an absolutely vile thing to say.'

'Well, I'm tired of the veiled threats.'

'*You're* tired?' Her eyes widened. 'But you're the bully here, Eve. You and Fen. Don't think I don't know that the two of you were in league from the very start. Yet you still choose to act the innocent. At least Fen didn't try to hide who she was.'

Eve couldn't defend herself without knowing exactly which of her and Fen's misdemeanours Mrs Parish was accusing her of. For the moment, she judged it was better to keep quiet than to inadvertently incriminate herself. Meanwhile, Mrs Parish swept on.

'Nobody likes to speak ill of the dead, but the truth is that Fenella Easton was a drunken slut. I'd always thought inviting the Eastons to Cleeve was a mistake. Gabriel certainly wasn't the catch he appeared – as unpopular with students as he was with staff. Your husband was the only one who tolerated him. But then, poor Peter doesn't have enough of a backbone to dislike anyone, does he? Even his disapproval of Fenella was milquetoast.'

Eve felt a welcome flash of marital loyalty. 'Leave Peter out of it. Just because you treat your own husband with contempt doesn't give you leave to insult mine.' The time had come for plain speaking. 'Was Fen blackmailing you over Tristan von Aldstine? Is that what you think I was "in league" with her about?'

To her surprise, the First Lady laughed. 'Oh, goodness, Fenella didn't have the discipline for a credible shake-down. Mostly, she treated my indiscretion as an enormous joke. She fancied she could use it to lord herself over me.

'I told you, didn't I, that my husband is rather alarmed by women? To be perfectly honest, I have no idea if his tastes have a more *masculine* bent, but the critical point is that Mr Parish and I have reached a happy understanding. Fenella Easton was never in any danger of spoiling that.'

Eve had to appreciate the irony. It sounded as if the Parishes' 'understanding' was similar to Gabriel's acceptance of Fen's escapades. Except that Gabriel was, in every way, in love with his wife.

'And even if Fenella was minded to make things difficult for me, she couldn't help shooting herself in the foot. Nobody would take her seriously, not with her history of drink and drugs and general mischief-making. It wasn't hard to uncover the real reason the Eastons left St Benedict's, either. To find out she'd been smoking a joint by the Lake was the final straw. Smack in the middle of exam season, in full view of anyone who might wander by! So I told her to go quietly. All she needed to do was talk to her husband and explain that Cleeve wasn't working out for her. It would be better for all concerned. Besides, she must have already been looking for an excuse to leave. Surely that's what her high jinks were in aid of. Pure self-sabotage.'

Eve considered this. 'All right. That might be true. But if you weren't fussed about Fen exposing your adultery, then what the hell are you doing here? Because I don't believe for a second that you're on the hunt for a missing gas bill.'

'Dear me, Eve,' said the First Lady gaily. 'Use your head. If I was worried that boxes of blackmail material had been stashed away here don't you think I would have come looking for them *weeks* ago?'

That gave Eve pause. The cottage had been unoccupied all summer. What, then, had drawn Madeleine here?

The First Lady had recovered her poise. She now looked graciously forbearing, as if Eve was a neurotic parent whose expectations must be managed and worries soothed. But she *was* hiding something. Or she was afraid of something.

Eve was sure of it, and that frightened her in turn.

ALICE

During the third week of Advent term, Bette Drummond had an emotional breakdown and was taken home for good.

I heard about it first-hand from Pa, of all people. He'd found Bette sitting in the dark when he was about to lock up the Chapel on Thursday evening, and she asked if he would hear her confession. He had gently explained that confession was a Catholic sacrament, but if something was on her mind, he would be happy to talk it through with her, or perhaps set something up with a female member of staff. He then reminded her that a grief counsellor had been drafted in to help students who were struggling to come to terms with the 'loss' of Mrs Easton (as Cleeve was officially referring to it).

Apparently she had got quite angry with him. 'I'm worried about the state of my *soul*,' she said. 'I thought that was supposed to be your speciality.'

Slightly taken aback, he invited her to say more. But then she burst into tears and ran off. She was then found in hysterics, ankle-deep in the Lake. 'It was rather difficult to work out what she was saying,' Pa reported. 'She'd had a bad break-up, apparently, and it seems this and the Easton business had sent her over the edge.'

So her housemistress put in a call to her parents overseas, and a relative who lived locally came to collect her that same night. Two days later Cleeve was informed that Bette wasn't coming back. She would be continuing her studies at a London day-school.

'I'm only telling you this,' Pa said on Saturday evening after he'd come back from a meeting with the Higher Ups, 'because I know you were friendly with her, and also –' he coughed and looked downwards '– that the two of you had a bit of a dust-up last term.'

Dust-up was putting it mildly. 'We'd moved on from that,' I said.

'Well, I'm glad to hear it. But now I worry there should have been some kind of earlier intervention. Bette Drummond was clearly in a very fragile, perhaps depressive state. Seeing her flail about in the Lake … in such distress …' His voice faltered. 'Why are such things so easily missed? It haunts me. I should have done more. We all should have.'

It felt disloyal, as well as cruel, to voice my suspicions about Bette's flair for drama. 'You mustn't feel guilty about this. I think Bette's stronger than she looks. Now she's back with her family, making a new start, I'm sure she'll be fine.'

Pa sighed. 'I fear Cleeve is not a good environment for sensitive girls.'

'I'm a sensitive girl.'

'But you're also a very sensible one, Alice. And besides, you don't attend Cleeve.'

'Right. I merely lurk in its corners. Like a squatter.'

This came out more bitterly than I intended. Pa raised his brows. 'Dear me, I hope you're not going to smash another water glass.'

In fairness, I think he meant it as a joke. Something to lighten the tension. But I wasn't in the mood. 'There's a lot of things that could do with smashing up around here,' I said, and set off to gatecrash the social.

———————————

It was the first social of term for the sixth formers and as such wasn't one of the big, more glitzy affairs when students from neighbouring public schools were bussed in to make up the numbers. Still, the Hall had been decked with fairy lights and a glitterball was winched up to dangle among the chandeliers. Murky oil paintings of headmasters past glowered down on the festivities, their frames festooned with rather tired-looking streamers.

I'd helped set the Hall up for socials on a couple of occasions, but this was the first time I was going to be in actual attendance. The housemaster on bouncer duty was Mr Riley. 'Oh,' he said. 'Ah. Alice. Hello. Er, what are you doing here? Does your, um, father know?'

'He gave his blessing,' I said, marching past.

Things were already in full swing by the time I got there. The assistant housemaster from Hawkins' was DJ, and The Prodigy was blasting from the decks. A rabble of boys were monopolising the dance floor to thrash about, butting against each other, stumbling and tumbling, and uttering primitive whoops. Their bow-ties were askew and their shirts half-unbuttoned. Meanwhile, the new crop of lower-sixth girls stood in slightly tense clusters, observing the scene. The upper-sixth girls were more nonchalant and looking self-consciously bored, except for those who were already paired up with boyfriends or snogging partners. Obviously no alcohol was allowed, and it was equally obvious that copious amounts of booze had been sourced from somewhere. Really, it was no different to the school disco at my comp, except that the girls' perfume smelled more expensive and the boys' hair flopped forward in sweaty hanks, rather than being gelled back.

Heads turned on my arrival. I suppose I didn't exactly blend into the background: I was wearing leggings and a boy's polo shirt from the lost property box, with one of my dad's scraggy old cardigans. Since last term, I'd rather let things slide on the fashion front. I went over to say hi to Moira, who was in charge of the snack table, and Janet, who was doling out the punch. Moira loves working the socials; she gives romantic advice to the girls and scolds the boys about their hair and posture. (She can get away with this, because she's A Character.) Janet likes the socials too, because, she says, they put her in mind of her own dancing days. 'What are you doing here, love?' they asked. 'Have some crisps,' and, 'You know, there's plenty of time for you to go change into a frock if you want to have a little boogie.'

I got a much warmer greeting from them than anyone else. Bette's girl-gang wrinkled their noses and narrowed their eyes when they saw me. I presumed Bette hadn't told them the whole story, but they knew enough to know I was persona non grata. A couple of the boys nodded at me blearily. 'Wotcha, Fishface!' said Julius Simmonds, going to slap my arse. I neatly sidestepped, so that he tripped over his own feet instead and nearly blundered into the punch bowl. His friends applauded. Moira and Janet rolled their eyes.

I spotted Henry standing under the portrait of Headmaster Dorkings, a nineteenth-century tyrant with a fearsome scowl. He was standing alone, sipping from a can of Coke and looking almost as stern as the portrait. Rupert and Nico had graduated and Bette had dumped him – in a way calculated to make rumours run wild – so perhaps he was feeling at a bit of a loss. Still, he looked undeniably good, all dark and brooding in his tux and spangled by the light of the glitterball. One of the bolder new girls sashayed towards him but after seeing him glower into his drink thought better of it and slunk back to her friends.

When he saw me, he nearly spat out his Coke. 'What are you doing here?'

'Looking for you. I heard about Bette.'

'What about her?'

'That she's not coming back to school. Pa told me just now.'

'OK.' He looked down at his feet, frowning. 'To be honest, that's probably for the best. She didn't seem … well.'

'Bette leaving has certainly made life easier for you.'

His head snapped back up. 'Look, I don't know what shit she's been spouting, but she's been acting extremely strangely for a long time. Whatever has been going on with her, I think it's bigger than our break-up. To be honest, I think she probably does need some professional help. So it's a good thing if leaving Cleeve means she's going to get it.'

'She wrote you a letter over the holidays. Didn't that explain anything?'

'God, that letter – it was more like a cryptic crossword. I couldn't make head or tail of it. Then she basically ran away whenever I tried to talk to her.'

A snogging couple wheeled into us, so that Henry's drink slopped. 'Sorry, bro,' the boy slurred. He was wearing tartan trousers, his cheeks were crimson, and his quiff was lank with sweat. I looked at the girl clinging to his shirttails in incomprehension.

'Let's get some air, shall we?' said Henry.

The fire doors were open at the back of the Hall. It was a chilly night, so most of the other people who'd wandered outside were keeping warm by prolonged groping. There was a staff member patrolling back and forth at a discreet distance, to check couples didn't try to sneak off into the night. Luckily, one of the benches was unoccupied. Henry took off his dinner jacket and draped it around my shoulders, an act more automatic than chivalrous. Cleeve boys had this stuff drilled into them far harder than algebra or Latin declensions.

The moon was high, painting the buildings with cold washes of black and silver. Cleeve looked older, more austere, at night. Behind the bright Hall windows, the party pulsed and roared. I had to appreciate the irony: sitting out here with Henry, his jacket warming my shoulders, his eyes fixed intently on mine, had once been a scene out of my most private Mills & Boon fantasies.

'So tell me about the last time you saw Bette,' Henry was saying. 'Is she still blackening my name?'

Might as well cut to the chase. 'She thinks you killed Mrs Easton.'

His jaw dropped so that he looked almost comical. Slack-faced and foolish. I felt glad. A criminal psychopath wouldn't react in such a way.

'What? *What?* Why? Why the *hell*—?'

'Because you were sleeping with her.'

'Oh no. Oh no, no, no, no, no, no.' He was shaking his head. 'No. This is seriously bad. Something has gone seriously wrong here.' He ran his hands through his hair. 'It was Lindsey. Lindsey! I had a – this one time – this one hook-up – with Lindsey Bates. That's all. Nobody else. Never. But you knew about Lindsey … didn't you? I mean, yes, I denied it at the time, but later – when Bette – when Bette—'

'Bette told me about the key to the Chapel storeroom, with the ribbon on it, that you'd given to Mrs Easton. Bette saw her with it.' But my voice faltered. It was only now striking me how circumstantial all of this was, how tangled and blurry our lines of communication had been.

'Fuck,' Henry shouted, so loudly that people paused their romancing to look over at us. He lowered his voice. 'Look. I don't really understand how this has happened. But at least some of the craziness is now making sense. When Bette confronted me and said she knew I'd cheated on her, she sounded *deranged*. As in screaming and swearing and crying. The works. She just *lost* it. I was in shock – I didn't have a chance to get a word in edgeways. I never dreamed that she'd got it so wrong …'

'It was because of the key,' I prompted.

'The key. Shit. Yeah … Rupert saw it in my room and asked me what the deal was. So I told him. Which I shouldn't have, obviously. It was a dick move. That was supposed to be something private between Bette and me. Rupert just laughed and said that since I wasn't making use of it, he might as well borrow it. And he took it off me. Just like that. I was actually really angry. I'd thought me and Rupert had become pretty good mates. But there wasn't anything I could do about it without, you know, making a massive scene.'

I swallowed. 'So it looks like Rupert gave it to Fenella Easton.'

We were both silent for a moment. Henry let out a shaky sigh. 'Jesus. I had no idea. I mean, I knew Rupert was seeing someone. Secretly. He said they liked sneaking around, for the kicks. But I never … He was having a rough time with his dad last term, and I think I was the only person he told about it. I don't have the best relationship with my father either. I guess I thought that's why he was acting out – risk-taking and all that. But …' Henry bit his lip. 'Him and Easton's beard? Sorry. Mrs Easton. That's so messed up.'

'Bette thought it was you. She thought the two of you had a lovers' quarrel in the cabin on Hazard Night and that you pushed Mrs Easton over by accident. She's been protecting you. She thinks she's helping you to escape justice. That's what the cryptic letter and general craziness has been about.'

Henry groaned. 'Poor Bette. I never meant – I never dreamed – if only I'd known—'

'And,' I said, pressing on, 'Bette knew you snuck out of Wyatt's on Hazard Night. That's why she deduced you went to the cabin.'

'I snuck out with Rupert's help. I was … running an errand. I was meeting Lindsey, in fact. But outside the Lodge, not the cabin. And not to hook up, either.'

'So what were you doing then? You and Rupert and Nico and the rest? I followed you guys to the cabin, remember. What's this all been about?'

Henry put his head in his hands. 'God, it all seems so tame in hindsight. It wasn't drugs or – or sex. It was poker.'

I let out a breath I hadn't realised I was holding. 'You were gambling?'

'It was Rupert's idea. Games night, he called it. He likes to have a flutter. But poker, so he kept saying, isn't about luck, it's about skill. And we're all so clever, so fucking *skilful*, us Cleeve boys. Right?'

His voice was thick with disgust. I kept quiet, listening.

'Lindsey had a Saturday job at Cleeve for a while, and that's how she bumped into Rupert. She cadged a fag off him and they started talking, and somehow it ended with her saying she could set up Rupert and his friends with some of *her* friends who liked to play cards.

'You know what that lot are like: Rupert, Niko, the twins. They're rich. Rich and bored. Joining a gambling ring with some local tough guys – it was a thrill for them. Something to boast about when they went home for the holidays and were hanging out with the chinless-wonder set. Plus they've got money to burn.'

'*You* don't,' I said bluntly. The summer before last, I knew, Henry had spent the holidays working in a tourist café in Hong Kong's Victoria Harbour.

'No,' Henry said slowly. 'But I wasn't there to play. Or not so much. Rupert subbed my buy-in. Basically …' He screwed up his eyes. 'My God. This is all so ridiculous. It would be laughable if it wasn't so … ugh. Anyway. Once Rupert met with Gary – Gary Bates, that's Lindsey's uncle – he could see it wouldn't do to be seen as a bunch of clueless posh boys. Which is what they – we – essentially are. So Rupert brought me in and hinted to Gary and his mates that I come from this Hong Kong triad family and that my dad's basically Asian mafia.'

I stared at him. 'You're kidding.'

'I wish I was. Rupert persuaded me it would be a laugh. And it seemed to work – Gary and Co. were asking me about triad initiation rituals and so on, all super respectful. So I made up some shit about Dragon Masters and blood oaths. It was funny at first.'

'And this worked, did it?' I folded my arms across my chest. 'You intimidated the Bateses into playing nicely?'

Henry's mouth twisted. 'No. They fleeced us, of course. Rupert lost the most, but the others weren't far behind. Niko ended up handing over his Rolex at the last game they played and he was freaking out because it was a birthday present from his sodding granddad.'

'Is that what your punch-up was about?'

'Niko said I'd turned the whole fake triad thing into a piss-take, and that's why Gary's crew felt emboldened to rip everyone off. Like it was all *my* fault. But I felt bad about punching him. I shouldn't have lost it like that. That's why I went to negotiate with Lindsey and her uncle, to try and recover his watch. That's when you saw us at Burger Biz. And we arranged for a handover on Hazard Night. It had to be late, because Lindsey was working at her bartending job earlier.'

'It sounds like you and your pals were in seriously over your heads.'

'Well, I might have been bullshitting about being triad, but that lot were play-acting at gangsters too. Lindsey told me that her uncle's mostly all talk, no trousers. Kneecapping a bunch of public schoolboys was way above their pay grade.'

'But you said Lindsey set Rupert up with her dodgy uncle in the first place! And when I followed you out to the cabin, it was Lindsey who was keeping watch. Why would you trust her?'

'I didn't have much choice. Look, I only ever went to three game nights, and the other two times it was that Kyle bloke on lookout. Lindsey was more like the host – fetching drinks, keeping an eye on the time, running through the house rules. I sat out most of the games, trying to look all triad-y and intimidating in a corner. It was pretty boring, to be honest. Lindsey came and joined

me, and we talked a bit. So, no, I didn't trust her, but …
I respected her, I guess.'

'Is that why you cheated on Bette with her? Because
of all that "respect"?'

He winced. 'I've screwed up a lot of things this year.
But you deciding that I'm an unreconstructed piece of shit
is one of my biggest regrets.'

'Why do you care what I think?'

'Are you kidding? Of course I care, Alice. You're one of
the only things – people – that make this place bearable.'
The intensity of his gaze made me uncomfortable, so that I
had to look away. 'Look, me and Lindsey had one drunken
fumble in the woods, and I felt terrible about it. That's all.
Lindsey didn't make trouble for me. For one thing, she
had her sights set elsewhere. She'd found out the Rolfe
twins' dad owns that high-end hotel chain, and she said
she wanted a job there that wasn't scrubbing toilets and
changing sheets.'

I resisted the urge to roll my eyes. 'I see. She said she'd
help get the Rolex back and all outstanding debts settled,
so long as the Rolfe boys wangled her a position front of
house.'

'Or in the back office. Like I said, Lindsey's smart. She
left school at sixteen but her grades were good. It's not right
that her only employment opportunities are working in
that burger joint and some seedy bar or doing shady stuff
with her uncle.'

'Doing shady stuff with her uncle seems to have worked out pretty well for her.'

I thought back to my encounter with her and Rupert in the Lavender Walk and how he'd made that crack about her having the shirt off his back. He hadn't seemed to bear a grudge for the poker-game stitch-up. I suppose as soon as Henry had helped to settle the debts, it didn't suit Rupert to dwell on the humiliation. The whole affair would be recast as a hilarious anecdote. Perhaps he and Mrs Easton had even laughed about it together.

Henry shook his head. 'Honestly, the whole business has been such an unbelievable mess …You can see why I didn't tell Bette about the gambling, right? I knew she'd freak out.'

'Except she came to her own conclusions instead. And they were a hell of a lot worse than a stupid poker game.'

He rocked back and forth, shivering. 'I just can't believe she thinks I'm capable of *murder*.'

'She wanted to protect you all the same.' Bette had savoured the drama. But she had acted out of love. Of that I was sure. 'Write to her. Explain everything. It'll be OK.' I wasn't so certain of this, but I tried to smile reassuringly. 'Have you seen, uh, Lindsey since Hazard Night?'

'No. But she called me, actually, not long afterwards. She must have scammed the school office into giving her my home telephone number. She was really upset. About Kyle. She said he couldn't have done it, that he's a bit of a creep, a loser, but he's not violent. She said he'd been stitched up. She said that's what Cleeve does best. She said the school's the "biggest load of gangsters on the block".'

'Shit.'

He nodded. We stared out into the darkness. For the moment, we'd exhausted ourselves.

'You know,' said Henry after a while, 'I only became tight with those guys – Rupert, Niko, the twins – because I thought it would impress Bette. Isn't that pathetic? I'm not making myself out to be any kind of victim, because that would be stupid, but one of the things I hate about this school is how there's times I hardly know which is the real me … and which is the person Cleeve has groomed me to be.'

The disco music was now oozing treacle, and the slow dances had begun. I looked back through the doors to the Hall, where couples rocked and swayed drowsily in the flickering light. I looked back at Henry, black and silver and beautiful in the moonlight.

'People do stupid things for love,' I said. 'At least you didn't kill anyone.'

'I wasn't even in love. I know that now.'

I barely heard him. It had struck me, with dizzying force, that the notion of Henry killing Mrs Easton wasn't the only implausible explanation for her death. After all our lies and muddles and confusion, I was starting to wonder if Lindsey was right. What if Kyle Henderson really had been in the wrong place at the wrong time?

And if so, what was I going to do about it?

228

EVE

The encounter with Mrs Parish in the Eastons' cottage left Eve badly rattled. Fen may have toyed with the idea of razing Cleeve to the ground, but if she'd intended to accomplish this through blackmail, Eve had to concede that Mrs Parish's extra-marital indiscretions were hardly thunderbolt material. Yet she couldn't shake off the suspicion that the First Lady was hiding something more.

Back at home, in the half-hour before she was due to collect Milo from nursery, Eve got out the diary she'd stolen from Fen's bedside and leafed through the pages, more slowly this time. There was something horribly poignant about a diary belonging to a person who had run out of days for good. The Monday after Fen's death, she had been planning on going to the cinema, and had written down the various showings of the film she wanted to see. She'd booked a dental check-up the following week.

Most of the earlier entries were similarly pedestrian. Coffee with Eve, the address of a picture framer, a note to remember somebody's birthday. Rationally, Eve knew there was no chance of finding an appointment for 'blackmailing Mrs P' or 'sexual delinquency with X'. Yet one thing caught her eye. On the day of her death, Fen had written the name Lindsey Bates. When Fen had met Eve in the Clock Tower, she'd said she was late because she'd been meeting with somebody – was that somebody Lindsey? In any case, Eve thought the name sounded familiar. There was a local family called Bates, Eve knew, and she seemed to remember there was something either bad or sad about them, maybe both. She called out to Peter, who'd just come in to change after rugby coaching.

'Do you know of a Lindsey Bates?'

'Doesn't ring any bells, sorry. Why?'

'Never mind.'

So she phoned Nancy, who thought a Lindsey might have worked in Housekeeping. Housekeeping confirmed that Lindsey Bates had been a temp in the Laundry the previous school year, and after Eve spun a story about finding a postcard half-addressed to Lindsey among Fen's things, HR found a home telephone number for her. A man answered with a grunt.

'Hello. Is Lindsey there, please?'

'She's gone, in't she. Moved up in the world.'

'Do you have another number for her?'

'No.' A dog was barking and a woman shouting in the background.

'Well, I'm phoning from Cleeve Col—'

He swore, violently, and put down the phone.

Really, Eve thought, she was chasing ghosts. She should return the diary to Gabriel. She should forget about the bright-green scarf in Fen's trophy box. She should stop speculating about both Fen's and Madeleine Parish's sex lives. She should reach out to her husband, engage with her child. Let sleeping dogs lie.

And yet, late at night, her thoughts seethed and churned. In the morning, the first thing she reached for was the diary again. Lindsey Bates might be a dead-end, but there was one other appointment in Fen's last weeks that wasn't immediately explainable. In the Tuesday two weeks before Hazard Night, Fen had a ten o'clock appointment with a Monica Danbury. In this instance, she'd scribbled an address and telephone number.

Eve dialled the number.

'Thank you for calling Fairview House Private Nursing Home,' said the recorded greeting. 'If you know the extension you are calling, please dial …'

Eve held for reception.

'Fairview, good morning,' said a sprightly voice.

'Hello, I wondered if I could speak to Monica? Monica –' she checked the diary '– Danbury.'

'I'm very sorry to say that Monica passed away last month.'

'Oh dear. My apologies – I didn't know.'

'It was very peaceful. Are you a friend of the family?'

Eve thought quickly. 'No, no, I was only calling because one of Monica's, ah, friends, had sadly died and I wondered if she had heard the news.'

'I'm sorry. Monica was suffering from dementia so I'm afraid it's unlikely she would have been able to process the information.'

Eve looked down at the diary. There was only one entry for Monica, which suggested the visit was a one-off. Surely Fen would have mentioned if she had an elderly relative or friend in a nursing home in the area.

Then she remembered that Fen *had* mentioned it – or rather, when Fen had once failed to turn up for something, she'd said she'd gone to see a friend in a nursing home. *Don't ever get old, Eve. Fucking horrible business.*

But getting old was still better than the alternative.

Eve realised that the Fairview receptionist was still talking, and asking her something. Since she wasn't quite sure what the question was, she mumbled something about mutual friends and Cleeve College.

'Ah, how nice. However confused she got, Monica always spoke of her time at Cleeve very fondly.'

That made Eve sit up. 'She was at Cleeve for, er, long?'

'Well, she was head matron there for a good few years.' The receptionist's professional tone had softened – she was suddenly chatty. 'There was a little obituary in the local paper if you're interested; I remember the family said they were sending it on to the school archives. It would be nice if there was a mention in the magazine or similar – I'm sure there must be lots of former students who remember her fondly. And the school chaplain came to visit her once or twice.'

The chaplain's visits made sense. It was the kind of do-gooding priests were supposed to go in for. But why was Fen visiting a former Cleeve matron?

Eve had had little to do with the Reverend Andrew Gainsbury. Although he was one of the handful of still-serving members of staff from Peter's school days, he had made no particular effort to welcome the Winslows to Cleeve. His was a benign yet impersonal presence, and if Eve ever thought of him, it was as part of the background stage-business of the school, like the chime of the Clock Tower bell or the faded Union flag that hung over the Memorial Arch. She had warmed to him at the vigil for Fen, where he had spoken with real feeling. But she struggled to remember anything he had ever said in chapel.

On her way to the Gainsburys' cottage Eve passed God's daughter, Alice, rushing off in the opposite direction. The girl had always been a loner – determinedly so, according to Nancy – but she seemed to have rather reinvented herself over the last year. Eve said hello and the girl waved distractedly. She still ran like a child: unselfconsciously, arms akimbo, hair flying. It must be nice, thought Eve with a pang, to be so carefree.

Or was she? Something niggled her about Alice, though it took her a moment or two to remember what it was. Fen had said something – something about an unrequited crush. Fen had had a keen eye for human fallibility and relished the clandestine; she was always startlingly well-informed about the secret dramas of school life. Now Eve found herself wishing she'd paid closer attention.

She met the chaplain on his way out, but he said he was happy to spare five minutes to look at Eve's newspaper clipping. Sure enough, Monica Danbury's obituary and a covering note had been waiting in her much-neglected in-tray in the Archives office. She showed the obituary to Reverend Gainsbury and asked if he remembered Miss Danbury – 'I think she was still working at Cleeve when you joined?'

'Yes, that's right. Last year, one of the staff told me she had been moved to a nursing home nearby and I went to visit a couple of times. I didn't know she'd died, poor lady, but it was clear the last time I saw her she wasn't long for this world.'

Eve tucked the clipping back in her pocket. 'Do you know of any reason why Fenella Easton might have visited her?'

The chaplain was startled. 'Fen went to Fairview? Really? I can't think why.' He frowned. 'Though, I suppose,' he said doubtfully, 'if there was no personal connection it may have been an impulsive act of kindness. She was very, ah, spontaneous, wasn't she?'

'Yes. Yes, she was.'

Eve thanked the chaplain and turned to go. She needed time and space to think, for the obituary wasn't the only discovery she had made in the office. She had also realised that the blue manila folder that Fen had been leafing through when she'd visited the archives was nowhere to be found. It should have been easy to locate, since most of the office folders were green, but Eve had looked everywhere to no avail. The only other thing Eve remembered about it was that Fen had said it contained old medical records. Could they have been records from Monica Danbury's time as head matron? Had Fen stolen the folder, and if so, where was it now?

Eve wanted to believe she was grasping at straws. She wanted to dismiss her fears as Peter would dismiss them: as a paranoid fantasy. That was why it had become of such burning importance to find out what, if anything, Fen had been investigating. Eve had to hope it was something as trivial as it was intriguing – only then could she reject any connection between her friend's appetite for other people's secrets and her death.

ALICE

I passed Winslow's beard on my way to meet Henry. She'd been more mopey than ever this term. Like she was before Mrs Easton arrived, but worse. Maybe it was just grief for her friend, but the word from Jenny in Housekeeping was that Mr and Mr Winslow were in separate bedrooms. Mrs Winslow was usually quite a neat, precise-looking person. Today it didn't even look as if she'd brushed her hair.

Not my problem, anyway. It was Saturday afternoon and I'd got back from swimming to find a note from Henry lying on the doormat. *Hi, I got an afternoon pass and am meeting RVA to talk about HN etc. Meet at the Lodge, 2, if you're free?* This left me with five minutes to get there, and even less time to think about the implications of the invitation. Flustered, and a little panicky, I shouted to Pa that I was going out, dumped my swimming bag, grabbed a coat and legged it down to the Lodge.

'Alice, hi. It's great you can make it.' Henry gave a quick smile as I skidded into view. 'I got a pass to go see my godfather – luckily Mr Winslow was too distracted to ask awkward questions.' He checked his watch. 'The taxi should be here any second.'

I had to take a moment to catch my breath. 'OK, so I know we're not meeting your godfather. But can you fill me in on the other stuff?'

'Right. Of course.' Henry ruffled up his hair. He was wearing a cable-knit cream sweater with navy chinos. His Ralph Lauren gigolo look, Bette used to call it, a little meanly. 'Rupert's on his gap year, but he's still at home. And he phoned me last night. It was kind of awkward, talking on the payphone with all the usual suspects wandering past, but from what I could make out, he's in a pretty bad way. It sounded like he'd been drinking. He told me about Mrs Easton but said he wanted to meet face to face to talk about his dad. And some stuff about Cleeve, back in the day. He lives locally so we're going to meet at the pub.'

'OK. Why am I involved?' I tried to sound business-like. Running after Henry in a mad dash, all sweaty and red-faced, can't have done me any favours.

'I'd like to get your take on things. Rupert and I were tight for a while, but seeing as he was hiding his dodgy affair the whole time ... Well. I'm not sure how real our friendship is, to be honest. But I also don't think he has a lot of people to talk to. Obviously, you don't have to come. I don't want to get you any more mixed up in this – whatever *this* is – than you want to. But … well … I could do with some moral support.'

'That I can do.'

Henry looked relieved. The next moment the minicab drew up and he opened the door for me – another well-practised courtesy that was as meaningless as it was charming. And I couldn't afford to be charmed.

We spent the journey staring out of the window, lost in our own thoughts. I was glad when Cleeve Woods were out of view. I hadn't walked there since Mrs Easton's death. I don't think anyone had, except for a few ghoulish sightseers. The school was going to tear down the cabin and put up some kind of memorial. Probably another bench.

The von Aldstines lived close enough for Rupert to have been a day boy, if Cleeve had allowed such things, and in less than thirty minutes we were pulling into the car park of The Rose & Crown. If someone had told me that the first time I'd go to a pub with people of my own age it would be with Henry Zhang and Rupert von Aldstine, I'd have thought they were out of their minds. I *felt* a little out of my mind, to be honest.

Most people were in the beer garden, making the most of the last autumn sunshine. Rupert was holed up alone in a back room, which was small and dark with brass horseshoes tacked over the fireplace. The table looked sticky and the paisley carpet was an indeterminate shade of brown. He was busily shredding a beer-mat, an untouched pint in front of him.

Henry had said Rupert sounded in a bad way and he looked it, too. His hair was lank and the ruddiness of his cheeks was rough and blotchy. His oversized rugby shirt hung off his frame. The figure I'd last seen sauntering along the Lavender Walk seemed like a ghost.

When we walked into the room his head jerked upwards. 'What the fuck, Zhang? Why *her*?'

'Because,' said Henry, 'she already knows about you and Mrs Easton. Because she's known all of us from the beginning. Because nobody knows Cleeve like she does. And you said you wanted to talk about Cleeve and whatever secretive shit went on, back in the day. Right?'

'All right,' said Rupert irritably. 'Don't get your panties in a twist. Fishface can stay.'

'I'm getting a drink. Alice?'

'A lemonade, please.'

Rupert rolled his eyes. An awkward silence fell. I thought back to Rupert's Arrivals Day at Cleeve. He'd been full of swagger even then. He and his dad, striding around to inspect the goods like the two of them owned the place. His skinny mother with the rictus smile and expensive tan trailing along behind.

Perhaps Rupert knew what I was thinking. 'You must be loving this,' he said abruptly. 'How the mighty have fallen and all that.'

I laughed – I couldn't help it. 'Mighty?'

He had the grace to wince. 'All right. So maybe I phrased

that wrong. I just meant that things shouldn't have turned out this way. Everything's turned to shit and I still don't really know why or how it happened.'

'Well,' I said tartly, 'I imagine it started with you and Mrs Easton.'

It was at this point that Henry returned with the drinks. He looked between the two of us nervously.

'OK, fine,' said Rupert, taking up a new beer-mat and resuming his shredding operation. 'Yeah, me and Easton's beard were screwing. It started before Easter, and then for most of my final term. A bit of fun to enliven the unrelenting tedium of the days. For both of us.'

He scowled at his pile of ripped-up card. Henry and I waited.

'At the time, I was going through some shit with my dad. I told Henry a bit of it. I told Fen some more. Not to make her feel sorry for me – just to, like, vent some steam. Because the thing about Daddy Dearest is that he loves to act the big man. School governor. Hotshot financier. Most popular man at the bar. But as it turns out, he's a fraud. Worse than that – a loser. And I only found out about the fraud part thanks to that mouthy bitch Lindsey and her low-rent gangster chums.'

Henry frowned. 'Lindsey isn't a bitch.'

Rupert let out a snort. 'Oh, yeah. I forgot I wasn't the only one with a dodgy side-piece. My apologies.' He made a la-di-da half-bow. 'Anyway. As you may recall, our poker nights ended up being considerably more pricy than anticipated. Since I didn't fancy graduating from school with both my legs in plaster casts, I went to get some extra cash to settle the debt. Except my bank account was empty. My allowance hadn't been paid in.

'It was exeat that weekend, and so I went home and asked Dad what the hell had happened to my money. He laughed in my face and said there wasn't any left. I didn't believe him. Then he poured himself another whisky and said he'd had one too many "whoopsies" at work and he was out on his arse. Hadn't even got enough cash to settle the last term's school fees. I ended up confessing the whole mess with the poker and the Bateses and the debt. He laughed *again.* Said he knew the Bates family from way back, and they were notorious crooks even then.

'Did you know my dad had some bullshit coaching job at Cleeve? It was after he'd been "let go" from Sotheby's and before he managed to latch on to Mummy and her trust fund. Anyway, while he was there some kid died on Cleeve's watch. The teenage daughter of one of the cleaning ladies or whatever. It was a suicide, but Dad said the family – the Bateses – tried to pin it on him in some way, make out he was responsible.

'He didn't tell me all the details, but he was very clear the Bateses were on a hiding to nothing. The way he put it, the girl killed herself and it was a damn shame, but he "wasn't her sodding nanny" so it wasn't on him. The point is, he told me this story like I was supposed to be *impressed*. Like, he was this major alpha who didn't get pushed around by anyone, let alone the local peasantry. He basically told me to learn from his heroic example and stop being such a pussy with the plebs.'

'Wow,' said Henry quietly. 'And I thought my dad was a dickhead.'

'To be fair,' said Rupert, 'it was probably the coke talking. I got Mummy to write me a cheque instead – Grandpa still slips her some cash from time to time. Maybe now she'll finally see sense and leave the bastard.' He took a deep swallow of beer.

Henry looked at me. 'Do you know anything about this? A teenage girl who died at Cleeve? A suicide?'

I hesitated. 'I heard something about a girl from the Laundry who hanged herself, but it wasn't at school. It was at a farm, I think, outside town.' I looked at Rupert. I felt sorry for him in spite of myself. 'When did your dad work at Cleeve?'

'He was twenty-five at the time. So twenty years ago. *Your* dad must have been around at the time too. God's been at Cleeve forever.'

'Maybe he was the one who told me about it.' Or Moira in Catering. Or Jenny in Housekeeping. Or else I'd simply overheard people talking about the death, before they saw me listening and shushed each other. Then along came

Lindsey Bates, with the revelation that Margaret Mumford's bench was a memorial to her cousin.

'But the suicide definitely didn't happen on school grounds,' I continued. 'Everyone would know about it and still be talking about it if it had. Listen, your dad said that the girl who died was part of the Bates family. Did Lindsey or her uncle ever mention her?'

Rupert shook his head. 'Not a word. Henry?'

'No. No, never. God – do you think the Bateses targeted Rupert deliberately? As some kind of *revenge*?'

I did wonder. Lindsey had described her cousin's death as a suicide but, moments later, had referred to Cleeve as a crime scene, which suggested she blamed the school in some way. The way Henry told it, Lindsey had fallen into conversation with Rupert outside the Laundry one day, and somehow their chat ended with Rupert and his mates fixed up with an underground gambling ring. It looked pretty fishy to me.

'Did you tell any of this to Mrs Easton?'

Rupert sighed. 'Yeah, and this is where it gets messy. I was feeling a bit sorry for myself one night and out it came. But then she wouldn't let it drop. She kept coming back to it, you know? Endless questions. I got pissed off and we argued about it. That's when she gave me back to the key to the Chapel storeroom.'

He stared into his pint.

'And then …?' Henry prompted.

'Then Fen died. And it was fucking terrible. I mean, Jesus Christ. We used to meet in that cabin to fool around. To think of her lying there, bleeding out, alone in the dark … and I had to pretend I was only a little bit, you know, upset by it. Like it was the same for me as anyone else.

'I mean, don't get me wrong – I wasn't in love with her or any of that shit. She was just different, that's all. Kind of wild. Fun. Not like all the Sophies and Georgias wafting and pouting around the place. I can't get her out of my head. I can't get past it. If anything, the more time passes, the worse it gets.

'Dad had a major go at me towards the end of the summer. Kept asking what the fuck was wrong with me, why I'd turned into such a massive loser. I'd cancelled my travelling plans, you see. Didn't turn up at my internship – basically told the bank to go fuck themselves. This is supposed to be my gap year, right? And so far I've spent all of it alone in my bedroom or in the pub.

'So in the end I told him everything about Fen and me. And he *lost* it.

'Now, I'd actually thought he'd find it funny, me and a gog's wife. He always boasts about what a big stud he was at Cleeve, chatting up all the maids and whatever, back in the day. But he was furious. As in apoplectic. He said Fenella Easton was an evil slut and that I'd got no idea what I'd got myself mixed up in.

'He asked me if I'd told Fen what he'd said about the girl who died and the family who tried to blackmail him. I tried to deny it but it wasn't any good. Apparently she'd, like, *accosted* him about it? And he hadn't known where the hell she'd got the story from, but now it was clear I couldn't be trusted to keep my fucking mouth shut.'

I held my breath. I'd seen Mrs Easton having words with Mr von Aldstine in the car park. I'd assumed it was just her being drunk and disorderly. This was something else. What kind of shit had she been stirring?

Rupert covered his eyes with his hand. His voice had a shake in it. 'Dad was ranting and raving, on and on. And finally he said, he said, "That bitch got what was coming to her."

'So part of me thinks that maybe *he* did it. Maybe he'd had some kind of fling with the girl who died, and that's why she topped herself. That's why the family said he was to blame. And maybe Fen found out. Confronted him. I don't know.' His voice was now so low we strained to hear him. 'He's a sack of shit. But I still don't want to think my dad's some kind of, like, killer.'

Henry and I exchanged glances. 'You told me your father was in Dublin the last week of school,' Henry said. 'He couldn't possibly have lured Mrs Easton out to the cabin on Hazard Night.'

'No,' said Rupert slowly. 'But he might have paid someone else to do it. He's always at Cleeve for something or other, and he's got fingers in a lot of fucking pies. I mean, he already told me he'd got someone to search the Eastons' cottage in case Fen had left an incriminating love letter or porny drawing or whatever. So he could've found out earlier who Fen bought her weed from and made some kind of deal. Maybe Kyle Henderson was only supposed to threaten her, get her to back off.'

'I don't think that's likely,' said Henry.

'Nor me,' I said. 'The Bates family knew Kyle. He was one of their hangers-on. If they thought your father set him up or paid him off or whatever then we'd have heard about it. But I think we should talk to Lindsey in any case. Once we find out the real story of the suicide, I'm sure there's a lot of things we can rule out.'

Rupert nodded weakly. Neither a lion nor a pirate, just a scared teenage boy. 'Yeah, thanks. Thank you, Alice. Because even if my dad's in the clear … it gets me, you know? Thinking of her. Of Fen. Alone in the dark, dying.' He covered his face with his hands. 'I can't get her out of my head.'

EVE

Eve was looking at the latest issue of the school magazine and a photograph taken at the finale of the Fox and Hounds game. Rupert von Aldstine was in the centre, the plastic fox mask pushed back on his pale mane, his grin irresistibly cocksure. The other players crowded merrily around, fox-tail scarfs tied flamboyantly around their heads, cheeks flushed and eyes bright. It was a scene as wholesome as it was privileged.

'Looks like a gripping read,' said Peter. He'd just returned from the final roll-call and looked dog-tired.

'Oh, it's quite the page turner.' Eve put the magazine down. The nights were chilly now, and Peter had laid a fire after supper. A working fireplace still seemed a wondrously quaint luxury to Eve. She smiled at her husband, remembering the first time they'd sat by the fire here, and at the same time tried to remember the last time they'd had a proper conversation. Either house business was even more than usually onerous, or Peter was still avoiding her. 'By the way, I've been meaning to ask: do you remember a woman named Monica Danbury?'

'Dimly,' he said. 'She was one of the matrons while I was here. Why?'

'She died recently. Her family sent in the obituary to the archives.'

'That's sad to hear. She must have been very old, though. She retired a year or two before I graduated.'

Eve wanted to tell him that Fen had visited Monica at the nursing home. But *Fen* was a trigger word. She dithered, and while she was dithering, Peter took the lead.

'Listen, Eve. There's something I've been meaning to talk to you about. I've been putting it off because I know it will upset you. It's upsetting to me, certainly. Shocking, in fact.' He paused. 'It's about Fen.'

'All right,' said Eve cautiously. 'What about her?'

'See for yourself.'

He passed over a crumpled piece of notepaper.

It was a drawing rather than a letter, hastily done in black ink, depicting a bushy-tailed fox, a woodland cabin and a clock face pointing to one. Fen recognised the cabin and also the fox. Although it had been lightly sketched in just a few flowing lines, the animal's head was like all of Fen's artworks. Indisputably vixen, it was also indisputably her.

'I intercepted it on the way to one of my students. One of the boys at Wyatt's – I won't say which one. I was retrieving something from his pigeonhole which had been put there in error, and the note fell out.'

Eve thought of the fox-tail scarf in Fen's trophy box. Green, just like the one tied around Rupert von Aldstine's arm in the photograph in the school magazine. No wonder Fen had found Madeleine Parish's affair with Tristan von Aldstine so amusing – 'too delicious for words', she'd called it. The note was merely confirmation of something Eve already knew, yet she had been resisting the knowledge for so long that she was still shocked into silence.

Peter was looking at her narrowly. 'The note is an invitation, or an assignation, rather,' he said, slowly and carefully. 'Time, place, person. Do you understand? The only reasonable conclusion to draw is that this boy and Fen … that Fen … Well. I'm sure I don't need to spell it out. Or do I?'

Eve shook her head.

'I found the note the evening of Hazard Night, while the students were at supper. I think that's why Fen was in the cabin the night she died. She had gone there at 1 a.m. to wait for this boy.'

It took a while for Eve to find her voice. 'What did you … what did you do when you found it?'

'Nothing.' Peter grimaced. *Nothing*. And that haunts me. That is, I made sure the note never got to its intended recipient. But beyond that I didn't know *what* to do. I knew

I had to inform someone of what had been going on, of course, but the timing was all wrong. The boy was leaving school the next day – leaving Cleeve forever. He was the victim in all of this. I didn't want to haul him over the coals on his last night. So I resolved to go to the headmaster in the morning. But then – in the morning—'

In the morning, Fen was found dead.

'And the boy Fen was supposed to be meeting definitely didn't know about the plan? He was back in Wyatt's from midnight?'

'Yes, of course. I made sure both Matron and Steve kept everyone under lock and key. Then I went to the Eastons' cottage. I didn't have a plan. I was in shock, I suppose. When Gabriel opened the door I'm afraid I lost my nerve. I babbled something about cleaning up the graffiti on the Lodge. He offered to help. Said Fen was off on one of her midnight wanders. And the whole time I had his wife's sordid little sex note literally burning a hole in my pocket.' He covered his eyes with his hands. 'Things could have been different. I know that. If I had found and confronted Fen before she went to the cabin—'

'Peter. Peter, listen to me. None of this is your fault. You were in an impossible situation, and none of it was of your making.' Eve pulled him into a hug but his body felt stiff and unyielding. 'I'm so sorry you didn't feel you could talk to me about this. My poor love. What a burden you've been carrying.'

He drew back from her. 'That's the thing. I've told you this shocking, terrible thing, and you don't even seem that surprised.' His eyes narrowed. 'Is it possible you already *knew*?'

'No!' Eve shook her head but she knew she looked guilty. 'No. Certainly not at the time. But ... more recently ... I began to wonder, I suppose. Fen had been so strange and distracted ... there were these hints ...'

Peter was stony-faced. 'Madeleine was right. You were complicit.'

Her whole body jolted. 'In *what*? Seducing a student? Are you *mad*?'

'Don't overreact – I'm not accusing you of any crime. But you and Fen were bad for each other. You should have set proper boundaries. You could have reined her in.'

'Enough. This is Madeleine Parish talking. You shouldn't listen to that woman. She's little better than Fen, believe me. If you only knew—'

'About Madeleine's indiscretion with Tristan von Aldstine? Yes, I know about that. She confessed it to me.'

Eve gaped at him. 'Why?'

'She told me that Fen had found out and was making life very uncomfortable – trying to make trouble of one sort or another. And I'll be honest: Madeleine suspected you were egging her on behind the scenes. She thought I might be able to persuade you to call Fen off. Of course, I told her there was no way you were involved.'

'Well, I knew Madeleine Parish was a hypocritical slut with terrible taste in men. But that's as far as it went, believe me.'

Peter sighed. 'Tristan's not a good man. I remember him from my school days, when he did some coaching. He was unreliable then, and a bit disreputable too, I'm afraid. Nothing seems to have changed there, and I certainly don't approve of Madeleine's choices. But blackmail isn't much better than adultery, to my mind, and a grown woman sleeping with a teenage student is an indefensible abuse of trust. There is no possible comparison.'

'I completely agree,' said Eve numbly.

'So I should hope. Once Madeleine found out about Fen's drug-taking she had enough on her to ask her to leave on the quiet. I felt very sorry for Gabriel. But he wasn't happy here in any case. It would have been the best outcome for both of them.'

This was more or less what the First Lady had told her when Eve had interrupted her going through Gabriel's desk in the cottage. Now Eve wondered if Tristan had belatedly discovered his son's involvement with Fen. Could he have asked his mistress to find and destroy any evidence?

'Eve?' said Peter, calling her back to the present. 'I know there's an awful lot to take in. I'm still struggling to come to terms with it myself. But I've thought long and hard about it all, and it seems to me that exposing Fen's affair with a student will only cause a great deal of harm. The important thing is that there are no more secrets between the two of us. Now that you can see Fen as she truly was, maybe your grief will ease and we can both move on from this. Together. Do you think that's possible?'

'Of course,' said Eve. The new gentleness in Peter's voice shamed her. She roused herself. 'You're right, and I'm sorry. I want this all to be over too.'

She took one last look at Fen's sly vixen eyes, and then she put the note in the fire.

ALICE

Henry was very agitated after our meeting with Rupert. Back at Cleeve, and under the Clock Tower, he did a lot of monologuing while pacing back and forth. The monologues were full of rhetorical questions, swearing and self-flagellation. His upset annoyed me: I wanted to keep a cool head. 'How the hell are we going to get hold of Lindsey, anyway?' he fretted. 'I had a number for her but she's moved on. It's like she's vanished off the face of the earth. If you ask me, it's really strange, no, *sinister*—'

'The Rolfe twins helped get her a job, didn't they? At one of their dad's hotels? We could start by looking at the staff directory.'

'Damn. Of course. Thank God for you, Alice – always one step ahead.'

'Have you spoken to Bette yet?'

'Bette?' He looked at me as if I was mad. 'What's she got to do with it?'

'She thinks you're the killer, if you recall.' I was thinking, in fact, of how Bette would have relished the intrigue of our morning. I didn't just miss our friendship, I missed being in the company of another girl in a kingdom of boys and men. Until Bette, it wasn't something I knew I was lacking.

'No, it's OK, I wrote to her, as you suggested. I didn't go into a lot of detail – it all sounded so mad on paper – but I did make it very clear that she was mistaken. About a lot of things. I haven't heard back.'

'I'm not surprised if that was the tone you took.'

'What tone?'

'Pompous. Judgy.'

'I'm not pompous. Maybe I'm a *little* judgemental.' He paused. 'I judge you to be unequivocally excellent, for instance.'

I looked back at him. The clock struck the hour. Boys were suddenly swarming everywhere, making their way between sports and clubs. Several looked at us curiously. Fishface and the captain of the cricket team – standing so close as to be almost touching, right in the middle of one of Cleeve's main thoroughfares.

And here was my heart, crashing and smashing and thundering in my ears.

'So show me,' I said. 'Show me how excellent you think I am.'

And Henry Zhang kissed God's daughter, under the Cleeve Clock Tower, for all the world to see.

I woke up very early on Sunday. I didn't trust my happiness, not quite yet, but it fizzed impatiently through my veins. I decided to go for a walk while the campus was still mostly quiet and undisturbed and try and focus my energies on our promise to Rupert. When I spotted Lindsey herself, smoking under one of the willows fringing the staff car park, it felt as if everything was finally falling into place. It was a foggy grey morning and seeing her figure emerge from the mist was an uncanny moment – as if the Fates had sent me a revenant.

Close up, Lindsey looked good. Different. She'd had her hair cut into a sleek bob and had either grown out her eyebrows or filled them in. She was wearing a plain grey tracksuit and her make-up was softer, but her signa ture mix of pugnaciousness and condescension was unchanged.

'Wotcha, Alice. How's tricks?'

'Fine, thanks. I'm surprised to see you here. I thought you'd moved on.'

'Home for a visit, aren't I? What your Cleeve wankers would call an *exeat*. My old neighbour, Tania, works in Housekeeping. Her car wouldn't start this morning so I gave her a lift.'

'That's kind of you.'

'I'm all heart, me.' Maybe she *had* softened. Certainly,

she was more affable. 'And speaking of hearts … How're your boys? How's the chink?'

I felt a wrench of heat, deep and pleasurable. 'His name is Henry. You know that.'

'Indeed I do, Alice. Indeed I do.' She smiled through a plume of smoke. 'I'm only joshing. These days I have to watch my mouth. Customer service is king.'

'I'm glad you're doing well.'

'So you should be. Cos I am.'

I braced myself. 'Lindsey … could we talk? I mean, *really* talk?'

Showing curiosity was beneath her, so she settled for a half-shrug of acquiescence. 'Pretend I'm listening.'

I moved closer under the shelter of the tree. 'Look, I know how you got your job. I know you're probably ace at it, too. But you twisted some arms to get it.'

To my relief, Lindsey seemed amused, not offended. 'Me and the lads came to a mutually beneficial arrangement, yeah. What's your point?'

'The point is that those poker games were rigged, right? Your uncle fixed it so the Cleeve boys were going to lose.'

'The house always wins, Alice. I told you that. First rule of gambling.'

'OK, the house may win, but some players lose more than others. Like Rupert von Aldstine, for instance. Can I ask … did you go after him in particular? Because of what you think his dad did to your cousin?'

Lindsey was very straight and very still. Her voice was soft as she tapped the ash off her cigarette. 'Now what do you mean by that, I wonder.'

'Not much.' I'd decided to be honest. 'I don't know enough to be sure of anything. But this is what I wanted to talk to you about: Margaret Mumford, Tristan von Aldstine ... and Fenella Easton.' I paused. 'I might be wrong – really, really wrong – and I hope that I am. But whatever happened in that cabin between Mrs Easton and Kyle, I think there's a back story, a story about Cleeve, that needs telling. What do you think?'

There was a long wait. I sensed the calculation going on behind Lindsey's eyes. She smoked and she calculated and she smoked some more. I wasn't surprised she was nearly always with a fag in hand: she smoked more elegantly than anyone I'd ever seen. Like an old-school movie star. 'All right,' she said at last. 'I'll tell you the same as what I told Mrs Easton. I don't know what it is you're sniffing around for, exactly, but here's my story.

'So my Auntie Trish, that's my mum's older sister, worked in the Laundry here about twenty years ago. She left school at fifteen, pregnant. The dad legged it, of course. All in all, washing Little Lord La-di-da's cum-stained jockstraps for a living was about as much as she could hope for. Because that's what most people round these parts hope for, don't they? Scrubbing Cleeve's floors. Cleaning Cleeve's toilets. Scraping away Cleeve's scraps. It's even sold as some kind of *privilege* for the likes of me.

'Anyhow. Auntie Trish's kid was called Peggy. It's fair to say she didn't have the best start in life. My auntie drank, had terrible boyfriends and wasn't much use for anything. Peggy was fifteen when she died. I never knew her; I've seen pictures is all. Mousy, but nice-looking. Long hair and freckles.

'Peggy got suspended from school a lot. Or maybe it was cos she was being bullied, I don't know. Whenever that happened, or when her mum worked a weekend shift, she'd come along with her to Cleeve. It wasn't strictly allowed, but people turned a blind eye since Peggy was mostly quiet and kept out of the way. But she had a crush on the assistant rowing coach. Used to follow him around like a little dog, people said.'

'Tristan von Aldstine. Rupert's dad.'

'The very one. Peggy was the quiet type – never had a boyfriend or anything like that. But my mum said Peggy had a crush on him, and Peggy used to tell my mum things that she wouldn't tell her own mother.

'Then one weekend, some of the boys went on an outing. To go to a village fair or some such bollocks. Rupert's daddy was supposed to be supervising. Peggy somehow tagged along. And that's when she did it.'

'Did what?'

Lindsey looked at me as if I was a moron. 'Hanged herself. That's when she hanged herself, Alice. They found her swinging in a barn. She'd used her own belt to do it.'

259

'I – I'm so sorry. Was there a note?'

'No,' said Lindsey. 'There wasn't. But it was hardly a big mystery, was it? Girl was depressed. Bullied at school. No dad, drunk mum. Now, Peggy wasn't ever supposed to have been on that sodding trip, but Von Arsehole and the other staff still should've kept an eye on her. It wasn't right, letting her wander off, a vulnerable kid like that. Especially as Von Arsehole had been drinking. People at the fair saw him getting tanked up.

'That's what my auntie said, anyhow. She said the school had been negligent. *They* said they hadn't no duty of care to somebody who wasn't one of their students or employees. My auntie couldn't prove anything. Von Arsehole had a massive strop and the school told her to fuck off, basically.'

'God.' I swallowed. 'And this is what you told Mrs Easton. The day before she died.'

'Yeah. Fact is, she was a nice lady. Different to the rest of the two-faced bitches on campus. She was proper upset when I told her. Cleeve couldn't care less. Look at that poxy bench. *Margaret Mumford, In Memoriam.* It was the Laundry staff and such who got it put up, but they weren't even allowed to pick the sodding words. Fuck. I mean, nobody called Peggy Margaret. *Ever.* Four cold, stingy little words for a whole life … Oh, and they gave my auntie the sack soon afterwards, together with a wad of cash she pissed away, as her drinking got the better of her. Blood money, she called it. A year later she was dead.'

None of this was my responsibility, yet I still felt the burn of shame. Lindsey must have sensed this. 'Not one of the stories they boast about, is it, when they're showing parents the feather beds and the gold-plated cricket stumps.'

'No.' I hung my head. 'Why do you think Mrs Easton was asking about this?'

'Oh, she was just being a nosy cow, I expect. She probably had some beef with Rupert's dad and was looking for dirt. He's a governor here, in't he? I know how this place operates. It's all Happy Families for the paying customer, then behind the scenes everyone's sharpening their knives for a stabbing.' Absently, Lindsey scratched at her jaw. 'I told the police some of this shit, for what it's worth. I told them Kyle wasn't violent, too. They didn't listen to me, of course. Us Bateses don't make great character witnesses.'

'I'm sorry,' I said inadequately.

She shrugged. 'I dunno. Part of me would like to believe Von Arsehole was part of some evil conspiracy to kill off my cousin and then Mrs Easton when she found out, but I can't really see it, can you?'

I shook my head.

'So why're *you* asking, then? What's my tragic family history to you?'

I couldn't tell her the truth – about Rupert and Mrs Easton, and his fears his father was a murderer. But I told her another truth, all the same. 'Cleeve is all I've ever known and I used to think I knew it inside out, for better

261

or worse. But ever since Mrs Easton it's as if I've overturned the rock under the rock. And there's rot, and stink, and black things squirming about underneath. And I can't look away.'

'Seems to me that looking the other way is what Cleeve does best.'

'Maybe you're right. I don't see how you can stand to set foot here.'

'Oh, Cleeve's home from home for me now.' The light glinted on her chipped tooth. 'The thing about me, Alice, is that I'm gonna be a winner and I'm gonna be rich, and depending on how quickly that happens, I'll be sending my kids or else my grandkids here.' Lindsey flicked her cigarette butt into the grass. 'And once they get here, you know what they'll do? They're gonna burn this place to the fucking ground.'

After Lindsey's story, I couldn't think of anything else. My thoughts buzzed and swarmed blackly. It didn't help that the next person I saw was Gabriel Easton, of all people. He was carrying boxes of books out of the cottage and into his car. Inevitably, I thought of the Eastons' Arrivals Day and Henry going to help Mrs Easton bring in her easel.

When Mr Easton straightened up from the boot of the car, he looked up and saw me. I felt myself go red. The fact that I, a Cleeve nobody, knew such a humiliating secret about his wife gave me an odd sort of power over him, but it was a power I didn't want to have. I felt soiled, and a bit sick, thinking about it. This forced me into making an effort at sociability that surprised us both. 'Hello, Mr Easton! It's nice to have you back. How *are* you?'

I spoke with a gush worthy of Nancy Riley. We both winced a little in the aftermath.

'Thank you, Alice. I'm ... ah ... rather up and down, to be honest. It's even harder than I thought, returning to this place.' Mr Easton cleared his throat. 'As a matter of fact, I handed in my resignation this morning.'

'That's a shame,' I said feebly.

'I think it's for the best. I'm glad I ran into you, though. I'm finally trying to tidy up the cottage and so on, and I found something that might belong to your father. Will you wait a moment while I fetch it?'

He ducked into the house and came back with a blue manila folder. 'Fen had stuck a rather, um, whimsical Post-it note on it. I had a quick look inside and I can't really see what it's about or why your father might need it, but I feel he should see it all the same. Will you pass it on, with my apologies?'

I looked at the folder. The Post-it note simply read 'God?' *God* was underlined heavily. 'Of course, I'll take it to him now.'

EVE

Eve dreamed of foxes all night long. Sometimes she was the fox, and sometimes she was the hound. Sometimes it was a game of kiss-chase, as a sly-eyed vixen darted through the shadows, always just out of reach. Sometimes it was a hunt to the death through the undergrowth, and it was her own body twisting desperately, last gasps of breath scraping her exhausted lungs.

But Eve woke up that Sunday morning with another image seared on her brain. It was of Madeleine Parish going through the writing bureau in the Eastons' cottage. Something had tugged at Eve's memory and now she was sure there had been a blue folder on the desk. In Eve's fragment of memory, Madeleine had pushed it impatiently to one side. It wasn't, then, what she had been looking for. But it *was* what Eve was now in search of. A blue manila folder, like the one missing from the archives. Where else would it be but Fen's house?

Milo's waking-up chatter was increasing in volume. Eve checked the time – just after seven. There was no sign of Peter, who must have gone for his morning run. Eve pulled on some clothes and went to get Milo ready for the day, hustling through his change of outfit and delivery of breakfast with even more than usual speed. Her whole body itched with impatience. Wiping the last dregs of Weetabix from Milo's chin, she thrust him in the buggy and set off for Hawkins House. 'So sorry to interrupt your breakfast,' she babbled to Nancy, who opened the door holding a cup of steaming coffee, her hair blow-dried and her blouse ironed. 'But could you bear to mind Milo for half an hour or so? I can't find Peter and something urgent has come up with work.'

Nancy blinked. 'At the archives?'

'At the archives, yes. An archive emergency.'

'Well, of course, anything I can do—'

'You're a lifesaver. I mean it. Thank you so, *so* much.'

Eve bundled Milo into Nancy's arms and headed to the Eastons' cottage. Her best hope was that the spare key was still in its hiding place and the First Lady hadn't confiscated it. *I can always break in*, she thought wildly. *Smash a window and stage a burglary.*

There was no need. As she reached the turn off to the Eastons' close, she saw Alice Gainsbury come out of the cottage's front gate. Alice was holding a blue folder – *the* blue folder – and as Eve watched, she loitered by the garden wall to flick through the contents.

'Oh, thank goodness,' Eve cried, hastening over. 'Thank goodness for that. I've been looking *everywhere*. Can I just—?'

And she snatched the folder out of the girl's surprised grasp.

'Excuse me,' Alice said indignantly. 'Mr Easton just gave it to me to return to my dad.'

'No,' said Eve breathlessly. 'It belongs to Archives. Fen borrowed it. I've been looking for it for months.'

The girl looked at her as if she was a lunatic. Maybe she was.

'I'm the assistant archivist,' Eve said, smoothing down her hair. 'The state of the filing system is bad enough without paperwork disappearing all over campus.'

Alice looked as if she was going to dispute this, but thought better of it. 'OK,' she said, frowning. 'If it's really that important … But why did Mrs Easton put a note for my dad on it?'

'Who knows, who knows,' said Eve distractedly. 'You said Mr Easton's back?'

'Here he comes now,' said Alice. 'I'll, er, see you later.' She moved slowly away, still casting doubtful looks over her shoulder.

Gabriel had, indeed, just opened the front door. He was holding a shoebox. 'Hello, Eve,' he said tiredly. 'I saw you from the window.'

Eve clutched the folder against her chest. 'Oh, hello. Hi. Welcome back. It's been such good luck running into Alice just now. I've been looking for this for a while.'

'Oh, the folder belongs to you, does it?' Gabriel said vaguely. 'That's good.' He came to join Eve by the gate, and put the shoebox down on the wall next to her. 'There's probably a few things of yours in here too.' It was Fen's box of beer trophies. 'I'm having a clear-out, you see. It's time for me to move on.'

'From Cleeve?'

Gabriel nodded, but didn't elaborate. 'Fen could be a touch light-fingered, I'm afraid. One of her little peccadillos. Most of it's junk, but there are a couple of things … Well. I'd be terribly grateful if you could look through and see if there's anything you can return to its rightful owner.'

Without letting go of the folder, Eve opened the lid and stirred through the jumble of things inside. It was, as Gabriel said and she remembered, mostly junk, but there was a silver bangle that she thought might belong to one of the music teachers and a spare key to the print room that Facilities was still searching for. Peter would like his whistle back, she thought. Her hand fell on the green polyester scarf. Rupert von Aldstine's fox tail. She looked up and, without meaning to, caught Gabriel Easton's eye. Knowledge flashed between them.

'Shit,' she said, dazed with certainty. 'You knew. You knew about Rupert.'

He looked away. 'God forgive me, I did.'

'You knew. You knew! You—'

'Fen confessed to me. She always does – did. She didn't name names but …'

'And what were you going to do about it?' Her shock had worn off: she felt only anger now. 'This wasn't a Cambridge post-grad. This was an eighteen-year-old boy. A student. At *your* school.'

'God forgive me,' Gabriel said again. His voice cracked. 'Please, Eve. You mustn't expose Fen's secret. You can't. It's too late for it to make any difference. If you felt any affection for Fen at all, if you can still believe in the good within her, please … you have to protect her memory.'

Eve's throat tightened. 'Are you concerned for her reputation or yours? You *enabled* her.'

She had known Gabriel Easton as the aloof don and then as the stricken widower. This was another man entirely: craven and stumbling.

'I know how tainted I am. How compromised. It gnaws at me. But – you have to see, to understand – when Fen died – my position –' His face looked clammy. Eve stared at him in disgust. 'My position was so precarious that I – I always knew the suspicion … the doubt … If it wasn't for Peter … he was so kind. Understanding. And now – please – I'm asking for you to be kind too.'

Peter. Eve had another flash of intuition, even more unwelcome than the last.

'You have to forget you know this.' Gabriel advanced on her. He was actually wringing his hands. 'It won't do any of us any good—'

She let out a sharp inarticulate cry, and fled.

ALICE

I found Pa in the Chapel, laying out the hymnals. He looked surprised to see me. I couldn't remember the last time I'd been in here outside of Sunday Service, and since last term I'd been a bit irregular there too.

'Hello, Alice. You were up early this morning—'

'Yeah, so I think Mrs Winslow's having a breakdown,' I announced.

'I'm sorry to hear that. What about her behaviour alarms you?' He carried on setting out the books, unperturbed.

'She's dashing around campus looking … well … like a maniac. And I had some paperwork for you from Mr Easton and she practically tore it out of my hand. She said it was VIP property of the archives.'

'Oh dear. I fear Eve hasn't been herself since her friend died. It's understandable, of course.' Pa sighed and scratched his beard. 'If she comes to this evening's service I can try and have a quiet word. The trouble is, people tend to think the

270

pastoral care offered by the chaplaincy comes with religious strings attached.'

I nodded distractedly. 'Mrs Winslow was arguing with Mr Easton, too. She grabbed the folder with your name on it and then she had some kind of row with him and ran off. I don't know what they were rowing about—'

'I should hope not, Alice. Eavesdropping on other—'

'But I think it was about Mrs Easton. Do you know why Mrs Easton meant that folder to go to you? Because she must have taken it from the archives, and then she'd stuck a Post-it with your name – nickname – on it. Like she wanted to talk to you about it, maybe. There was hardly anything in it, just notes from a matron and some old detention slips. About a game the boys had been playing?'

'Ah.' Very slowly and carefully, my father placed his stack of hymnals on the pew. 'I see.' He bowed his head in thought. Or maybe it was prayer. The silence lasted a long time.

'See what?' I eventually prodded.

'"The secret things belong unto the Lord our God: but those things which are revealed belong unto us and to our children forever ..."'

Pa very rarely quotes scripture in conversation. And when he does, he tends to use a slightly ironic, half-mocking tone. He sounded mocking now, but there was a bitterness, too, that I hadn't heard before. Then he sighed.

271

'The truth is, Alice, I was the person to deposit that particular folder in Archives, though it's unlikely Mrs Easton could have known this. I expect she saw my name amongst the papers. They date from my first year in Cleeve.'

'So twenty years ago. Two years before I was born.'

Twenty years ago, when Tristan von Aldstine was assistant rowing coach, my mother was still alive, and Peggy Mumford was soon to be dead. The shadowy hush of the Chapel suddenly seemed oppressive. It had a new waiting quality – as if an invisible congregation had assembled on the pews.

'That's right,' my father said quietly. 'Twenty years ago. Back when Cleeve, marriage, the idea of fatherhood … even my faith – back when all those things were new to me. New and shining. It seems a long time ago but it isn't, really. Not in the scheme of things.'

I sensed the invisible congregation listening intently, leaning in.

'As for the folder under dispute … If it's the one I'm thinking of, you should know that the headmaster of the time asked me to dispose of the papers it contained. His instructions weren't explicit, but we both knew what he meant by them. Nonetheless, I chose an alternative interpretation of the task. I didn't destroy the papers. I buried them in the archives instead.'

The ghost congregation held their breaths. My voice was a whisper. 'What needed burying at Cleeve, Pa?'

'Ah, Alice.' My father's head sunk even lower on his chest. 'It was more a case of who.'

EVE

Eve felt as if she was going mad. She knew she must look it, flying here, there and everywhere about the campus. The boys, especially the squits, were always being told to slow down. Running was unseemly. She had thought how childish Alice Gainsbury had looked racing around the other day. Now here Eve was, haring back to Wyatt's, breathless and dishevelled, in case Peter had come home.

She found the boarding-house side alive with the sound of flushing toilets and slammed doors, tinny music and male laughter. Steve, the assistant housemaster, could be heard shouting something about toast. Sunday morning was in full swing. But Peter wasn't there.

He'd intensified his training regime over the last few weeks and was talking vaguely of marathons. Today he must have gone on one of his big runs. There was a fifteen-mile circuit around the Lake, up Hunter's Hill and then back through Cleeve Woods, and if he'd set off just before Eve got up, he would be well along the woodland trail by now. She'd go and intercept him there. This was not a conversation she wanted to have anywhere near the boarding house – or in Cleeve itself, for that matter.

Setting off at a jog herself, she headed towards the woods. She took the path that avoided the cabin, with its sagging crime-scene tape and horror-movie decrepitude, but even in her agitated state, she was able to appreciate the scenery. Dew still beaded the brambles, and light had begun to pierce the morning mists so that the lower tree branches were bathed in a milky translucence. The leaves had a coppery tint; a fertile odour of wet grass and mud hung in the air.

Eve reached a fork in the path. One trail led deeper into the woods, the other one out to the main road. She heard Peter before she saw him: the ragged yet controlled breathing, the rhythmic thump of his feet. When he emerged from the mist, she was struck by how exhausted he looked and how grey his face was under its sheen of sweat. He was also leaner and more sinewy than he'd ever been; if he'd been one of the students, somebody would have taken him aside by now and told him he was overdoing things. The neglect, she thought guiltily, was hers.

When Peter saw her, he gave a start. 'Eve!' His breath rasped painfully. 'Is everything all right? Where's Milo?'

'He's with Nancy. He's fine.'

'Then what are you doing here? Has something happened?'

'Yes. I suppose it has. I don't mean to ambush you, but I need to ask you something, and it can't wait. It's about Gabriel Easton and the night Fen died.' She licked her lips. Her mouth had gone very dry. 'Peter. I have to ask: did you – did you fudge the timings on Hazard Night to give Gabriel an alibi?'

His expression didn't change. But his long silence was confirmation enough.

'*Why*, for God's sake?'

He was still silent, but he began to shake his head slowly.

'Gabriel knew about Fen and her student lover. Did you know that?'

Peter swallowed. 'He … he suspected her of being unfaithful. He confided that to me, as we were cleaning up the graffiti. But he didn't say anything more. He refused to be drawn on it, in fact.'

'And what about the message from Fen in your pocket? You said you never showed the note to Gabriel. Is that another lie?'

'No! No. I never revealed I knew who Fen was sleeping with, let alone showed Gabriel that disgusting note. It was cowardice, really. I knew that as soon as I spoke to the headmaster in the morning the Eastons would be gone. Perhaps I should have warned Gabriel what was coming … but it wouldn't have changed anything. Or so I thought.'

'Look, I know Rupert von Aldstine was the boy in question. And so does Gabriel – because Fen told him herself. Is there *any* way Gabriel could have known Fen had invited Rupert to meet her in the cabin later that night?'

Peter wiped his sweaty face on the hem of his T-shirt. 'If he did, it wasn't because of me.'

'But you gave him an alibi – you lied about what time he stopped cleaning the graffiti with you! You gave a false alibi to a man who had both motive and opportunity to kill his adulterous wife! Christ, Peter. Don't you see how serious this is?'

'I do. But I also know Gabriel didn't kill Fen.' His voice was stronger now. 'I was the one who broke the news of her death to him, remember. Nobody could have faked that kind of despair. I'm as certain of it as I've ever been of anything in my life.'

In normal circumstances, it would have been the police who told Gabriel the news. But when the walker who found Fen's body had run to get help at the Lodge, the porter on duty had phoned the headmaster before the emergency services. And it was the headmaster who had tasked Peter with informing Gabriel. Peter had always said that Cleeve looked after its own. Which meant, Eve thought bitterly, that no matter how extreme the circumstance, Cleeve was a law unto itself.

'When did Gabriel ask you to lie about the time he left you on Hazard Night?'

'It wasn't as blatant as that. He started crying – saying everyone would always believe he'd killed his wife, that it didn't matter that he was innocent, that it wouldn't even matter if he was exonerated – he'd never escape the suspicion. That his life was over, essentially. Gabriel never asked me to lie outright. I felt terribly sorry for him, that was all. And once Kyle Henderson was taken into custody … well, I thought no harm had been done.'

'No harm!' Eve stared at him in disbelief. 'What if that man – Henderson – is taking the fall for Gabriel's crime?'

'Kyle Henderson belongs behind bars. He'd been pushing drugs on the kids in town. He's an associate of the local crime family. He—'

'He could still be innocent of murder.'

'You're wrong,' said Peter flatly. 'You need to let this go. Gabriel didn't kill his wife.'

'Neither of us can be sure of that.'

'Let the dead rest, Eve. It's time for us to get on with our lives. I thought you wanted that, I thought we agreed to that, remember?'

'This changes things. It changes everything.'

'I have to get back. I'm on study-skills supervision.'

'Peter!'

He turned away and began jogging in the direction of the main road – taking the shortcut back to school. It was just like every other time he'd turned his back on her. Every other time he'd prioritised supervision, service, duty. The endless supply of difficult, needy boys and their difficult, needy parents. The endless summoning of telephones and bells. There was always somewhere else he had to be, someone or something else he had to deal with, before he could turn to her.

So Eve raced after him and furiously grabbed him by the shoulder, yanking him back. He was startled and nearly fell, making her stumble too. She dropped the folder, which she had almost forgotten about, and the few flimsy papers fell out onto the damp ground.

'Shit!' She bent down and began gathering them up. Automatically, Peter bent to help her. He held one up and peered at it.

'Where did you get this, Eve?'

'From Fen. That is, Fen had the folder. I don't know why. I haven't had a chance to read through it properly yet but—' She shook her head. She was a little shocked by her own violence, and regretted the loss of control. She looked Peter in the face and tried to smile. 'Sorry for lunging at you. I didn't mean to trip you up. Here, let me.' She took the paper from his resisting hand. 'Oh, look. Your name's on here. On a detention report! And here's me thinking you were such a goodie two-shoes. So what's this about, golden boy?'

He was looking very tired again. 'I've never been a golden boy, Eve. I'm not golden and I'm not good.'

Eve felt herself soften some more. 'Look, I understand why you wanted to help Gabriel. It's just the sort of thing you do. He manipulated you, though. Just like Fen manipulated me. Together, we can put this right. We can go back to the police and explain that when you gave Gabriel his alibi you were confused, in shock, mistaken. Tell them about Fen's affair. Tell them that we've only just found out that Gabriel knew about it. Of course, it's still very likely that he's innocent. But let's do this properly. It will be better for everyone, in the end.'

'It's too late for that,' said Peter. And he began to weep.

THE CHAPLAIN

'The boys called it the Fainting Game. The first the faculty knew about it was when the head matron grew concerned about a number of students presenting with the same symptoms. Back then, there weren't matrons in the individual boarding houses. There was one central sanatorium.

'It was mostly the younger ones, first formers up to third years. Since the start of Trinity term, there was steady trickle of boys showing up at San with bloodshot eyes, complaining of headaches and blurred vision. Some of them had bruised necks, too. Matron kept a record and had a quiet word with the boys' housemasters.

'Lord knows how the craze started or who was the instigator. I subsequently learned that things like this sweep through schools from time to time. They called it the Fainting Game at Cleeve, but I gather it's called other things elsewhere. Perhaps you'll have heard of it – the Choking Game or Blackholes or the Pass-Out Challenge. It seems to have been around more or less forever. The goal is a very simple one: kids temporarily asphyxiate themselves to get high.

'There are different methods. Players can hyperventilate until they get light-headed, then hold their breath until they pass out. Or someone helps them out by giving them a bear hug, pressing on their chest, covering their nose and mouth. Sometimes the players faint; sometimes they have seizures. It gives them a rush that's supposed to be like taking drugs.

'Once the matron voiced her concerns, we staff members were told to keep our eyes out. Then I caught a group of third years in the act. It was during the free period between junior supper and prep, and they'd congregated in an empty classroom and were taking turns to hyperventilate. It all seemed rather silly, to be honest.

'I put the boys involved into detention. One of the housemasters found a few of his boys doing the same thing shortly afterwards. They were put into detention too. Everyone was given a stern talking to and told how stupid they'd been. In hindsight, though, it's clear we didn't take the issue as seriously as we should have. There was less awareness of these fads back then, and a shocking ignorance about the dangers. Mostly, we were relieved it wasn't some kind of drugs issue. We treated it as more of a prank that had got out of hand. And that, you see, was a fatal mistake.'

THE HOUSEMASTER

'I know I probably idealise my schooldays. But I haven't forgotten the miseries of them either. I remember we were always proclaiming how bored we were. Bored to *death*. It was partly an affectation, but the seventies was a dreary decade, on the whole. And we were more institutionalised at Cleeve than students are now.

'Boredom was only a part of it. Being a teenager is a frenzied business – in the hormonal clutch of your treacherous body, constantly second-guessing your own ungovernable mind. You're always looking for an outlet, an escape. And an institution like Cleeve is founded on the principle of repression. I mean, these schools were established to provide adolescent boys with seven years of *no* escape – no alcohol, no sex, no rebellion or experimentation. Just sports, basically. Things are changing, thank God. We live in more enlightened times, and the public school system is adapting accordingly. But in the meantime, I'd be the first to admit that a lot of damage has been done.

'As everyone knows, repression has never worked very well, has it? Drugs and alcohol still find a way in, even in the most controlled environments ... Kids still act out, take stupid risks ... That's what the Fainting Game was about. For us younger students, especially the designated 'good' ones, it seemed like a risk-free way of getting round the system and finding a cheap thrill.

'It started after one of the boys in the year above talked about playing the game at a house party over the holidays. It felt innocent and edgy at the same time. Once we started, we'd boast of how far we could go. We'd black out, feeling this euphoric rush – seeing actual stars shooting under our eyes. Our whole bodies would fizz. Then we'd come to, on the floor, and look up to see a ring of laughing faces, clapping hands. We felt like rock stars. And we looked after each other. We were careful – or so we thought. The euphoria we were feeling was addictive, though we didn't know it at the time.

'We told each other we weren't doing anything wrong, but we knew the game would get us in trouble, all the same. That was part of the thrill, of course – the danger of discovery. So we took ourselves to the brink, time and time again.

'When teachers became suspicious, and some of us got caught, people lost their nerve. We knew we were under surveillance and it was harder to sneak off. Then the older, cooler boys decided the game was childish. They went back to obsessing about girls. It seemed the craze was over almost as quickly as it had flared up.

'I hadn't played the game for weeks, in fact, when the summer exeat weekend came around. The school emptied out and it was just us Leftovers again. There were always a handful of us on these occasions – usually foreign students and kids isolated because of family illness or domestic drama. Sometimes it was just a scheduling issue. Parents were more careless back then.

'Most of the faculty were on holiday too. The ones left in charge didn't really know what to do with us, so the chaplain said he'd take us to a local fête. There were five of us boys and then a girl, the daughter of one of the laundry maids.

'Her name was Peggy. She was the same age as me: fifteen. She wasn't anything like the girls we knew from other boarding schools or as friends and family. She was a townie, for one thing, but she was also monosyllabic and always hunched in on herself, with her hair hanging over the face. We tolerated her, I suppose is the best one could say. And we used to laugh amongst ourselves at the way she'd go bright red whenever Tristan von Aldstine came into view.

'He'd come to help coach the rowing team. He'd been a big rower in his own schooldays and he'd also crewed for his college. I wasn't a rower so I hadn't had anything to do with him, though I knew he was popular with the big names on campus, having been one himself. Then, as now, I mostly kept out of his way.

'Anyway, the chaplain asked him to drive the minibus to the fête. There were six of us going: Thomas Plummer, Arjun Kumar, Ollie Davies, Frederic Bouchard and me. And Peggy. The chaplain included her as a kindness, because her mother was working in the Laundry that weekend and I suppose there was nobody to look after her at home.

'Peggy was a Leftover too.'

THE CHAPLAIN

'I felt sorry for the Mumford girl. Of course I did. She always looked so lost, and you could hardly get more than two words out of her at a time. She must have been intimidated by Cleeve, and that was only natural, but it was more than that, I felt. She was one of those poor souls who seem to walk around in a cloud of enduring defeat.

'As soon as I said she could come to the fête with us I regretted it. I didn't have a licence then so I'd asked Tristan von Aldstine to drive. There was hardly anyone else around, so I didn't have much choice, but I had always thought him as a bit of a thug. And poor Peggy had a crush on him, that was plain to see. If she'd been older or more obviously attractive it would have been an issue. As it was, he was as contemptuous of her as he was of everything else he deemed beneath his notice. Everyone knew he was merely killing time at Cleeve before some relative or family friend found him another made-up job to keep him out of trouble, or married him off to some nice girl with a trust fund. And so it proved.

'The boys were a motley bunch: a lone sixth former, one fourth year, two third years and a first year. It was hard for them, knowing everyone else was enjoying a summer's break away with their families. I suppose I was rather resentful too. My wife had gone to visit her parents, and there was barely another sensible adult left to talk to on campus.

'The village fête was about six or seven miles away and took place in a couple of fields belonging to a local farmer. It was a decent size: all sorts of tents, a music stage, as well as a riding course and a handful of fairground rides. Within the first ten minutes of our arrival, the sixth-form lad, a boy called Thomas Plummer, managed to trip over a hay bale and sprain his ankle. I took him to the first-aid tent, only to be told that the sprain might be a fracture and he needed a trip to Casualty. A kind local offered to drive us. So off Thomas and I went and, somewhat reluctantly, I left Tristan in charge. I said they should stay for two hours, and if I wasn't back by then, Tristan should take everyone home to Cleeve.

'It was the seventies: health and safety, and safeguarding in general, wasn't taken as seriously as it is now. Even so, Cleeve had its rules. On any outing or field trip, a register was supposed to be taken every hour. I put the register for the outing in that archives folder. It was typed out with the date, the location, the names of the boys and staff members present. I forgot to add Peggy Mumford's name, but at some point she wrote it in herself. It was a small act of self-assertion, I suppose. *Remember me.*'

THE HOUSEMASTER

'The fête was underwhelming. We'd got the measure of it in about five minutes. Then Thomas Plummer busted his ankle and the chaplain had to take him off to Casualty. Von Aldstine was left in charge. He went to get a beer from one of the refreshment tents, found a sunny deckchair and a discarded newspaper, and told us to piss off for the next two hours.

'So there we were. Arjun, Ollie, Frederic, Peggy and me. We were none of us particular friends – we weren't even in the same year groups – but we were stuck with each other. I don't know who suggested we play the Fainting Game. We didn't included Peggy explicitly in the invitation but she was there, and I suppose we knew it would be rude not to include her. Just for that afternoon, she was one of us. Resentful, bored and abandoned.

'Boarding-school life makes you expert at sneaking around unobserved. So we sloped off from the main event and found an outbuilding in the farm that was suitably neglected looking. Then we showed Peggy how the game worked. I had the first go. I hyperventilated for about thirty seconds or so, then Arjun came behind me and squeezed my neck. I came to flat on my back, and everybody cheered. We were suddenly best of friends.

'Peggy had a turn. She looked prettier with her hair off her face. It was the first time I'd seen her even slightly animated, except when Tristan made her blush. Freddie, the French boy, was the one to give her a bear hug, and I remember being jealous. I think we all were. She was enjoying the game. Perhaps it was the first time she'd been included in something.

'It was a hot day, and the shed was a bit smelly, and after we'd all had a turn, someone suggested we should go for ice cream. Peggy said she'd prefer to stay put and could someone maybe bring her some water? The rest of us set off. I told the others I was going to stop off at the Portaloos, but then I couldn't find my wallet. I realised it had probably fallen out of my pocket in the outbuilding, while I was playing the game. So I went back to get it.

'Peggy looked pleased to see me. She said she was going to have another go at the game. She said she wanted to try something different and did I think her belt would work? I wasn't as alarmed as I should have been – back at school, a couple of the more daring players had had success with using the belts from their dressing-gowns, tied onto the bar inside our closets.

'The shed was used to store some old bits of farm machinery and Peggy thought she could loop the belt over this rusty pole thing. She was positioning a wooden crate and chattering away, like a completely different person. She asked me to hold her up, after the noose tightened. For safety, you know. So I did – the second she began to struggle. Her breasts were pressed tightly against my chest. I could smell her sweat and a trace of flowery shampoo in her hair. And there we were, the two of us, alone in that closed, dark, animal-smelling place ... Peggy's flailing limbs, the softness of her body relying on the strength of mine ... I was a late developer and an innocent. It was the closest I'd ever been to a girl.

'When she took the belt off from round her neck, however, she was annoyed. She said it hadn't worked because I'd taken the pressure off too soon. This assertiveness was a shock to me. Peggy Mumford was bossing me about, as if she wasn't a girl, and a townie, but an actual peer. I suppose the attention had gone to her head. Then she looked at me, and she could see I was excited. More than that: *aroused*. She blushed too, but then she gave this funny little smile. She said, *Don't get any ideas, shrimp*.

'Then Peggy stuck her head through the noose for a second time and hopped off the crate. I heard the gasp as the belt cut off her air; I saw her legs kick and her hands scrabble at her throat. But this time I wasn't going to intervene too soon, I told myself. This time I'd give her a high, yes, but I'd also give her a fright – to remind her who was in charge. The gasps grew hoarser. I watched, mesmerised, as the thrashing of her body slowed to a twitch. Her breath was a rattle. That's when I came to my senses. It was like being sluiced with ice-water. I tried to support her body, drag her free of the noose, but she was heavy and I was panicking. In less than ten seconds it was over. I couldn't save her. Her lips had gone grey.

'I was terrified. Sick. Shaking. I thought everyone would think I'd killed her. I never meant for her to get hurt. Or rather, I never dreamed –

'Well. It was all too late, either way.

'So I ran away. I just … ran. When I bumped into Arjun by the ice cream van, I thought he'd see what had happened all over my face. But he didn't. He was too busy bickering with Freddie about his Flake. The others had wandered off. They'd lost interest in the game, forgotten about Peggy waiting for her water. Tristan von Aldstine was on his third pint and chatting up one of the pony-club mums.

'It was so strange, being in the middle of the fête, in the sunshine, with a brass band playing and everyone milling about eating ice cream, not a care in the world. And all the while there was that poor girl with the grey lips, hanging from a belt in that squalid little shed … I even thought for a moment I'd imagined the whole thing. Maybe *I'd* been the one with the belt round my neck. Maybe I'd passed out and hallucinated Peggy being there at all.

'Eventually, the chaplain returned with Thomas on crutches. He found von Aldstine asleep in a deckchair with a sunburnt nose, and the Cleeve students scattered to the four winds. It took a while to round us all up. We'd all had a bit too much sun and eaten too much sugar – everyone was groggy and crochety. I said I had a headache. It wasn't until we were straggling back to the minibus that somebody thought to ask "Where's Peggy?"'

THE CHAPLAIN

'When the girl's body was eventually found, it was a moment of pure horror. The shadows had only just begun to lengthen – it had been such a golden afternoon … Any violent death is a tragedy. But the suicide of such a young girl, a child almost – the darkness felt unfathomable. I remember trying to pray, and it was like attempting to speak in a foreign language I'd only ever seen written down.

'There was never any suspicion of foul play. Never. Even so, something about the Cleeve boys made me uneasy. They were, naturally, traumatised. Most of them were in tears when they heard the news. Their shock and sorrow was real. But to my mind there was also something … furtive … about them. And I noticed that even before the crying, a couple had bloodshot eyes.

'Tristan von Aldstine looked shifty too. It was obvious he'd been drinking on the job. It was also obvious that he'd provided no supervision whatsoever, to Peggy Mumford or anyone else. That register had never been used.

'He and the boys gave witness statements to the police. They all said the same: that Peggy had been very quiet but she seemed to be enjoying the fête. Nobody could be sure of what time she wandered off. Almost immediately, the suicide narrative was established. Soon everyone was talking about the girl's troubled home life and difficulties at school, her crippling shyness. We all became social workers.

'All the same, I wondered if anyone would ask questions. Many of the Cleeve teachers and medical staff had talked among themselves about the Fainting Game. We'd all heard about the boys with bruised necks. I waited for someone to bring this up. But everyone stayed silent. As silent as those boys.

'I found Peter Winslow in the Chapel one night. He was sitting alone in the dark, praying with what I can only describe as a ferocious intensity. Again, one might say this was a natural response to the tragedy. Nonetheless, I wondered some more. I tried to visit the girl's mother, but she wouldn't let me near her. She was swearing and spitting and making all kinds of threats. But I heard that she told the police and the press and anyone else who would listen that her Peggy would never have left her. That Peggy wasn't depressed. She was just … quiet.

'So I went to the headmaster. I'd gathered the medical notes from the head matron and I showed them to him, along with the detention reports, detailing what the boys had been up to. Some of them were the same boys who'd attended the fête. I said that we had a duty to talk to Peggy Mumford's family and the police about the possibility that she had died by accident, in the course of playing a game. A game she had most likely been introduced to by students at Cleeve. Her family deserved to know that there was another possible explanation for her death.

'But Headmaster Gray ... Well, he's dead now. I'd always thought him a decent man. Certainly, he looked after his students with a fatherly care. Even now, I still believe that the well-being of his boys was his primary concern, rather than the reputational damage to the school, though he was frank that this was something he had to consider. Peggy's family had already made a lot of noise to the press about negligence. And he said the boys in question were all good students, which was true. Fine boys with bright futures ahead of them. We had a duty to protect them, not expose them to suspicion and hearsay and cross-examination by the police.

'And I had no evidence. None at all. It was possible, the headmaster conceded, that Peggy may have overheard our students talking about the game and decided to experiment for herself. But there was no way of knowing that for sure. No way, certainly, of bringing the unfortunate girl back to life. It would be better for everyone if I disposed of my few bits of paper and let everyone move on with their lives.

'Putting the paper trail into Archives was a sop to my conscience. I told myself I would return to the matter, by and by, when I had some distance and clarity on the issue. I would pray for guidance, and it would come.

'But it never did. In time, I stopped praying too. Or rather, all my prayers seemed to be in a foreign language again – if there was an answer, it was untranslatable too.

'Then all these years later Fenella Easton somehow got hold of the folder and its record of the Fainting Game. She must have already heard about Peggy Mumford's supposed suicide. There are plenty of old timers who could have filled her in. So I suppose she heard the story about the hanging, and then recognised the names in the folder and the dates on the Fainting Game reports. And I think we can be sure her curiosity was not an idle one. Why else go to talk to the old matron? Why else make a note to ask me about the documents? Fenella was a clever, questioning, rebellious woman. The kind of woman who is dangerous for a place like Cleeve.

'"So whoever knows the right thing to do and fails to do it, for him it is sin." This, then, is the sin that's kept me here all these years. I'd like to believe "and the truth shall set you free" but it's never that simple, is it? Out of the frying pan, into the Lake of Fire.'

THE HOUSEMASTER

'We Leftovers never talked about Peggy Mumford or the Fainting Game. Not one word. Back at school, there was a ghoulish fascination with the suicide, but by unspoken consensus we kept our mouths shut. She'd been on the minibus with us, and that was all.

'Arjun, Ollie, Frederic – they must have known that the hanging was most likely an accident. To this day, though, I don't think it occurred to any of them that one of us could have been directly involved. I suspect the chaplain always had his doubts, mind you. I could see the question in his eyes, even after all these years, when I returned to Cleeve. But he never said a word. Nobody did. We absolved ourselves of any responsibility, any guilt, and so did the school.

'*In loco parentis*. That's what Cleeve was to us boys. It was my – our – watchful and loving parent. And now I'm a father too, I know first-hand that parental love is the most selfish and ruthless of all. It means you are prepared to protect your own against all reason, at all costs.

'And Peggy Mumford wasn't one of Cleeve's own.'

EVE

The trees had begun to thin out, and Eve could hear the occasional car murmuring along the road ahead. They had walked together, through the pearly mists and beneath the lacing branches, as Peter told her his story. His and Peggy Mumford's.

When Peter finished, he came to a halt under a beech tree. Eve remembered the first time she set eyes on him, at that house party. He had been talking to another guest by the fireplace. She had noticed his clear eyes and his diffident smile, the watchful care he took in listening to his companion's story. Public school, someone told her, and she'd fancied she could see that, too, in the straightness of his bearing, and the particular way he'd run his hands through his hair. Even his self-effacement was posh, she decided. *Not my type*, she had thought. But she had kept looking at him, all the same, and when at some point somebody made the introduction, and he had greeted her with such guileless pleasure, she had

had a feeling of great relief. *Oh*, she had thought. *So it's you, after all.*

Now she was looking at him again, and his eyes were still clear, and his smile was still diffident, and his bearing was still straight. Nothing had changed, and this terrified her.

'That's not where the story ends, though, is it?' she said.

'No,' said Peter. 'It ended with Fen.' And he took her by the hand.

Eve felt the warm, familiar press of his flesh, the hardness of his wedding ring. His touch should have disgusted her, she knew that. She should have flung his hand off, recoiled from him, run. Instead, she gripped him tighter.

'How did Fen find out about Peggy?' she whispered.

'Rupert told her because his father told him.' Peter was quite calm. He had picked up the loose sheets of paper from the ground and returned them and the folder to her with careful courtesy. Now he looked at the light breaking through the mist and smiled a little. 'I think she must have asked around, too. But it was finding the records of the Fainting Game in the archives that allowed her to piece it all together. That was very unlucky. Fen wasn't the kind of person to let anything go.

'As you know, I had thought her a malign force in school for some time. Madeleine Parish came to the same conclusion and had privately told her to leave the morning of Hazard Night. However, after I'd intercepted her note to Rupert and

301

went storming over to the Eastons' cottage, it was clear she hadn't said a word about their ejection to Gabriel. He was in enough of a state as it was. All he would say was that 'Fenella's been up to her old tricks', and what kind of man was he, anyway, to keep letting her get away with it. No wonder he was relieved when I gave us both an alibi.

'It was a spur-of-the-moment decision to go to the cabin and tell Fen to get the hell out of Cleeve. I suddenly couldn't bear the thought of her being in my school, my *home*, even a minute longer. The damage she'd done – I mean, for God's sake, Rupert is big on bravado, but he's a troubled boy underneath it all. Fenella Easton was a predator.

'I surprised her, that's for sure. The way she looked when I opened the cabin door – it would almost have been funny, in different circumstances. As it was, the circumstances were irredeemably squalid. The place was hardly a love nest. Empty beer bottles, some ancient stained mattress on the floor.

'Once Fen had got over her surprise, she didn't try and deny anything. In fact, she laughed in my face. She said there's no one so prudish yet so sex obsessed as an ex-public-school boy. She and Rupert were consenting adults; *she* wasn't his teacher. And she said I'd better keep my eye on you, Eve: that you weren't the kind of woman who'd submit to mummification by inches.

'I kept my cool. I told her that she and Gabriel were finished at Cleeve, and that Gabriel's career would be finished too if they didn't leave quietly. I told her that if she made a fuss then Cleeve would have no choice but to inform Gabriel's other places of work that his wife was an abusive drunk with a habit of seducing her husband's students. He'd have no choice but to get rid of her.

'She was furious, of course. Fen said if Cleeve was going to try and bully Gabriel out of his job without providing a glowing reference and proper compensation, then the school had another think coming. Two could play at the blackmail game, she said.

'I laughed. I knew she didn't have a leg to stand on.

'That's when she lost it. She started ranting on and on about Cleeve. How the school was emblematic of everything that was wrong with this country, how it and the establishment it served were rotten to the core. It's nothing I haven't heard before, of course. This was standard staff-room chat in those sink-estate comps I worked in.

'But then Fen played her trump card. She told me she'd worked out the real story of Margaret Mumford's death and how Cleeve had "suppressed the evidence", as she put it. It was Rupert who'd tipped her off, but she claimed she'd found witnesses – and documents – to back up her findings. She was convinced that all the Cleeve boys at the fête were involved in Peggy's hanging, and that the death was some kind of sexual hazing ritual. She made it sound even worse than it was. She said she'd go to the papers – tell them that the Fainting Game was an exercise in autoerotic asphyxiation, that it was all about public schoolboys interfering with poor peasant virgins. And that the school had instigated a criminal conspiracy to cover it up.

'It was a nonsense, of course. But it still took me back. For a nightmare moment, I was back in that stinking shed, Peggy's breasts crushed against me. Her breath rattling. My own breath a frantic gasp.

'I said no one would believe her, and there was no credible evidence, but Fen was hysterical at this point – shining her torch into my eyes as if it were a dodgy police interrogation. She began to laugh manically, saying that this would be her legacy to Cleeve: exposing the school for the evil tyranny it truly was. Creation through destruction, she said. Art is violence, she said, and it would liberate us all. She was just ranting and raving, on and on. Her spit was all over my face. She had her teeth bared, like a wild animal. So I gave her a shove – just to give me some space, that was all. Just to put a little distance between us. And the floor was wet, because of the leaky roof and the rain, and she went down harder than I ever expected, hitting her head against the corner of the metal locker as she did.

'I heard the crack, I saw the blood.

'Another limp body. Another dark shed.

'That's when I ran. Again.'

They were at the edge of the trees now. Eve could smell exhaust from the road as well as loam from the earth, but her vision was blurred by tears that hadn't yet fallen. She

304

felt that they would perhaps always be suspended there; an endless veil between her and the rest of the world. Peter and his voice seemed very far away. It seemed as if she had been alone in this foggy wood forever.

'I am most dreadfully sorry,' said Peter, kindly and patiently. The teacher breaking bad news. The housemaster offering comfort. 'Please let everyone know that.'

A car had crested the hill and was humming swiftly through the mist.

Peter stepped out in front of it.

EVE

The aftermath was, in a bleakly inverted way, not dissimilar to childbirth. Eve felt drugged with shock to the point that life became an almost out-of-body experience, but although the toxins swirling through her blood slowed everything down, and put everything at a distance, they failed in every way to numb the pain. Lights were too bright. Voices too loud. Every surface, every touch, seemed to be serrated and drew blood. And, like childbirth, there was no way through this catastrophic agony other than to keep on pushing, no matter the tearing of flesh, the shredding of mind.

But she had a child. She had a son. Her and Peter's child. And her work to care for and protect him and find ways, despite everything, to bring him joy was enough – just enough – to make her survival meaningful. That was why it was important to tell her lies well and to make them strong.

On her last day at Cleeve, Eve took Milo for a final walk around the Lake. He loved to feed the ducks. 'Daddy loves the ducks too,' he told his mother. 'Does heaven have ducks?'

'Yes,' she told him. 'Masses. So every time we feed the ducks, we can think of Daddy feeding angel-ducks with heaven-bread and sending the crumbs down through the sky. Look,' she said, pointing to a scrap of leaf dancing in the wind. 'There's one now.'

It was a dark cold day and, much to Eve's relief, the environs of the Lake were deserted. It was a shock, then, to turn and see Alice Gainsbury walking purposefully towards her, bundled up against the chill.

'Hi,' the girl said awkwardly. 'I heard you were leaving today. So I came to say goodbye.'

'Thank you. That's very kind.'

Alice shifted her weight from one foot to the other. She was nervous, Eve noted distantly.

'I think,' said Alice, even more awkwardly, 'that maybe you and I were asking some of the same questions these last few months.'

'Yes,' said Eve, very slowly. 'Yes, I believe we were. And I hope you understand that, despite everything, I have to keep some of the answers to those questions to myself.' She looked over to where Milo was gleefully tearing up hunks of bread. Then she looked back at Alice. For the first time in a long while, she felt almost calm. 'Do you think you can forgive me?'

'But you … but you didn't do anything wrong.'

'Maybe. Maybe not.' Eve was cold; she hunched her shoulders and rubbed her arms. 'It's strange … I hated this place for such a long time. And yet I've ended up inadvertently protecting it.'

'It's not that strange,' said Alice.

So they stood together in silence, watching Milo feed the ducks.

ALICE

When the worst of the storm was over, I went to meet Lindsey Bates in a café in town.

Lindsey had got there ahead of me and I paused a moment in the doorway, watching her sip her coffee. She was wearing a smart black trouser suit and her nails were short, with a French polish. I thought of the first time I'd seen her, swigging Diamond White with the two skanks at the bus stop, but though the changes in her were more obvious, I felt mine went almost as deep.

'Wotcha, Alice.'

'Hello, Lindsey.'

I sat down and we looked at each other for a long moment. Then I pushed over Pa's blue folder. 'This is it. In all honesty, I don't think there's anything to be done with it, even with my dad to explain. As you know, Mrs Winslow told the police that her husband confessed to killing Mrs Easton because they were having an affair. So at least Kyle Henderson's a free man. But as for the rest ... it's only guesswork that Mrs Easton found out what happened to Peggy, and that Mr Winslow likely had something to do with your cousin's death too. Mrs Winslow won't come out and say it and there's no proof – either of Mr Winslow's involvement *or* the school's cover-up.'

Lindsey took this calmly. 'The way I see it, Eve Winslow's got a kid to think about. She won't want him growing up thinking any more badly of his dad than he has to. Maybe she wanted to keep Rupert out of it, too. Still, she left you the folder, didn't she?'

I nodded. After Mrs Winslow had gone, she posted the Fainting Game folder back to me. The note inside read *For Peggy Mumford's family.*

'Not that it's going to do any good.' I looked down at the table. 'I'm sorry. I'm sorry I can't change anything.'

'Wasn't your mess to clear up, Alice. Don't you go feeling bad.'

'But my dad – what he guessed … what he knew... All those years of never facing up to it. All those years of treating his job as some kind of *penance*.'

Lindsey snorted. 'Seems to me that Cleeve College was a pretty cushy penitentiary. Your dad wasn't moved to save souls in some third-world shithole, was he?'

Pa had taken early retirement. He was renting a cottage in the countryside and said he was looking forward to catching up on his non-theological reading. I worried about him, but whenever I expressed this, he'd bristle his brows

310

at me and quote something about making a way in the wilderness and streams in the wasteland.

I suppose I looked rather glum. 'Ach, don't mind me,' said Lindsey. 'He'd've tried to do his best by you.' She thought for a moment. 'I don't know much about the Bible, but from what I hear, it's big on turning cheeks in some parts and taking out eyes in others. Three people died, that's clear. But who and what got avenged, and how the forgiving and the forgotten fit in ... Well. I'm glad it's not my job to untangle it.'

By a twist of fate – or act of a capricious God – it was Tristan von Aldstine and his Range Rover that killed Peter Winslow. Mrs Winslow had testified that her husband had stepped into the path of the car with suicidal intentions. Even so, when the police tested Mr von Aldstine's blood they found traces of cocaine as well as alcohol. He received a criminal record and a driving ban, but was spared jail. The judge was told that in the wake of the accident he was suffering from post-traumatic stress.

Cleeve was in meltdown. Mrs Winslow might have thought she was protecting the school by not exposing Peggy Mumford's story, but I'm not sure it made a whole lot of difference in the end. The tabloid headlines of 'SEX AND DRUGS BLOODBATH AT TOP PUBLIC SCHOOL' might as well have been written in six-foot flaming letters above the college gates. Headmaster Parish resigned, and the trickle of parents withdrawing their children became a flood. Within a year, the school was forced to go fully co-ed and open up to day pupils, which – said the old guard gloomily – was the *real* nail in the coffin. I thought about Lindsey's ambition to send her spawn to Cleeve, and so bring it down from the inside. It seemed rather unnecessary now.

'You know,' I said, 'your kids can do a lot better than Cleeve.'

'So can you, Alice.'

Suddenly, I wanted to cry. I suppressed the urge, as I often did these days, and got to my feet. 'Thank you. I hope you're right.'

'I always am, aren't I?' Lindsey smiled her sleepy smile. Her gaze was still cool, her tooth still chipped. 'You take care of yourself, Alice.'

I nodded back at her. 'Take care, Lindsey.'

Later, I heard that Eve Winslow had reverted to her maiden name and was living in Bristol. Nancy Riley had kept in touch, and she told me that Eve had found work at the university there.

The next few years were busy, first with my law degree and then the move to London. Henry had got a job at an engineering firm in the Midlands, and I spent a fair amount of time shuttling back and forth on the train to visit him. One Sunday afternoon, my train was held at a station. I looked out of the window, and just a little way down the platform I saw a thin dark woman I thought I recognised, with a small sandy-haired boy. They were playing some sort of card game together while waiting for their train. The boy was laughing.

My train began to pull away from the station. Something made the woman look up, and our eyes met. I hesitated a moment, and then I waved.

Down on the platform, Eve hesitated too. Then she smiled and waved back.

ACKNOWLEDGEMENTS

Thank you, as ever, to my editor Sarah Hodgson, to Hanna Kenne, Emma Dunne and the team at Corvus, and to my agent, Sue Armstrong. Writing would be a lot less fun, and full of many more pratfalls, without you.

My own school days were a sadly tame affair. So thanks also to Gordon Bourne and Louisa Wilton for sharing their expert knowledge on how to break out of a boarding house at night, as well as several other shenanigans that may or may not have made their way into this book.

Thank you to Ali, always.